DEAL

AKASH MISHRA

Copyright © Akash Mishra
All Rights Reserved.

This book has been self-published with all reasonable efforts taken to make the material error-free by the author. No part of this book shall be used, reproduced in any manner whatsoever without written permission from the author, except in the case of brief quotations embodied in critical articles and reviews.

The Author of this book is solely responsible and liable for its content including but not limited to the views, representations, descriptions, statements, information, opinions and references ["Content"]. The Content of this book shall not constitute or be construed or deemed to reflect the opinion or expression of the Publisher or Editor. Neither the Publisher nor Editor endorse or approve the Content of this book or guarantee the reliability, accuracy or completeness of the Content published herein and do not make any representations or warranties of any kind, express or implied, including but not limited to the implied warranties of merchantability, fitness for a particular purpose. The Publisher and Editor shall not be liable whatsoever for any errors, omissions, whether such errors or omissions result from negligence, accident, or any other cause or claims for loss or damages of any kind, including without limitation, indirect or consequential loss or damage arising out of use, inability to use, or about the reliability, accuracy or sufficiency of the information contained in this book.

Made with ❤ on the Notion Press Platform
www.notionpress.com

"I would like to express my sincere gratitude to my amazing parents for their unwavering support and motivation in every situation life has presented me. I could not have achieved this without your constant encouragement and belief in me. Mom and Dad, your love and support mean everything to me. Thank you for everything."

Mom and Dad, I love you.

Contents

Contents

Contents

Acknowledgements

I would like to express my heartfelt gratitude to everyone who supported me in bringing this book to reality.

First and foremost, I would like to thank myself for not giving up despite many problems. I would like to thank my family and friends for their constant support and suggestions, and I am grateful to have you in my life.

I would also like to thank my editor and proofreader, Afreen Nazeer, for your expert guidance. Your insight and suggestions helped shape this book into its best possible form. Your attention to details was invaluable and I am grateful for your contributions to the final product.

To all of you, thank you for your invaluable contributions to this book. I am deeply grateful for your help and support, and I couldn't have done it without you.

Prologue

This story revolves around Akash's life and a life-altering "deal." Everything about his life will change irreversibly, from his dreams to his relationships.

Akash is a fortunate boy, blessed with a good life, a happy family, friendly parents, wealth, and a vast business with abundant properties. Despite his family business, his true passion lies in music. His dream is to become a complete artist - a singer, writer, and performer.

He is striving to have his name recognized among the world's top musicians and is diligently pursuing his dreams. Some of his albums have caught people's attention, but his life will change when he signs a deal with his father.

He has a very good relationship with his father but only point of disagreement between them is the family business. His father wanted him to succeed him in the family business, but Akash had his own aspirations to create his own legacy. However, his father desired his son to learn about his business, its tricks and tactics.

Akash's life took a turn when his father presented him with a completely unexpected proposition. He wished for Akash to work under Tanisha, a highly intelligent and impressive businesswoman who leads her own startup company.

Despite initially refusing, Akash eventually agrees to sign the deal after witnessing his father's deteriorating condition and realizing his business's importance.

This story will depict Akash's journey after he signs the agreement. What will happen? Will he succeed on this test or fail this life exam? Will he grow to have strong feelings for Tanisha, or will his passion diminish in the face of this test? Or, he will lose himself in this whole process.

1

Chapter One

Aryan sat before the top officials, all eyes fixed on his hand holding the pen to sign the deal. However, he looked at his father, knowing he couldn't sign. Despite this, he held the pen with courage, facing the moment he had always run from. There was no turning back now.

Aryan was tense and looked towards his father, but he was nowhere to be seen. Instead, all he saw was a businessman who cared only about closing the deal, even if it meant damaging their relationship.

Aryan is being coerced to join his father's business and must abandon his dreams, as his only hope - his father - has clarified that signing the deal means his dreams, love life, and personal identity will be put on hold for three years until he achieves the set goal. You won't be able to go back to your previous life if you fail. Are you brave enough to sign this deal?

Aryan appeared bewildered and attempted to leave, but his father blocked his way. "You're not going anywhere until you sign this deal," his father warned. "Otherwise, witness the destruction that you alone have caused."

Upon hearing this, he felt a sense of despair wash over him. He picked up the pen once more and signed the deal, resigning himself to his fate. As he handed over the papers, he said, "It was a pleasure doing business with you, Mr. Rajnish Kumar Mishra." The

CEO looked at the papers, seeing his son's signature, and seemed to be lost in thought.

All his shareholders seemed annoyed in an instant. Aryan had signed a regular deal, which was not the reason they had gathered, instead of the main company papers. The group applied pressure to the CEO, urging him to convince Aryan to sign the company deal. As they approached the CEO, armed forces stopped everyone in their tracks. The CEO, holding a stack of ordinary deal papers, was ecstatic as he signed his first successful deal with his son. Although their relationship wouldn't be the same, the CEO remained composed and stated, "I got what I want," before departing.

Eight months back,

The CEO of the 'Divine group,' Rajnish Kumar Mishra, has an only son named Akash, who lives abroad to learn and practice different music. Akash frequently performs in music concerts, leaving him little time to visit his hometown.

Akash's father supports his career and checks on his health often, while Akash never inquires about his father's health or dreams as he is too busy chasing his passion. Akash was unaware of what was going to happen in his life as his father's DIVINE grew wider, and he was expected to take full responsibility. However, he was unhappy doing so and found happiness pursuing his passion.

The CEO, who lives alone and is busy with work, was reading articles about new business ideas on the way to DIVINE. He read a magazine while waiting to discuss his upcoming project with the company. He stopped mid-conversation upon receiving a notification on his phone. Upon seeing the news headlines, he shifted to the company portfolio and discovered new business ideas that caused a nearly 10% loss in his shares.

He looked around and inquired if anyone had heard about the new technological advancements that have taken over the market. Our company couldn't provide it to our clients and now they are giving the business to new startup companies, even though we have been running the contract for so many years.

Everyone who knew nothing remained silent. The CEO called the lawyer and brokers to buy all new startups under DIVINE, gaining control and recovering losses in a few hours. Additionally, he initiated DIVINE, a new technology evolution program. One company declined to sell their shares or idea to the DIVINE group, which the CEO disregarded since he still has much to learn about new technology.

The CEO skipped the business summit where companies were nominated because he had already made all the decisions. He went to see his son instead. After returning, the CEO visits his office to find his new prize missing, and upon searching his wall of fame, which is adorned with medals and prizes that DIVINE has gained, he calls for a meeting and asks, "Where is my new prize?"

Observing everyone's silence, he angrily grabbed one of the skilled staff members and demanded to have his reward returned to his wall of fame. I won't repeat myself. The CEO removes his hand, and everyone suggests strategies and projects to him, but he only cares about getting back what he lost. Just as his anger was about to erupt, an unknown person entered the meeting room and walked confidently towards the CEO, taking a seat next to his chair. The CEO's eyes were emotional when the unknown person asked, "Hey, Dad, can you show me around your office? I've never been here before."

The CEO walked him through DIVINE with great enthusiasm, pointing out every detail, before departing to visit other locations. For the past few days, the CEO has put all his work aside and is spending time with his son. They are visiting various places and reminiscing about the old days, and the CEO finally feels like he is truly living his life.

Walking to Akash's room later at night, the CEO noticed him resting and took a moment to admire his impressive collection of musical and expensive items. Eventually, his gaze fell upon a framed photo of Akash's late mother, who had always dreamed of providing her son with a better life. Our son is living a life that exceeds the wildest dreams, the CEO mumbled.

He walked to DIVINE and went straight to his cabin. He sat on his chair and spent the whole night staring at the wall of fame. The feeling of missing one award kept him up.

2
Chapter Two

Next day,

The office staff walked into a beautifully decorated DIVINE and were pleasantly surprised by the sudden blast of music that everyone loved. The CEO walked into the main hall, where familiar music was playing, and everyone was dancing. He discovered Akash had organized a sudden party and joined in the fun. Although an old-fashioned CEO, he attended a party to support his son's music. To his surprise, more business tycoons and an immense crowd joined the party, showing their love for Akash's music.

Finally, the crowd moved to the back of the office, where all the business tycoons were waiting for the award ceremony organized for DIVINE. As soon as the CEO took the stage, every businessman stood up in pride for the one who recovered his credit back in just one week. Now everyone was gathered to celebrate his success.

The CEO was overjoyed to finally have the award back in his possession, as it held a special significance to him. It wasn't just any gift, but a divine symbol of pride that his son had given him. His gaze fell on his son, who was beaming with pride and cheering him on from the crowd. The CEO's announcement of bonuses and share-profits was met with cheers and applause from the staff and business partners.

With tears of joy in his eyes, he walks towards his son, proudly showing him the prize. "We did it," Akash exclaimed, his voice ringing with triumph. "You have claimed your reward, and now you stand victorious. None can stand in your way, for you are invincible."

The CEO asked, "How did you manage everything?" while listening intently.

"Everything has been taken care of," Akash replied with a smile, "and right now, I want to celebrate my father's success before I leave tomorrow." Listening to this, the CEO joined the company celebration with his son. Akash sneaks out of the party at dawn, watching as the CEO and the other guests continue to enjoy themselves.

Next day,

While watching the news headlines covering the DIVINE group's success celebration, the CEO's phone buzzed with a message promising a final, special gift on the way. The promise of a grand feast and flowing alcohol was in the air, as the CEO invited all to join. Meanwhile, the CEO was the only one left waiting for his specific gift. In an instant, a stranger barged in, throwing and smashing things with a rough attitude. The CEO observed everything in silence before receiving another text that read, "here's your present."

The waiter arrived carrying a covered plate, piquing the CEO's interest. When the CEO uncovered the plate, they found a simple handmade cake. As the CEO was about to taste a piece, the woman dramatically threw the plate away, finally gaining the CEO's attention. As the CEO looked closely at the girl, the girl asked him, "What does it feel like when someone takes away the bread you earned with pride, the only source of food for your family?"

"Who are you?" asked the CEO, peering at the girl with a curious expression. "And why are you doing this?"

Tanisha, CEO of 'FAITH', said she was there because of his son's dishonest actions which made her lose everything and you are celebrating this? By not confronting me directly and resorting to this, he has shown a lack of courage in my eyes, even if he feels proud of his actions. The CEO took a piece of cake and got on his knees, looking around at the mess she created. He seemed happy as he spoke, "Can you explain why I value this cake more than the expensive materials you ruined?"

Despite having everything, I couldn't afford the simple cake my son made for me. The taste and smell of it brought a flood of emotions I haven't experienced in years. I would like to express my gratitude to you for creating a situation that led him to visit his hometown and this company that even his father couldn't persuade him to. He showed up unexpectedly and presented me with a gift that I will always cherish, but then left without a farewell this morning. Any idea why?

The CEO continued, noticing Tanisha's clueless expression. Perhaps he's hesitant to confront his father once he learns of the methods, we use to achieve this success. Sometimes, in the business world, we must shatter others' dreams, even if the prize is insignificant. My son learned this bitter lesson in a single day. He did what he felt was right to restore my pride, but in doing so, my identity as a successful businessman was lost in his eyes, leaving me with nothing.

The CEO's eyes were filled with emotion as he spoke, his smile conveying the depth of his words. Despite paying a high price for my success, everyone in this place seems to revel in their accomplishments, and even in the midst of my own failure, I find solace in the fact that someone still believes in me enough to bake me a cake.

After telling this, he threw the prize and took a big bite of cake, and everyone stood still. As she listened to his story, Tanisha felt a pang of regret for misjudging the CEO, who had opened to her about his pain.

The CEO noticed her guilty expression and confronted her. She replied, "I can't forgive your son for taking everything from me just to please his father. Although I respect his decision, he damaged my work, my reputation, and my pride. Your son may have inherited everything, but I earned this power and position through hard work and dedication. I offer this gift to you as a gesture of goodwill, as I have no desire to ruin your son's gift, which he gave after destroying my world."

She picked up the fallen prize and put it on his desk. Despite everything that had happened, she couldn't bring herself to hate him because of his son's devotion to family. "When it's about family..." she paused before continuing. "Let this be a great gift not only from your son, but from mine as well."

Her eyes filled with tears as she said, "I hope your son develops a big heart and learns that genuine success is not about taking, but about giving something valuable to others."

Finally, he loses to me. CEO, your son can buy your happiness at any cost, but you can't enjoy it despite having this success. Your son has connected us unintentionally, but you have a loving relationship with him, and I have a hateful one. I will wait for him, as I owe him more than what he gifted me. Enjoy your son's gift until then.

She watched as the CEO cut another slice of cake and offered it to her, but she declined. The CEO agreed and said, "My son really brought us together in a way nothing else could. I'm filled with happiness since he gave me a simple yet invaluable gift- you, my dear. I don't want to see you as a business rival. Instead, I hope you'll be my daughter for life."

As everyone looked on in surprise, the CEO praised Tanisha's assertive attitude, admiring how she stood up for her rights regardless of who held the power. The CEO expressed a deep respect for her pride, and even said aloud if her parents were proud of them.

With tears streaming down her face, she finally let out the grievance she had been holding onto for so long. "FAITH" wasn't just a name to her, it was a symbol of the trust her late parents always had in her. The CEO comforted her by gently touching her head as she listened intently to his words. He expressed his newfound appreciation for his son's gift, which gave him a sweet daughter he had always dreamed of.

The CEO gripped her hand and declared, "From this moment on, you are my daughter. You will never be alone again." Tanisha's voice trembled as she spoke, "You have only one son and to everyone else, you are a godfather. Please treat me the same. I don't want to be betrayed again. If it happens, this time I will spare nothing, not even you, my godfather."

Just as she was about to leave, the CEO's guards stopped her, showing that he had more to say. She turned around and saw him holding a plate, waiting patiently. As she caught sight of the piece of cake, a small smile tugged at the corners of her mouth. She couldn't stop thinking about the plate's cost. It was equal to six months of her employees' salaries and one-third of her company's profits. She had invested that money in helping the elderly, youth, and hungry children. Despite all that, the cake was too little for her, and she suggested they continue the party with the staff.

The CEO accepted responsibility and promised to revive everything that was lost, with three times the original amount. Tanisha was left stunned by the CEO's gesture of offering her a bite of cake. She tasted it and seemed lost in thought for a moment before silently taking the plate from his hand and leaving.

The CEO was amused by her childish act and couldn't take his eyes off her until she left. Coming to his senses, he burst out laughing at the thought of the prize for getting her to take just one bite. The CEO was impressed by her clever trick that helped her earn three times more than what she had lost in a single day. He asked his PA to gather all the information regarding her, wanting to know every detail. With a grateful heart, he finally sent his son a text message, thanking him for the gift. "Don't stop now," CEO said, "the party is still going strong."

3

Chapter Three

After few days,

The CEO was surprised as he reviewed her achievements. In a short time, she had defeated him twice before, and he reminded her to stop crying, which had cost him three times. He then calculated how much her smile could cost him.

With his mind racing, he swiftly ordered his board members to prepare a new project file. Without hesitation, he then invited rival business partners for a meeting, and this time, he invited startup companies as well. They reviewed his new file, knowing that no competitor would dare to boycott his set limit. Despite this, he raised his shares to 15%, unsure if it was the right move. As he waited, he sensed the terror in the air as he made a sudden, unexpected move that no one was prepared for.

The market fell a couple of days later, but the CEO refused to lower his prices. Instead, he used his son's trick to recoup his losses, which ended up causing everyone to suffer great losses. The CEO searched for a specific person at the business event but couldn't find her. He asked his staff for help and learned that she had declined his meeting invite. He left the event soon after.

A few days later, a business summit was held, where all the businesspersons gathered to overcome the loss caused by the CEO, who also attended the summit. As they examined the reports, everyone was taken aback to see that FAITH was still soaring, unaffected, and they turned to the CEO for an explanation. The CEO had no answer why they were tricked into leaving FAITH behind.

With the office empty, the CEO sat down to review the reports in solitude. Suddenly Tanisha appeared and said, "You won't find what you're looking for in that report. It's all inside you."

The CEO said, "I don't know how we'll bounce back from this, but I'll figure it out soon."

During the meeting discussing new projects, a staff member suddenly pointed out that Tanisha invested almost 30% of the company shares in a new startup. Though the CEO disregarded her, he held onto those parting words: "What you are looking for is within you."

The CEO struggled to decipher Tanisha's business tactics, even when she dropped subtle hints in their conversations. Eventually, he disconnected from the outside world to take a break.

Tanisha's company took over the market, and yet the CEO remained absent. Tanisha planned a corporate event where all the businessmen came together to celebrate her success. Unexpectedly, a stranger approaches Tanisha to offer congratulations. Upon seeing the stranger and his connection to DIVINE, everyone else is shocked, but Tanisha greets him warmly instead of asking him to leave.

He was 'Gajraaj' the one who betrayed DIVINE by leaking confidential information to Tanisha, resulting in her attempt to overthrow the CEO. He turned to Tanisha and spoke in a serious tone, "We have some pressing matters to deal with."

The stranger asked for the remaining amount after everyone left, but Tanisha informed him they had already transferred the promised amount. He cuts in, his tone demanding, "Miss, your success far outweighs the measly dimes you've given us. I think it's only fair that I receive half of your success as repayment for our support."

Tanisha got so mad when he threatened her that she hurled her wine glass and yelled, "You can't just destroy me like that!" No one can challenge the power and pride I have earned through my own efforts. Insulted, he pulled out his tablet and warned her that she would regret ignoring his offer.

He started the process, and suddenly everyone received a notification. They turned to the projector side and found their shares falling drastically. It shocked them to discover that Tanisha had invested 50% instead of the agreed-upon 30% without their consent. It was a move to win over the CEO, who was her real opponent.

Gajraaj warned her that if she didn't transfer him half of the profit the company had earned, she would regret it. With a nod of agreement, she started the transfer. The transfer was finally done, and to Gajraaj's surprise, Tanisha had given all her shares to the CEO and crushed her tablet in anger. "You are an immoral person," she said with venom. "You tried to drown a king out of jealousy, but he bows to no one. If I lose, everything will be ruined."

As everyone's eyes were fixed on the projector, the CEO's shares rose rapidly, much to Gajraaj's dismay. He tried to intervene, but his efforts were futile, and he ended up shouting in anger, calling Tanisha foolish. You've got no company, no power, and still smiling?

Tanisha said, "I happily gave everything for my people and partners. They won't suffer for my mistake. Their future is safe now. And I've got one more surprise for you." She transferred the entire amount to the CEO's firm.

He couldn't take it anymore and ordered Tanisha to be taken down, even with her guards protecting her. Eventually, Tanisha was left with only a few guards and was surrounded by her rivals who still wouldn't quit. She got scared and closed her eyes. Then she feels a touch on her head and sees the CEO and his squad taking over the summit.

CEO noticed Tanisha was scared, so he gave the termination letter to Gajraaj that his staff handed him. Gajraaj asked, "I did what you wanted, so why this?"

The CEO said, 'You did great. You did exactly what I wanted. You can go now.'

Gajraaj wanted to oppose upon hearing this, but the CEO's armed forces took him hostage. Gajraaj, while on his knees, challenged the CEO by stating that his days were numbered and he would eventually be replaced. He argued that he, not the person chosen by the CEO, should be the new successor of Divine's heritage, as it was not fair. `

The CEO replied, "You messed up thinking you could take me down. I knew your intentions from the beginning. I let it happen to teach my daughter a lesson. Never trust anyone without knowing their true intentions. You proved to be a great example for her."

Before he leaves, the CEO stops and says, "Hey, it's not right to let you go without a reward for what you did. Why don't you take it?"

The CEO calmly returned the FAITH shares to Tanisha, reinstating her as the successor of the business. "How can you be so serene after losing?" Gajraaj asked.

The CEO boasted, saying that being the best was always his goal, and he had achieved it. Thanks to your cunning tactics and betrayal, FAITH went from being an independent firm to becoming a franchise of the DIVINE group. You thought eliminating FAITH and betraying DIVINE would be simple, but in doing so, you gave me the precious gift of FAITH.

My daughter has finally learned her lesson, so she is now the co-director and successor of DIVINE group. She has full authority to make profit decisions when I'm not around. He turned towards Gajraaj and made a public declaration that Tanisha would be his successor, and that she would be protected at all costs.

CEO turned to his partner and said, "You asked Tanisha why she's still smiling even after losing everything?"

She gave everything willingly, without a second thought, to help those in need and protect her partners' futures. Even after losing everything, she remains the best businesswoman and now inherits DIVINE. Above all, she is my daughter, a title she earned with pride.

The reason I'm here is that I know fully that once you complete your task, you'll eliminate her. However, you're currently powerless, a mere zero.

After hearing the CEO's decision, Gajraaj said goodbye and departed with his companions. As she held her godfather's hand, Tanisha couldn't help but think about how much she had underestimated the CEO, who had chosen her as his successor over his own son.

She felt a tight grip on her hand, causing her to turn and see the CEO struggling to maintain balance as everyone cleared out. The CEO's condition deteriorated rapidly, and his doctor administered a booster dose to stabilize him. As time passed, the CEO still didn't feel his strength returning, so he turned to the doctor, who wore a grave expression.

The CEO angrily administered himself another dose and injected it into his body. As he did so, he felt his strength slowly returning. After a few minutes, he left the place. Tanisha understood the CEO's illness, and this was the reason he makes sudden decisions. When she was leaving, everything had changed - her driver, car, and guards were all replaced by the CEO, leaving her shocked.

4
Chapter Four

Tanisha's anger intensified as she realized she no longer had control over her life. She hopped into her car and drove to her villa. When Tanisha arrived at the office the following day, she found that employees, staff, and new shareholders of DIVINE and FAITH were all mixed, making her feel like she was being controlled by the CEO and she yelled at everyone to leave.

All of them left, except for Tanisha, who still holds on to the hope that her employee will return someday. She keeps coming to the office to work on her new project, but nobody turns up. She walked into her cabin and was surprised to see guards and partners filling the room. As she approached, she realized the CEO was seated in her chair, reviewing her latest project.

The CEO calmly refused the new idea, stating that it would not be profitable for DIVINE and therefore could not be approved. She listened to him, her jaw clenched in anger, and finally replied, "Take whatever belongs to you. I want nothing of yours."

The CEO responded by saying that everything earned from FAITH belongs to him and advised her to work under his command for an easier time. Saying this, he left with his staff. Once again, Tanisha found herself alone at her company, remembering the day when she sacrificed everything to protect her people, but none of them came back.

Despite losing her savings, Tanisha continues working on her new project. Finally, she invested all of her savings in the project and was ready to launch it worldwide using the FAITH server. While uploading, the network suddenly shut down. She checked the server station and found it had crashed. She went outside to search for a Wi-Fi connection.

Just as she reached the fuel station and resumed uploading, Gajraaj took her tablet away from her suddenly. Despite being intimidated by his presence, Tanisha bravely asks, "Do you even know whose project this is? Why do you want to ruin it?"

He burst out laughing upon hearing this and taunted, "If that's true, why are you alone and empty-handed? You must have rejected everything the CEO offered you and now you'll regret it." She threatened him, saying if he did anything wrong, it would be worse for him.

After hearing her threat, he yelled, "Whose name did you try to threaten me with?" You also despise him and have already relinquished his authority and protection, but your new project allows me to retrieve everything that the CEO took from me because of you. Tanisha tricked him by warning him that his actions could turn everything in favor of the CEO and what he holds right now could be his downfall.

"You don't understand," he said, "the CEO is a master manipulator who took advantage of us both." I am no longer willing to accept the difference he set for us, and I am taking steps to change it. Suddenly, CEO's team arrived and intervened by placing an audio machine in front of Gajraaj. The CEO greeted Gajraaj as an old friend and questioned his eagerness for success that isn't his. The CEO expressed he intervenes because he still cares for him.

Despite Gajraaj shooting the device, the CEO continued to speak through the station speakers, warning against acting foolish and the consequences that may follow. Suddenly, the guards surrounding him, as well as the CEO's guards, aimed their weapons at him when Gajraaj fearlessly pulled out his gun and aimed it at Tanisha. The CEO's voice was stern as he asked Gajraaj whether he valued his family more than revenge.

Gajraaj's eyes turned to the screen, where he saw his family held at gunpoint. With a scowl on his face, he takes out his frustration by firing at the tablet. He chuckled while Tanisha let out a triumphant yell, "Your daughter is safe, but her project didn't make it."

Tanisha, frustrated with her failed attempts to fix the tablet, becomes consumed with thoughts of revenge. She impulsively grabs a gun from the guards and begins firing recklessly. When the magazine runs out, she realizes that the CEO's guards have saved Gajraaj, and he is still alive.

With a fierce expression, she grasped a blade and strode towards him. He yelled desperately to the CEO, his voice shaking with emotion, explaining that he had kept his promise not to hurt his daughter, but she was now breaking the code and he needed help.

Tanisha's anger flared up at the sound of the word "daughter". He couldn't bear to look at death up close and shut his eyes, only to open them and find the CEO standing there. I am the one who ruined your work, not him. Please, take your frustration out on me instead.

Annoyed by his words, she held the blade dangerously close to his heart. She saw the CEO's grip loosen from the blade and felt a rush of adrenaline as she prepared to take revenge. With tears in her eyes, she hesitantly inserted the blade and let out a scream. "I hate you," she cried, "Every time you appear, destruction follows. You called me your daughter, but this time, you hurt me more than your own son. I will never forget it."

Your family gave me the worst gift ever, and it seems like being your friend won't do me any good and being your enemy won't bring me any success either.

She held his coat and said, "You could've saved my work, but you didn't because you still see me as guilty for your son's actions."

As she said this and left, the CEO remembered her tears and suddenly plunged the blade into his partner. Despite being in pain, Gajraaj laughs and warns, "It's not over yet. You have much more to see. Your daughter is leaving without security. Run, or your successor will be dead soon."

After uttering those words, he lost consciousness, and the CEO instructed his guards to take him away while he went to find Tanisha. The CEO, desperate to protect his daughter from danger, drove recklessly and crashed into several cars before stumbling towards a group of hostile hooligans, his strength and vision impaired. Tanisha got scared, and the CEO took the gun to protect them, but he stopped and said no one can harm his daughter except him. The moment he finished, he collapsed and was rescued by the CEO's guards.

5

Chapter Five

The CEO slowly regained consciousness and felt the soft breeze from the trees surrounding the hidden bungalow. "Is my daughter alright?" was the first thing he asked, his voice trembling with worry.

As Tanisha locked herself away, she couldn't help but wonder what would happen to her family if she didn't make it out alive. Her heart ached as she thought about the family she grew up with, now separated by distance and grief.

Out of nowhere, a text popped up on her phone from her secret PA, whose identity was known only to Tanisha.

Tanisha, upon receiving the last copy of the ruined project, resolves to work on it again. She unlocked the final account left by her mother, hoping to honor her wishes to use it only in the most desperate of times. As she prepared to transfer the funds, the ringing of her phone interrupted her. She walked to the entrance of her villa, wondering who could be calling her at such a critical moment.

As the car pulled up, Tanisha saw her sister-in-law Urvashi step out, someone she had always had a cold relationship with. Moments later, her heart swelled with emotion as her niece Mayra stepped out of the car, looking just like her late brother. Tanisha ran towards her with tears in her eyes.

Mayra was taken to the USA following an accident that resulted in the deaths of her grandparents and father on the day she was born. She's an introvert and when she met Tanisha for the first time, she felt scared and held onto her mother. Tanisha ignored her niece's refusal and took them to their room. As she was leaving, Urvashi asked her directly why they were there and what Tanisha had done this time.

Tanisha chose not to respond and left quietly, spending most of her time at the office to avoid any further conflict. Tanisha tries to connect with Mayra, who appears introverted and lost, despite her mother's failure to help her overcome her fears.

For the past few days, they had been silent, not speaking to each other until the day Tanisha was about to enter the villa. Urvashi broke the silence with a pointed question, "What have you done to our family bank account? Can you explain where you spent almost a third of its money so suddenly?" Tanisha sat in silence, her eyes downcast, struggling to find the right words to make Urvashi understand her situation.

Tanisha looked lost, so Urvashi sat beside her and spoke in a calm voice. She wanted to make one thing clear: neither she nor her daughter will suffer due to any of Tanisha's decisions. They were already suffering from a decision Tanisha made in the past that couldn't be undone.

I request that you refrain from debiting any additional funds from our family account, which you have already used for your project. I expect it to be returned to me within three months, with interest. I understand that you may have invested in the project based solely on FAITH, which motivated you to continue operating our family business, but I am unsure how long you can maintain that motivation for success.

Urvashi's departure left Tanisha's mind buzzing with a new idea. She immediately instructed her PA to launch the new plan, which would fall under the parent's company FAITH. This new venture, called TRUST, was entirely owned by Tanisha.

Despite making sudden changes to her project, she waited anxiously for a few days until her hard work finally paid off. Her project once again scored a chart buster and defeated the CEO, but he was nowhere to be found to congratulate her. Instead, she walked straight to DIVINE, proud of what she had accomplished for the company. As the CEO arrived with his partners and saw his daughter receiving the prize, he showed no expression and began to leave.

Tanisha raised her eyebrows and asked, "Aren't you curious about how I won this time as well?"

As the CEO's partner spoke, his voice shook with anger and betrayal. He accused her of deceiving everyone by launching the project under FAITH and reaping all the profits for TRUST. Since FAITH is now a franchise of the DIVINE group, you knew there would be no opposition. You cleverly used the DIVINE background to achieve success. We will make sure to reveal your truth during the press conference.

The CEO whipped around with a look of anger at the sound of the interruption, causing everyone to freeze. However, a few professionals persisted and demanded to make their points.

Without our permission, she secretly transferred all the profits to TRUST, which is not a part of our franchise. The CEO responded, granted.

If you say yes to her eco-friendly project, DIVINE will lose a lot of money. The CEO said, "Okay."

FAITH is like a franchise family, and if something goes wrong, it will be a bad look for DIVINE. The CEO said, "Agreed!"

She doesn't know our stuff, our vibe, or our moves. So how can we let her in on our clients? CEO said, "Sure thing!"

With the CEO's full approval, Tanisha now has a team of DIVINE group employees who are not only skilled but also well-versed with the company's rules and strategies, standing behind her, ready to work according to her orders. The CEO is clearing everyone's doubts by providing everything at once, but suddenly someone questions their trustworthiness.

The CEO's voice echoed through the room as he yelled at the crowd, claiming ownership of DIVINE and asserting his authority over everything within it. Tanisha noticed the CEO's annoyance and spoke up, "I was the one who questioned this. Do you still have faith in me?"

The CEO's voice carried an edge of annoyance as he spoke, although most of his staff and partners remained staunchly opposed to his decision. The CEO, determined to make everything right, finally asked the lawyer to hand over the contract to Tanisha. She cleared her throat and read it out loud, stating, Tanisha Malhotra, the CEO of FAITH, transferred her ownership to Rajnish Kumar Mishra, Founder and CEO of the DIVINE group of companies.

The announcement made earlier was verbal, but now I am transferring the FAITH rights to Mr. Rajnish Kumar Mishra through a contract that I fully understand and agree to. This will make it an official new franchise of the DIVINE group.

Tanisha, who had been left in a corner by the CEO, could finally take control after the CEO played his last card and she signed the contract, accepting her role as the successor of the DIVINE group. She took a moment before leaving to carefully place the prize on the CEO's wall of fame.

With tears in her eyes, she turns to the CEO and tells him that although he tried to correct his son's mistake by offering her the position of successor, she cannot be like him and make the same mistake.

Although I've sworn to act as your successor until your son takes over, I'm struggling to follow through. If you truly want me to fulfill your wishes, then this will be our final meeting. Being around you only reminds me of my wrongdoing and fills me with guilt.

She continued while holding her breath and asked, "I am not asking for much. Can you do this much for me?"

The CEO, who was cold-hearted, asked if she still looked up to him as her godfather? Tanisha responded by wiping her tears and saying that she no longer respects him. From now on, he is only the

CEO of DIVINE and the new owner of FAITH, and nothing more.

6

Chapter Six

Tanisha's time in DIVINE began as an unsuccessful entrepreneur, but she left as a triumphant successor. She hopped into her new car and headed straight for her new office, TRUST, which the CEO had already arranged as a gift. The CEO observed the contract in silence, considering whether she had sacrificed ownership of DIVINE to her despised son. He couldn't decide if this victory would take everything from her or if her loss would reveal that she had much more than she ever wanted. Finally, she revealed to everyone that all she cared about was her pride and success.

The CEO noticed a habit in Tanisha that he didn't see in his son, and although it hurt Tanisha, he was happy to finally connect her to his family. He noticed her tear-stained signature just below, grabbed the award from the wall of fame, and departed.

As she approached Villa Urvashi, her anger grew at the sight of Tanisha's newly changed staff, guards, and cars. She couldn't help but ask how Tanisha could put a black mark on their family's faith by willingly handing over FAITH to the CEO, whose son had already caused them so much harm. You've made a mistake, and now you've lost your last opportunity to reunite with your family and now we are leaving.

Tanisha listened silently before storming off to her room, where she locked the door and began breaking things in a fit of rage. Tanisha had been locked up for two long days until Mayra stumbled upon the key and unlocked the gate. She waded through the cluttered mess to reach Tanisha, her hand reaching out to take hers.

When Tanisha saw Mayra, she immediately made her sit down and relax. Tanisha had tears in her eyes, but Mayra lovingly wiped them away. Feeling comforted by Mayra's care, Tanisha hugged her tightly and drifted off to sleep. Urvashi quietly left the room when she saw them resting together.

Tanisha took Mayra to her mother's room as the evening settled in. Later, Urvashi led her by the hand to the dining room, where she encouraged Tanisha to eat something. Before Urvashi left, she expressed her concern for Mayra's future and the well-being of their small family, emphasizing that she didn't want to abandon them.

DIVINE group's record-setting success became the talk of the business world following that day. Tanisha has already taken the reins of every DIVINE group meeting, overseeing all business affairs with her fixed share, assigned by the CEO, on every proposal. She gained the funds and, upon her return, she repaid Urvashi with interest, stating that it was tenfold what she had borrowed. Urvashi was leaving with the money when Tanisha proposed, "Why don't you all stay here as a family? I'll pay you even more."

"I want written consent for it," Urvashi replied firmly, "and if the contract is breached for any reason, we will leave immediately."

Tanisha listened carefully and replied, "Thank you for staying. You're an important part of our family, and I won't let anything come between us."

The CEO locked himself in his palace and stopped visiting his son, consumed with thoughts about a decision he had yet to make that would affect his son's future and ultimately bring everything to an end.

Tanisha received a text message with the tracker location as she was leaving for TRUST. Upon arriving at the dark villa, she followed the directions to the basement where she was met with the sight of an immense crowd gathered around Gajraaj, who was on his knees and at gunpoint, waiting for their master. As Gajraaj cried out for help, Tanisha rushed towards him, trying to figure out what was happening.

Gajraaj shouted for help, "Please help me or he'll kill me! Tani......" Then a gunshot went off and blood smeared on Tanisha's dress.

As she stumbled outside, the bright sunlight momentarily blinded Tanisha, her mind still reeling from the live assassination she had just witnessed. Tanisha approached the villa, her movements sluggish and lifeless, causing Urvashi to intervene, "Don't let Mayra see you in this state."

Witnessing the sight of her blood-soaked self, Tanisha hugged Urvashi, and to comfort the scared Tanisha, Urvashi tried to calm her. However, Tanisha fainted unexpectedly.

7
Chapter Seven

"I will let no one harm my daughter," the CEO declared before pulling the trigger on Gajraaj.

Thinking this Tanisha shockingly awakes, being impatient. She saw Mayra sleeping next to her and feels calm thinking about for whom she was going through this much pain, now rest in her arms.

From then on, Tanisha and Mayra spent most of their time together. Tanisha isolates herself from all members and projects within the DIVINE group, relying on her secret PA to provide updates on internal politics and projects that require her attention. Her suspicious nature made her turn rude towards everyone.

After much deliberation, Urvashi concluded she needed to intervene to prevent Tanisha from causing major financial losses to the company and her shares. During dinner, Urvashi mentioned, "I've been considering supporting you in your new project."

"I'll take care of everything else," Tanisha assured her, "but you must stay and watch over Mayra."

Urvashi speaks up accusingly. "Ever since that day, you've been acting weird and rude to everyone, and it's not okay. As a shareholder, I reserve the right to come to the office whenever I want."

The idea of Urvashi joining TRUST made Tanisha uneasy, as she knew the organization dealt with situations that could be overwhelming and dangerous.

Tanisha was in a meeting when she received a text message, which she ignored. Later, she received an audio link with the message "the small truth behind your biggest failure". She played the audio and listen to it.

As Tanisha listened in on the covert conversation between the CEO and Gajraaj, she felt her anger boiling over. In a fit of rage, she ordered the immediate reversal of all ongoing projects against the DIVINE group.

The anniversary day,

During the 25th anniversary of the DIVINE group, Tanisha announced an exciting new project. Investors who contribute a large amount to this project will receive a minute share of the board members of the DIVINE group, making them profit sharers instead of just investors.

Most of the shareholders invested in the project, and she invested 5% of DIVINE shares among the new shareholders. However, she set a condition that the project must be eco-friendly and must be invested in its initial stage. In case of failure, the DIVINE group would cover all their losses. She signed the contract without the knowledge of the CEO.

Tanisha dropped the project cost a few days after the product launch, which resulted in increased sales but failed to earn the promised profit. As a result, the investors started questioning the DIVINE group's decision. Meanwhile, Tanisha was reviewing the downfall of the product when she received a text that read, "I am coming for you."

As Tanisha read, she turned to the glass side and saw a fleet of cars, trucks, and buses pulling up to the main door of the company premises. Tanisha's eagerness to meet the stranger was in stark contrast to everyone else's terror. She received a video link with a warm message that said, "Please accept my good wishes."

As she clicked on the video link, she was immediately confronted with the devastating destruction of the DIVINE group premises. She watched as heavily armed forces stepped out of their vehicles and aimed their weapons at TRUST, yelling for everyone to back off.

After breaking down the doors, they stormed into the building and took everyone hostage, finally reaching the CEO's cabin. Upon entering the cabin, they were met with the sight of Tanisha sitting calmly, her eyes fixed on them. She had already texted, "I'll come alone wherever you take my people," and offered to surrender herself as a hostage.

While everyone else was corralled onto the big buses, Tanisha found herself slipping into the back seat of a stranger's luxury car. As they reached FAITH, the air was filled with the sound of people unloading. Tanisha's eyes were fixed on the building when she noticed a masked man stepping out to greet her. "finally, we met!"

She ignored his words. "Beautiful, isn't it?" the stranger mused, gesturing towards the view. "If you support us, we can take on the CEO, and in return, I can get your company back."

As he spoke, he extended the antique gun towards Tanisha, who reflexively aimed it at him. "Silly girl," the stranger laughed. "This could have been a great deal for both of us."

He walked back to the company and said, "You're only responsible for wrecking your own dream," before closing the door.

Once the door locked, all the army and weapons turned towards FAITH. Everyone ran away to save their lives except Tanisha, who stood before FAITH and aimed her gun at the general. Without warning, a triple-armed force appeared from behind, already in the process of taking down the enemy. However, the general remained focused on his target, Tanisha, and ran towards her without hesitation.

In an instant, the field transformed into a battleground, filling the air with the sound of clashing weapons and kicking up clouds of dust. The general, upon seeing his entire crew dead, let out a blood-curdling scream. Suddenly, the CEO appeared, standing between Tanisha and the general, and swiftly slit the general's throat with a dagger.

When Tanisha saw the CEO's anger, it reminded her of the master who assassinated Gajraaj. The CEO's voice boomed as he yelled at the general, "You all have made a big mistake this time. Despite knowing that she's my daughter, you tried to target her. Death is the only reward for such actions."

The general, with a bloody mouth, laughed and revealed that Tanisha was not the actual target. Instead, their boss would finally take down the CEO, with the help of Tanisha who led them to this spot.

While Tanisha listened to the lie about her, the CEO suddenly shot the general. Tanisha saw the reflection of someone pointing a gun at the CEO and wanted to help, but the CEO made her stand on his back while he pointed the gun at the person. Before he could react, a bullet was fired.

Tanisha hesitantly looked at the terrace side where the masked man, giving a victory sign, stood against the backdrop of the city skyline. Upon seeing the CEO's unstable state, Tanisha felt a surge of anger and frustration. She watched as he struggled to regain control and could not stop her from firing at the masked man.

Tanisha started crying and said, "Don't leave us, old man. We gotta get through this together."

8
Chapter Eight

After a few days,

There was a lot of sadness after the CEO's death. Akash, the new CEO of DIVINE group, struggled to stabilize the company's losses. In addition, DIVINE faced a multitude of rivals, with Tanisha being the most vicious of them all. After the CEO's death, she not only dismantled the DIVINE group but also drove Akash to his death, leaving him with insurmountable debts and causing the downfall of DIVINE's pride.

The CEO jolted awake from a strange dream and found himself in a hospital bed. As he looked around, he felt a sense of calm wash over him, knowing he was still the CEO of the DIVINE group. Tanisha remained by his side throughout the ordeal. However, one day, the CEO's phone rang, and it was his son on the line.

Tanisha nervously looked at the CEO and put the call on loudspeaker, "Father, I'm sorry for leaving without telling you. I hope everything is well. I wanted to apologize and confess that I don't want to stay in the palace anymore where we still grieve for my late mother. I apologize for my rudeness towards you, but you have always been there for me. I want you to know that you mean everything to me. I am fortunate to have a father like you who is never upset over a small matter. That's why I did what I thought was right to restore your success, and I have no regrets about it."

Tanisha leaned in, listening intently to Akash's words. "I'm sorry for what I did to make you happy, he apologized. It was a sleepless night after I realized I had caused harm to the company, its workers, and the CEO, despite my lack of knowledge about them. I wanted to apologize, but fear kept me from facing her. I doubt she'll ever forgive me, but I'm content knowing I gave you something of value. Even if it means enduring more hostility, I'll do it with a grateful heart. Wishing for a lifetime of joy and endless smiles."

As the CEO remained silent, Akash called out to his father twice, father, are you there?

Tanisha hesitantly answered, hello! She was about to share the CEO's health status when he suddenly grabbed her hand to stop her. "The CEO is in a meeting at the moment," Tanisha continued, "but I'll notify you as soon as he's available."

Akash paused for a moment before speaking, "I don't know who you are, but my father always answers my calls. Since you picked up his personal call, I trust you and request that you look after my father until I return."

After hanging the call, Tanisha looked at the CEO who seemed to be attentively listening, even though he was resting. Tanisha comforts the CEO as he sheds tears, reassuring him that he has an amazing son who cares deeply about his happiness. She tells him that if she were in his son's shoes, she would have done the same for her father. Tanisha silently left after kissing the CEO's forehead.

Tanisha recalled Akash's words and threw the things angrily. She wondered if he was the obedient son but the worst opponent whom she will always hate. Suddenly, CEO's phone rang and Tanisha answered it. It was his son, who had returned to his hometown and was asking for the location.

Akash noticed a sports car following him for a while and sped up his speed. Soon they started racing and Akash managed to leave the other car far behind. The roar of engines surrounded Akash as more sports cars joined the fray, creating a path for the one he had abandoned.

When Akash arrived at the DIVINE group, he saw the same sports car parked there. He ran his hand over the smooth curves and said, "I really like this car." He barely finished speaking when he heard a voice say, "Your wish is granted." He turned around to see his father greeting him.

A *few moments earlier,*

"I am finally back in my hometown. Just send me the location."

The CEO woke up to a sound and immediately got out of bed, ignoring the pain and treatment he was undergoing. He had to meet his son. Before leaving, he turned to Tanisha and asked, "Did you cover everything up as if nothing happened?"

Tanisha replied... yes!

Present time,

The CEO spoke, his voice laced with amusement, "You almost had me there, but being a seasoned businessman, I know how to turn a loss into a win." The CEO gave Akash a new gift by throwing car keys towards him and hugged him tightly.

Out of curiosity, Akash opened the company gate and admired the new interior design, which seemed to erase all traces of the past. Meanwhile, the CEO received a text from Tanisha asking if he liked the view.

When Akash visited his hometown for the second time, he had a serious purpose. He was suspicious that his father was hiding something. On the other hand, the CEO appeared restless as he thought about his two children, who were complete opposites of each other. Tanisha avoids Akash, and he can't bring himself to speak about her involvement in his wrongdoing.

The CEO and Akash set out to invest in a property one day and arrived at their destination. Without warning, Akash abruptly changes course, leaving the mundane meeting behind. The CEO's mind kept wandering back to his son's strong desire to pursue a different career path after their meeting.

He stumbled, lost in thought, until Akash steadied him with a hand on his shoulder. "Do you need to leave quickly, too?" Akash asked, noticing his instability. The CEO smiled as he listened, leaning forward in anticipation, and then asked, "If this is true, then what?"

Akash brings the CEO to their favorite restaurant, but the CEO abruptly leaves after answering a phone call. He arrived at TRUST and was met by a line of his employees, standing shoulder to shoulder, creating a barrier between Tanisha and her team.

After greeting the DSP and a few higher officials, the CEO asked for clarification on why they had decided to interrogate Tanisha without his approval.

The newly recruited interrogating team responded, mentioning the recent brutal assassination that took place in FAITH, and their suspicion of Tanisha. It is suspected that Tanisha handled a pre-planned assassination that was carried out by your armed forces. Could you shed light on the reason behind this turmoil?

In response, the CEO queried if there was any proof to back up the statement.

The officials played the CCTV recording, revealing Tanisha openly firing her gun and leaving behind vehicle prints. The CEO took a slow drag of his cigar, seemingly indifferent to the unfolding scene. In an instant, he had the higher officials on their knees, held at gunpoint.

The CEO's voice was filled with anger as he issued the threat, "I dare anyone to enter my premises and prove me wrong."

The senior official listened to his direct threat and quickly handed over all the proof to the CEO, who proceeded to destroy them right in front of them.

The CEO stated that he sees no evidence of guilt and expects them to not interfere with his affairs from now on. They can take it as a humble request or a straightforward warning.

Every official had their say, and finally the CEO addressed the newly hired officer who was still glaring at him with anger. The officials pleaded with the CEO to forgive Yogesh Singh, who was newly recruited and unfamiliar with their authority, and requested an apology.

"Train this young man to stand by my side," replied the CEO confidently. He then looked at the young man and advised, "Son, always be quick to adapt to new things. It's better to stay on the winning side."

After settling all his business affairs, the CEO finally arrived at his palace and hurried to the dining table. The food was served hot, and he noticed that Akash was missing. Upon looking around, he found a note that read, "It was great to have dinner with you, but I didn't get a chance to say this to you..." After reading the note, the CEO left.

Tanisha's mess has been taking up the CEO's time, leaving him with little opportunity to spend quality time with his son for the past few days. After much searching, the CEO found a solution for the troubled project, though it could only recover half of the loss and more work was still needed.

The announcement of the business summit came unexpectedly, catching everyone off guard. The CEO was determined to boost work productivity and often worked long hours with no rest. He decided to take a break in his cabin, but while resting, his mind concocted an unconventional plan that he acted upon without seeking advice.

As Tanisha noticed the CEO's sudden move, she checked her shares which were invested in his plan. She immediately called her PA, who confirmed that she was also taking the risk with the CEO. Despite the short notice, the CEO took steps to mitigate the risk. PA's confidence made Tanisha think that there would either be two winners or TRUST would suffer terribly.

9
Chapter Nine

The business summit day,

The CEO and his crew were attending a summit when some rivals approached and said, "We used to be partners, but now that your new successor has taken over, we are rivals, and you do nothing when it comes to your so-called daughter. You made the sacrifice of giving up a valuable franchise to ensure her safety. What made you choose Tanisha as your successor instead of your son?"

The CEO had been quiet, anxiously waiting for his score that had been kept confidential until now. It was the first time he was eager for the outcome, regardless of whether it was successful.

Everyone was left stunned by the product's success when they saw the result. The CEO noticed his shares remained stagnant despite a rapid increase in product sales. Upon logging into the company portal, the CEO was taken aback to find that all the profit earned was owned by TRUST.

Seeing which he feels stabbed. Despite Tanisha being the only one with access to the enterprise portal, the CEO cannot accept that she may have orchestrated the downfall of DIVINE group. As the shares continued to rise, excitement filled the room, and everyone began to applaud the CEO's decision.

The CEO shared that his friend's trust in him was the key to his success despite the challenges. He didn't judge or lose faith in me and finally recommended a plan that converted the losing game into a profitable one. My heart swells with pride whenever I say his name, Akash Mishra, my son. The CEO played his son's new composition, the notes echoing through the room and bringing the story to life.

Back when the CEO felt asleep in his office,

As the CEO rested in the cabin, he felt a gentle touch on his hand. "It's been so long since we last sat together," he complained, his voice tinged with patience. As I think about my father, I remember how he always made time for me. However, now it seems like he's lost in his own world. It's only then that I realized he has another family to take care of, the DIVINE group, whose success I wholeheartedly respect.

Akash meticulously studied the blueprint, carefully reviewing the strategy and plan. He then took a pen and began adding new, innovative points to the plan. When he was satisfied with his changes, he quietly left the changed plan for the CEO's approval.

The CEO's eyes were bright with excitement as he examined the blueprint that Akash had created in mere seconds. Akash gifted this success to the CEO once more, resulting in him being recognized as the best businessman. The CEO's phone beeped, and he read the text with a smile on his face, "Dad, I'm proud of your success and excited to finally have some time together to catch up."

As the CEO was leaving, he suddenly felt lightheaded and needed to steady himself, but before he could do anything, his nose began to bleed. He got dizzy and put his hand up for help. He thought his son was there, and the CEO said, "we will surely spend some time together if not today then tomorrow, but we will surely do." saying this CEO fainted and was taken to emergency.

10

Chapter Ten

One month later,

Akash sat in his car outside the company, contemplating the rightness or wrongness of his decision. His phone beeped, and he saw a text message that read, "Wishing you the best of luck on your new journey!"

Akash muttered to himself while reading, "I'm only doing this for you, Dad." As he stepped out of the car, the hot pavement burned the soles of his shoes. He stood at the entrance, reading the company name "TRUST" and wondered if they could provide him with the hope he desperately needed. With a deep breath, he walked through the doors for his job interview.

Before 1 month,

As Tanisha reminisces the words CEO spoke to her, "we will surely spend some time together if not today then tomorrow," she suddenly opens her eyes and turns to the other side as his son enters the room. Akash found his father lying unconscious and noticed the sound of his shallow breathing and spoke, "Thank you for being there for my father, miss."

The CEO quickly grabbed Akash's hand to stop him from approaching. Akash had a small gift in his hand, which he had brought as a token of appreciation for Tanisha's contribution. "I brought this especially for you," he said, "for all that you have done for us. Please accept this."

As Akash made his way towards her, Tanisha couldn't help but fixate on the sensation of his presence drawing nearer. Akash sat outside the ICU, unaware of his father's condition. Meanwhile, the CEO regained consciousness and asked the doctors about his health status.

"You're running out of time," they replied, their tone filled with concern. As the CEO held the knife to the surgeon's throat, they explained that they were still working on improving immune and strength levels beyond the current cycle. However, an alternative medication had been prepared, but using it would result in unbearable pain, almost to the point of death.

The CEO injected himself with the injector and soon felt a searing pain that had left him doubled over. The CEO's silence was unsettling, and a few staff members cautiously approached him. Suddenly, he erupted in a fit of rage, smashing everything in sight. As soon as they saw the scanner, his heart rate increased, and he felt a surge of energy.

The doctor attempted to inject a tranquilizer, but the CEO intervened, relishing the feeling of power. The CEO stepped out of the ICU and greeted his son, remarking on how long it had been since they last sat together.

The CEO was making dinner when Akash asked, "Dad, do you want to talk about anything?"

The CEO dodged the question by cracking jokes and then got Akash to help him cook. They stayed up late chatting, and that's when Akash shared his music ambitions and goals. The CEO sat alone and watched a hospital clip, feeling content when he learned that Tanisha had encounter Akash and was feeling positive.

Akash jolts awake in a cold sweat, heart pounding from the nightmare. Just as the CEO was leaving for the meeting, Akash shared his dream, "I had a dream where I lost my ability to play music."

The CEO inquired, "So, where exactly did you find yourself?"

"As a CEO, my role is to make decisions and attend meetings," Akash replied, "but there's an aspect of this dream that I feel needs to be changed."

With a curious tone, the CEO stopped and sat next to Akash asking, "What is it?"

Isn't it too early to transfer everything to an untrained successor who doesn't know how things work in the business? Akash asks. The probability of failure is high for the successor, even if they are the offspring of a highly successful person like you.

The CEO asked what he and Akash would do in a similar situation, indirectly including himself.

According to Akash, a CEO must be fully prepared and trained to work in the worst situations, which is why a successor should learn how things work and develop learning strategies before taking on full responsibility.

Listening to Akash's suggestion CEO looked at his wife portrait and said, why don't we try your suggested idea?

Upon hearing this, Akash broke out in a fit of laughter and commended his father for his improved sense of humor and left. As the CEO held his tablet and studied Tanisha's image, he felt a sense of relief knowing that his son's plan could finally bring them together. The CEO reassured himself that he would make his son's dream come true, just like he always had in the past.

11
Chapter Eleven

After a few days,

The CEO walked into Akash's room and exclaimed, "At last! I've made your dream a reality." He handed the file to Akash, his voice serious as he spoke of the impending situation. "We're going to face this too, soon," he said. "That's why I've decided to go with your plan. Let's see if it works."

"You're joking, right?" Akash asked, looking stunned.

Akash could see the CEO's lack of reaction, but he stood firm in his decision. "I never liked your business," he stated firmly, "and I won't be a part of it, NEVER."

Returning the file to the CEO, Akash left in anger. Akash and the CEO are sitting silently in the hall later at night when Akash breaks the silence by asking why his father is so concerned about DIVINE.

"It was your mother's final request," the CEO replied softly.

Your mother's support and dedication played a pivotal role in shaping me into the successful business tycoon I am today. Even though you don't enjoy running a business, you still manage it with ease. Seeing you handle things just like your mother did makes me feel less alone. Now, I don't have to worry about who will take care of you and DIVINE, the only remaining gift from your mother.

Upon hearing this, Akash tightened his grip on his father's hand and vowed to keep her mother's promise alive through any circumstance and asked for some time to decide. As Akash left, the CEO heard a voice from behind asking why he had portrayed his wife as a businessperson when she wasn't one.

The CEO responded, "to make him the next DIVINE successor."

Aditya responded, "but he hasn't agreed yet."

After listening to the old caretaker's negative response, the CEO turned to Aditya, whom he has always respected for looking after Akash since he was born. "There will be no alternative for him," the CEO declared. He knows he should reject the offer, but he cannot bear to disobey his mother's last request.

When Akash returned to his villa after a day of partying, he was clearly upset. He spoke with the CEO, explaining that his surname alone would make it impossible for him to get an internship like anyone else.

With a serious expression, the CEO handed him the file and said, "Not anymore." Akash was taken aback by the level of detail his father had already managed, and it signaled the start of his new life.

12

Chapter Twelve

Entering the TRUST,

Upon arriving at the main hall, Akash saw a diverse group of individuals, including employees, trainees, and job seekers, all patiently waiting for their turn. When Akash's turn finally came, he appeared in rugged jeans, a funky t-shirt, and a ponytail, as if he were dressed for a concert instead of an internship.

The service desk noticed something unusual and asked him to wait in the room for his turn. As Akash walked to the waiting room, he noticed a girl he thought he recognized from a bar but wasn't entirely sure. He put on his headphones and rested until he realized he was the only one left in the waiting room. Suddenly, he saw the same girl enter the next room and decided to follow her.

As soon as the power went off while they were alone in the room, Akash suddenly kissed her in the dark. She resisted, but he persisted, kissing and biting her lips and neck passionately. As the lights flickered on, Akash was taken aback to see a completely different girl in front of him, as the original girl was nowhere in sight. As he walked back into the waiting room, Akash could still taste the sweetness of her lips.

After a while, an announcement was made asking everyone to gather in the main hall. When Akash turned, he saw Tanisha in front of him, standing aligned and staring at him with anger. He noticed her faded lipstick and bite marks on her neck, and in response, he grabbed her waist to pull her closer.

Akash stands firm, unwilling to leave Tanisha, even with armed guards nearby. With a gun in her hand, Tanisha's rage boiled over until her personal assistant interrupted her with news of an email from the CEO. The message contained a warning about a new intern named Aryan Mishra and the potential consequences of mistaking him for someone else.

"I am Aryan Mishra," Akash said, lifting his hand in greeting and mentioning that he was a new intern at TRUST, referred by the CEO.

Akash's thoughts went back to the day when the CEO gave him the file and told him he could no longer be referred to as his son. He also added that Akash had to give up music for a year to make the plan work.

Akash's laughter echoed through the room as he playfully called over to the staff, "Can you tell me what my name is?"

Staff replied, Aryan Mishra.

The CEO responded, stating that nobody knows your identity. Akash examined his new identity while the CEO stated that great success requires numerous sacrifices.

Present time,

Akash, who goes by Aryan Mishra now, was held at gunpoint. As she lowered the gun, Tanisha spoke the fateful words, "You may have had a reference from the CEO, but you're terminated on your first day."

"My princess, the day isn't over yet," said Akash. "Your threats don't scare me," Akash said with a smirk. "I still have hours left until midnight to use your company name."

"I'll give you an extra 12 hours until tomorrow afternoon," Tanisha said, with a challenge in her eyes.

When Akash saw the girl who stopped Tanisha, he immediately realized it was the girl he had met at the club. She sauntered over to

Akash and commented, "You look much better at night. See you at the party." She gave a mischievous wink and a smile before leaving.

Akash promptly contacted Aditya and instructed him to prepare everything for tonight's party.

As soon as Tanisha arrived at the villa, she rushed to the bathroom and turned on the shower, still fully clothed. She examined the bites on her skin, which had turned a sickly greenish-black, and in her fury, she smashed the glass in front of her.

Just as she was about to ban Akash from any future jobs in the city, her phone rang. After a brief conversation, she decided to delay the ban until Aryan completed his dare. Meanwhile, Akash was outside of the TRUST building, waiting. Suddenly, a group of people with heavy items barged into the premises with him.

Akash's crew set up everything on the terrace, and he turned the entire building into a party with lights, launching his new composition live from TRUST. Once the party location is posted, it begins to draw in viewers and visitors. The site's credibility is so impressive that it attracted high-profile celebrities, causing a massive crowd within an hour. This made headlines and forced the police to maintain order in the city.

Officer Yogesh Singh arrived and stopped the party by shooting the loudspeakers one by one. As soon as the police arrived, people scattered in a hurry. Finally, Akash and his crew descended the stairs. "I want to know who planned this party without permission," Yogesh asked in a stern tone.

Aryan's crew steps up and takes the blame for themselves. When Aryan remains silent, Yogesh handcuffs him and says, "We have caught the main culprit." Upon Tanisha's arrival, Aryan gave her a victory sign and departed. Tanisha noticed the time and saw that it was almost 12 o'clock, which made her leave angrily after realizing she had lost.

13

Chapter Thirteen

"We have some business to do," Yogesh says as he stops the car. Ignoring Yogesh, Aryan took out some weed and smoked a few puffs. Afterwards, Aryan told Yogesh that everything was going according to his plan and gave the weed to him. As Aryan surrendered, Yogesh blew a few shots and noticed something foreign that wasn't readily available. He asked, "If it's not legal here, how did you get it?"

"Everything has a price," Aryan replied with a hint of cynicism. As Yogesh listened, Aryan's staff handed him a bag full of cash. "I know what I'm asking," Akash said, "but I want you to file an FIR against me and TRUST." Upon listening to the details, Yogesh realized he could finally get revenge on TRUST and deemed the deal worthwhile.

On the next day,

As Tanisha approached TRUST, she saw a massive swarm of fans and reporters. Just then, the police arrived with Aryan in handcuffs. Aryan, who was wearing his TRUST intern tag, was surrounded by everyone eager to know the truth about the previous day's events. According to Yogesh, TRUST has achieved outstanding success in recent days, and to celebrate, Tanisha Malhotra, the CEO, organized a grand event.

Tanisha didn't show any annoyance as she listened to the false story and asked, "How was the success party for you guys?" We put together this event as a way to encourage and uplift our employees.

Tanisha handed Aryan his appointment letter with a smile, leaving him confused. She quickly clarified, "Don't think you got this on your own. I made it happen."

"What did you get in return?" Akash asked.

She gripped his collar, her eyes blazing with anger. "You think you can just walk away after what you've done to my company and me? I want you to suffer every day you work here."

Aryan carefully plucked several flower stems from the flask, weaving them into a beautiful crown of roses, which he silently placed on her head. "You hate me for what I did to you," he said, his voice heavy with regret. "But I promise to stay by your side until you ask me to leave. Consider it my gift to you, a way to ease your pain. I won't ever oppose you again."

Tanisha reluctantly released her grip on Aryan, who had taken her anger in stride and was poised to toss the crown. However, Aryan stopped her, remarking that throwing it would only enhance her regal bearing.

As Aryan was leaving, he was suddenly pulled into the dark room. Aryan pulled her close, his lips meeting hers in a deep, passionate kiss as they remained locked in their embrace. "I did everything to keep you close!" she exclaimed, her voice filled with desperation. Aryan paused, carefully listening, and finally learnt the truth behind Tanisha's acceptance of his internship.

It was she who suggested to Tanisha, her voice tinged with a hint of malice, "If you want your revenge so bad, then keep him close. No one could touch him, as he's the nephew of the CEO."

While learning this, Aryan was silently leaving. "Be cautious of Tanisha," she warned again, "as you've already wounded her pride."

Aryan replied, his voice filled with a mix of uncertainty and trust, "If this happens, then I have you looking after me."

Once again, as Aryan left, he realized he had forgotten to ask for her name, and when he turned around, she had vanished. Then, he walks to the main area where everyone appears terrified as they look at him. Feeling strange, Aryan turns and sees his Team Leader.

When he looked at the leader's ID, he saw the name Akash Anand. Since Aryan couldn't use that name anymore, he went to the smoking zone and casually smoked weed, with Akash joining him.

Aryan extended the weed to him, promising it would provide a refreshing release from the burdens weighing on his mind. As Akash took 2-3 shots, he felt a surge of amazement, emboldening him to introduce himself, "I am Aakash Anand, the team lead responsible for training new joiners."

Aryan replied, "In that case, you will be my team leader too."

After a brief conversation, Akash departed for work while Aryan remained, anticipating an assignment that never came. Finally, he departed with everyone, who had all been waiting for the company transport, except Aryan, who left in a luxury car straight for the bar. Lost in the energetic atmosphere of the party, Aryan sought solace in a private chamber. There, he found his girl eagerly waiting, and their desperate kiss filled the room with passion.

As she reached villa Tanisha, she entered the spacious hall area and, after a while, caught sight of Mayra. As Mayra placed the flower crown on Tanisha's head, a sense of joy washed over her, and she couldn't help but smile. After Mayra had rested, Tanisha led her to Urvashi's room.

Urvashi's face lit up at the sight of Tanisha, and she couldn't help but praise her, "You look like a true princess." As Tanisha stood before the mirror, she couldn't help but notice how stunning she looked, realizing that it had been a long time since she had seen herself this way.

14

Chapter Fourteen

When Aryan woke up, he felt a sense of loneliness wash over him as he realized his angel had already left. Upon reaching the palace, Akash spotted his father, who was eagerly waiting for him, and exclaimed, "Finally, I got what you asked for!" and handed the appointment letter to the CEO.

Akash continued, "the CEO of TRUST Tanisha, she doesn't appear to be a typical CEO. Instead, she exudes elegance fit for a princess." Showing no reaction, the CEO simply said, "hoping you will succeed what you have started," and promptly left.

It had been a few days, and Akash was still waiting for some work to be assigned to him. Frustrated, he made his way to the CEO's cabin, only to find that Tanisha was not there. Aryan noticed Tanisha in front of him, and her annoyance grew as she saw him occupying the CEO's chair, giving him an air of authority that made her feel like the CEO had taken over the entire organization. In a fit of frustration, she flung the chair, shattering the glass.

Aryan smiled at her act and said, "you love watching me being a puppet, don't you?" He faces the broken glass while standing on her back, from where she used to monitor him.

With annoyance in her voice, she tightened her grip on his collar and asked, "How dare you sit in my chair?"

Aryan stared into her eyes, his concern evident, and asked, "I can see the pain in your eyes. Is there any way to heal your wounds?"

Angel's presence immediately diffused the tension as she stepped in to address the situation. Tanisha asked, "You are eagerly waiting for some work assigned to you, isn't it? Until this moment, you were comfortably seated, but now you must stand at the entrance, akin to a watchman, welcoming everyone and helping to repair the broken glass."

Upon hearing this, Aryan quietly left to lend a hand in repairing the glass, but unfortunately, his offer was met with reluctance, and everyone abandoned the task. When they returned from lunch, they were surprised to find the glass had been repaired.

Aryan, who may forgo his lunch but never his weed, calmly exhales a cloud of smoke, oblivious to the old person sitting nearby, struggling to breathe. On his return, he stands at the entrance, feeling a deep sense of humiliation that keeps him rooted in place until nightfall.

On the next day,

Aryan arrived late for work and found Tanisha and all the employees standing outside the office. He stands at his place, greeting everyone entering TRUST. However, when he wants to leave for refreshment, the guards stop him, but he can't resist his craving for weed. In the restroom, he exhaled a cloud of smoke, triggering the fire alarms and causing the water supply to gush. As he leisurely walks back to his place, others scramble to safeguard their work.

Knowing it was Aryan's fault, Tanisha's voice echoed as she yelled, "You're fired!" While listening, Aryan left silently.

When everyone arrived at the office the next day, they were surprised to see that all the systems and files had been restored. They went back to work, but were interrupted by the sight of Aryan sleeping near the cafeteria. As he woke up and grabbed a coffee, he noticed Tanisha and she questioned, "I fired you yesterday, why are you still here?"

While under the influence of drugs, he scans his surroundings and notices that all systems are suddenly functioning. He then receives a text from an unknown person stating, "everything is resolved."

Aryan claims full credit for the repairs, saying that although he was fired for making a mess in the office, everything has been resolved and he is still an intern here.

Just as he was about to leave, guards blocked his path and confiscated his narcotics. Tanisha instructed, "Make sure he doesn't leave his place, or you'll all lose your jobs," and then she walked away.

With a smile, he stands, reflecting on the CEO's words. "Where you are posted, she's the hardworking lady I truly wanted on our team. While working under her, try to persuade her and learn from her expertise."

She appears annoyed seeing him smile from the cabin while Aryan, who had been standing all day, finally sits after everyone leaves. When Tanisha saw him resting, she told the guards not to disturb him. When Aryan woke up, he found himself in darkness, alone and trapped in a building. Desperate to escape, he searched for a light source as his phone battery neared depletion. In a state of panic and fear, he attempted to save himself, eventually losing consciousness.

Tanisha, engrossed in her work, eventually comes across him lying unconscious. It is at this moment that she remembers he is the CEO's reference, prompting her to abandon her cabin and search for him. Upon finding him, her efforts to revive him are unsuccessful.

While trying to wake him up, it reminded her of the day she held her dying family members, evoking strong emotions, yet she manages to bring him back. As soon as Aryan regained consciousness, he immediately held her tightly and said, "Please don't leave me alone, it's too dark in here. I felt like I was almost dying."

Despite almost hating him for his past actions, she holds him back to calm his fear, while Tanisha, becoming emotional, has no one but him. Silently crying, she held him tightly, releasing all her pain. As dawn approached, she quietly slipped away, leaving him peacefully asleep.

When she got back to the office, she noticed Aryan was alert and wearing the same clothes as if he hadn't been to his place. He stands at the main gate, greeting each person with a smile, giving roses and gentle hugs, except for Tanisha, who walks past him with her security and goes to her cabin. Aryan embraces all with a smile, including employees, guards, and working staff.

Aryan went in suddenly, clutching a single red rose. Without even glancing at his face, Tanisha questioned, "What are you up to now?"

Aryan replied, "I chose to share the overwhelming feeling of love and care that enveloped me last night while I was trapped in the darkness." I witnessed a girl, in the midst of her own agony, deciding to prioritize my well-being.

She paused her work, her ears attuned to his every word as she listened intently. He went on, "I require your aid in finding that girl."

Listening intently, her anger grew, and she dashed the stuff from the table. Facing the other side, she could feel Aryan's presence as he walked closer to her, as if drawn by an invisible force, stopping just an inch away. Hesitant and protective of the truth, Tanisha forcefully pushed him away, her voice filled with anger as she yelled, "How dare you get so close to me?"

Aryan replied calmly, his voice tinged with curiosity, "I don't know what happened, but after last night, I am eagerly yearning to catch a glimpse of those mesmerizing eyes that were by my side."

With a determined look in his eyes, he placed the rose on her desk and declared, "I will find that girl, no matter how difficult it may be."

As he leaves, Tanisha slowly looks into her own eyes, filled with self-hatred for the mistakes she made in the past, both towards her family and her company. Realizing the harsh truth, she shatters a glass in anger before storming out. Aryan, sneaking into the smoking zone once more, managed to conceal his weed in various areas of the company. The first hiding place was in the garden near the smoking zone, a spot he chose after much deliberation.

On returning, he saw girls flocking to him, drawn by his gentle demeanor. He flirts with others, but still searches for his missing soul and ends up being intimate with female employees. The conclusion of his quest takes place in a dark office room, where his angel intentionally ensnares him, leading to a passionate and uninhibited encounter. On the other side of the wall, Tanisha could sense every sound and movement in the other room, prompting her to leave without making a sound.

15
Chapter Fifteen

Aryan was late the next day and wasn't allowed into the company, but he stubbornly stood at the entry point. Suddenly, several businessmen entered the premises and were allowed to enter by the guards, but he was not, so he left.

Tanisha and her crew, at the meeting, sense something strange. When they look towards the glass side, they see the entrance completely obstructed by high-end luxury cars. Aryan, holding a tablet, puts on headphones and cranks the music to the maximum, unveiling his new composition. He opened the gate where Tanisha and her partners were waiting, calmly taking off his headphones and asking, "How was the meeting?"

They all seem annoyed and leave the deal after listening, while Tanisha leaves angrily and commands, "You made a big mess today. It's now your duty to get me the same deal or don't enter the premises after this."

The following day, Aryan went to the office and saw the same vehicle that had come the previous day for the deal. Upon entering, he noticed everyone anxiously waiting for him. A man gave Aryan a file and said, "Our boss loved your composition and wants to complete the deal, but first, we need you at the company's celebration." Handing the deal copy to Aryan, he left.

Aryan was surprised by how everything was done automatically, prompting him to go straight to the CEO's cabin. Keeping the file he was leaving and seeing no one around, he checked the company recording to find the girl. In his search, he stumbled upon an unfamiliar folder housing his private recordings, saved in a different directory, which startled him and made him wonder why she hadn't terminated him.

Tanisha arrived unexpectedly, her composed expression betraying any irritation she may have had, and inquired, "Did you manage to find the clip I saved for you?"

Despite listening intently, he still couldn't fully comprehend her words. Despite her concern, she continued discussing the deal details, stating, "The rival party appears impressed with you, so I want you to negotiate a higher deal than what we initially agreed upon. If you performed well, I will spare your internship. Otherwise, you will be reported to the police for exploiting my female employees."

She handed him the precise details of the deal, her voice firm as she said, "Get ready, because you have a lot more to do than just fucking my employees."

As the night fell and everyone gathered, Tanisha and her family attended the cooperate celebration. Aryan, dressed in his funky attire, stood out from the rest of the crew. Mesmerized by the music band, Aryan couldn't resist and joined them.

While getting along with the musician, he taught them a few notes. To test their skills, he took out his tablet and played his recorded music, capturing everyone's attention as they started practicing without permission. Aryan, who came for a deal, ended up partying and saw Tanisha leaving angrily.

He saw her and recalled her threat, so he searched for the dealer who was standing with a girl. Finding the girl alluring, he came to a halt, their surroundings becoming a blur as they indulged in drugs. Just as they were about to get intimate, he abruptly halted, yearning for his angel's affection, and swiftly departed from the venue. Tanisha, who had already set bait, now patiently waits for him to fall into her cunning trap.

The next day, as Aryan arrived at the company, he was immediately instructed to report to the CEO's cabin. As he entered the room, he noticed her waiting anxiously, her eyes fixed on the unsigned contract as they had discussed.

"Why isn't the deal done yet, even though you played well with the CEO's daughter?" she asked, her voice filled with frustration.

Upon the revelation of the girl's identity, he is taken aback and she promptly exits to the main hall before he can provide an explanation. As the crew waits for the visitors, he stands with them, observing the familiar party girl. Aryan, intending to leave quietly, when a senior crew member invites him to a meeting. Aryan, who is unfamiliar with meetings, is now confronted with a pivotal one that will determine the fate of his internship. Deep in thought, he enters the room.

When he arrived, he saw only Tanisha and the girl sitting there. They started the meeting upon seeing him, with Tanisha patiently waiting for Aryan to join. He glanced at the set limit and immediately raised it by 25%. Tanisha remained unresponsive, prompting him to finally increase it to 50%. The moment he did this, Tanisha intervened and asked, "Can we agree on this limit?"

The girl immediately responded, "This is beyond our set limit and if you really want to get this deal done at your limits, then I need to indulge in this project, or my father won't agree to this deal."

Upon hearing this, Tanisha immediately agrees. Aryan, in a hurry, was leaving after seeing the deal done. Suddenly, he heard the girls say from behind, "I want Aryan in return." Continuing, she turned to the other side and said, "I want him in my team, where everything will be tailored to his preferences. If you agree, we can finalize the deal."

As Tanisha listened, she added a few points to the deal, her voice filled with determination. "I'm glad you accepted our offer," she began, "but if you're only doing this deal for my intern, it means that TRUST's role isn't necessary anymore. Before signing, I need to clarify my position. If this project succeeds, we will divide the profits in a 50-50% ratio. However, if it fails, only you and my intern

Aryan will bear the loss; TRUST will not be responsible for any losses incurred."

Upon listening to this, the girl objected to the deal. As Aryan watched the meeting go beyond Tanisha's imposed rules, he felt trapped between the looming threat and the deal. He immediately requested a moment alone with the girl from Tanisha. As soon as Tanisha left the room, the girl immediately approached Aryan and picked up where he had left off the day before. However, he insisted on agreeing to the deal first before allowing her to proceed, causing her to storm out of the room in anger.

Aryan felt that his first deal was unsuccessful as he left the room where he witnessed Tanisha and the girl shaking hands. Everyone congratulates Aryan for sealing the deal, and he finally shakes hands with the girl.

By the way, my name is Yashmita. Mr. Aryan, it was a pleasure doing business with you. Tanisha appears happy after witnessing the deal, prompting Aryan to silently leave for the smoking zone. Out of frustration, he quickly starts smoking weed until he notices a nearby old person. This time, the old person is upset and angrily reprimands him for smoking.

16

Chapter Sixteen

Despite never experiencing such treatment before, Aryan stays strong and carries his stress. Finally, the old man angrily leaves. Aryan followed him until he arrives at his house. There, he discovers his wife, who is ill, and his daughter, who is in college. He struggles to manage their expenses, paying for his wife's treatment and his daughter's education. Unable to afford both at once, he asks his daughter for some time. Seeing this, Aryan departs for his palace.

Quietly entering his palace, he made his way to his room, where he noticed the CEO sitting next to him, asking, "Did your day go well?" Akash immediately inquired, "Do I have any account in India that allows me to spend freely?"

Looking into his son's eyes, who, for the first time, radiated selflessness instead of selfishness, he saw a glimmer of hope in his father.

After taking one card, Akash's face lit up with joy, and he embraced his father tightly. The CEO, alarmed by his son's strange behavior, urgently emailed Tanisha to gather all of Aryan's official information. The next day, when Aryan arrived at the office, he was greeted by a new team and an unfamiliar employee. Yashmita was waiting, eager to start work. However, before diving into tasks, Aryan wanted to meet Tanisha, who unfortunately was absent from the office that day. Disappointed, he then searched for an old man, but he too was absent.

Returning to work, he noticed a group of new faces, mostly girls, among whom Yashmita stood out as the most eager for an opportunity. After working on the project for a while, he abruptly left and wandered around, until he unexpectedly ran into Akash Anand. Engaging in a brief conversation, he greeted his team. Suddenly, Aryan got an idea and waited.

The next day, Aryan waits for Tanisha who is still missing. This prompts him to execute his plan and involve Akash Anand and his team for his new project. He also asks Yashmita to help, and she agrees on his terms. Despite trying to work on the project and almost avoiding the girls, Aryan still has to confront Yashmita. However, he is ultimately saved by his angel entering the room.

Aryan attempts various tricks to avoid Yashmita, but also collaborates with Akash Anand on their project. When he becomes trapped again, he reaches out to Yogesh for help. Yogesh frequently takes Aryan out from the TRUST. Both Akash and Yogesh readily offer their help whenever Aryan needs it.

Yogesh called Aryan, telling him that he was going to pick his mother from the airport. Aryan, without informing Yogesh, headed to the airport and arrived just as Yogesh was about to leave with his mother. They all went to an expensive restaurant for dinner.

Yogesh and Akash suggested he should refrain from doing this as they could go elsewhere. Aryan, who treated Yogesh's mother like his own, enjoyed the dinner and played his composition to make the night memorable. The restaurant's popularity soared as a result, but seeing the uncontrollable crowd, Aryan and his friend left the spot.

Yogesh, Akash, and Aryan had a great night at Yogesh's house and before leaving, Yogesh hugged Aryan and expressed gratitude for his help with his mother. Aryan quickly interrupts, saying that she's his mother too, and he puts his whole heart into everything he did.

When Aryan visited TRUST the next day, he saw news headlines about the previous night's party. Akash proudly introduced him as his new friend and was about to post party pictures. Aryan asked him not to, so Akash deleted them. Suddenly, Tanisha angrily visited the office and waited for Aryan. When he entered, she asked if he had any explanation for Yashmita refusing to work with them due to his partying instead of focusing on the project.

Noticing his silence, she commanded, "I called her to finalize the deal and this time I want it done, no matter what."

Yashmita enters and Aryan, overwhelmed with stress, embraces her tightly, kissing her intensely. Tanisha walks away, leaving them alone and the recording still on in the meeting room. Aryan, not stopping this time, fulfills Yashmita's wish and promptly leaves the room, heading to the smoking zone, where he smokes quickly until he feels a touch on his shoulder. When he turns, he sees an old man standing in front of him.

Aryan threw the weed and apologized this time upon seeing the old man. Abruptly, the old man apologized, admitting, "Sir, I'm sorry for yelling at you last time. I got caught up in family issues, but today I find you because my salary will be paid next week." He joined his hands and pleaded, "Please don't complain about me or they'll fire me."

Witnessing his helplessness, Aryan instinctively reached out and hugged him tightly. He saw in him the resemblance of his caretaker Aditya, and said, "You're like a grandfather to me. No need to say sorry, feel free to vent on me whenever you're stressed."

The old man and Aryan were getting along well until a guard arrived, asking for the car to be made ready. "Whom do you work for?" Aryan asked the old man.

He replied, "Tanisha mam, even after retiring, gave me this job; she is someone who helps the needy seeking no personal gain."

Aryan had a sudden realization while listening and then resumed working. He attempted to log into the company portal but encountered an issue. As a result, he visited the CEO's cabin where Yashmita and Tanisha were already waiting for him.

"Please grant me access to the company portal," Aryan asked.

"First," Tanisha said, "submit all your formal documents for verification."

Shortly after, he mailed her all the documents. Tanisha told, "To login, you need to sign the consent form first, and then new users can access in 15 minutes."

He quickly grabbed a pen and rushed. Aryan signed the form without reading it, which Tanisha took with her before leaving. After a while, he logged into the company portal and instead of working on Yashmita's project; he started preparing a new plan where everyone else left the office, but he continued working and even took a quick nap.

Tanisha walks to his table while he's working, but when she sees him resting, she looks at the plan, adds a few points, and leaves quietly. Upon waking, he noticed new points added, which triggered a familiar fragrance, compelling him to hurriedly search for her, but once again he couldn't find her anywhere. Coming back, consulting no one, he posted the plan on the company portal and left.

17
Chapter Seventeen

The next day, everyone saw a new assignment posted under Tanisha's name. She glanced at Aryan, who acted nonchalant, and then instructed the rest of the team to work on the new plan. Witnessing her approval of his work, he decided to show his appreciation indirectly by preparing cupcakes and sweets for everyone in the office cafeteria. Aryan and Akash took the filled trolley of sweets and started distributing them to the staff.

Finally, they visited Tanisha to give her sweets. She ignored them, but he left the dish on her desk and was about to leave. Suddenly, he noticed a little girl bump into him and fall. He held her hand, gave her the sweets with a smile, and was leaving when he saw a new girl. He stopped and asked, "Have I seen you before? Are you new here?"

In response, she said, "yes!"

Aryan offers her a taste of the cupcake and then wishes her good luck on her new day. By the way, what's your name?

she replied, "Urvashi, and you?"

Aryan was about to introduce himself but was interrupted and taken away by the crew. Later, she entered the CEO cabin and found Tanisha sitting with Mayra. When she saw Urvashi, she asked, "Why did you come here so suddenly?"

Urvashi responded, "I came to see your new establishment and I must say I'm impressed by the enthusiasm your employees have for their work."

Tanisha appeared shocked and abruptly left her cabin upon witnessing everyone enjoying Aryan's dish. She shouted to halt everything before searching for Aryan. Walking outside, she angrily saw Aryan sitting with her driver, spending time and sharing a meal with an old man. She was about to intervene but was stopped by Urvashi. She overheard their conversation where Aryan patiently talked about his family and expenses before handing out packets of sweets and leaving for work.

When he came back, he saw Tanisha holding Mayra and leaving. He stopped in shock and asked Tanisha, "I didn't know you were the mother of such a beautiful daughter."

He asked the little girl to stop and went inside to get the packet. When he returned, they had already left, which upset him. Urvashi took the packet and reassured him she would deliver it to Mayra.

He calmly holds her hand and asks, "I met you today and already asked for help. Even if you couldn't deliver this packet, it means a lot to me that you wanted to help." By asking this, he left Urvashi pondering his concern.

Upon arriving at the villa, Urvashi presented Mayra with a cupcake. Tanisha, curious, asked why Urvashi would do so since Mayra never eats such things. However, before Tanisha finished speaking, she witnessed Mayra taking the cake and tasting it herself.

While both remained motionless, watching her until she was full and fell asleep, she took Mayra away and asked Tanisha, "what is the name of the person giving dishes to everyone?"

Tanisha mentioned that he is the CEO's nephew who took FAITH from her, and then she took Mayra from Urvashi to her room. Urvashi was left pondering about his care and background, which nearly tarnished her family's pride, causing her to lose sleep.

The next day at the office, Aryan discovers that the new plan has been implemented and will launch in an hour. Upon seeing everyone leaving, he also departs for the site. Upon reaching the bank, he notices his suggested insurance plan has been released, prompting him to purchase its first unit.

Tanisha arrived with her family and Mayra ran towards Aryan, who held her carefully, shocking both Tanisha and Urvashi. The old man suddenly pushed Aryan, saving him from a rushing vehicle. Aryan got bumped hard and felt injured. Witnessing this, everyone rushed to save him. Aryan seemed shocked by the old man's accident.

Tanisha paid no attention to anything and swiftly escorted Mayra away from the site. Urvashi witnessed Aryan's injury, ignored him, and stormed off in anger. Later, when Aryan regained consciousness, he rushed to the aid of an old man, taking him in his luxury car for treatment. Taking the patient to the ICU, Aryan remains motionless. Shortly after, the patient's family arrives with Tanisha, who immediately starts cursing him without hesitation. Aryan, with his shirt stained by the blood of an old man, appeared lost and blindly walked towards the dark room, ignoring everything.

Tanisha follows him, believing he fears the dark. When she turns on the flash, she discovers him sitting alone in the darkness. When she noticed he was cold, she turned off the flash, but he didn't react. Sensing his vulnerability, she gently touches him, and he immediately tightens his grip on her waist. The sight of his pain brings back memories of the accident, where she was also broken. She decides to support him and refuses to leave until he finds rest.

Aryan wakes up after some time, hearing the doctor's voice telling him the old man is safe now, and immediately heads to his friend's workplace. Yogesh calmly confronts Aryan, who smokes excessively due to stress. Suddenly, a girl accidentally bumps into Aryan's car and gets hurt. When Yogesh sees this, he helps her first. Instead of thanking him, she angrily asks about parking in the wrong lane. The fight escalates, and Yogesh, worried about Aryan, angrily asks lady cops to take her away, resulting in her yelling angrily at him.

Aryan, who rarely cares, immediately takes her to the hospital when he sees her hand bleeding. Afterwards, he asks Yogesh to drop her off and apologize for his mistake. Upon his return, Yogesh appeared annoyed with the girl and decided to share his day with him to improve his mood. The quiet Aryan caught sight of Urvashi leaving and instinctively sprinted towards her, urgently questioning, "Are you alright?"

Knowing he's the nephew of the CEO, her anger grows, and she yelled... don't get closer! You almost killed my only child. Anything could have happened to her if that old person hadn't saved her.

Aryan's expression turned to shock as he discovered she was Mayra's biological mother, leaving him at a loss for words. In a sudden moment, he spotted an old man with his family, their hands clasped together in front of Aryan, expressing their heartfelt thanks, "Thanks to you, my family and I were saved from a crisis as you covered all my medical expenses."

Aryan immediately takes everyone's hand, stating, "No need to thank me, credit goes to Mayra."

Urvashi appeared shocked while listening, but Aryan quickly held her hand and greeted her. She is Mayra's mother, and because you saved her daughter, all your medical expenses are now covered by Mayra's foundations.

The old man's wife asked them to join a small celebration in their neighborhood, and Aryan agreed. After they left, Urvashi angrily questioned the new story, stating they don't have any Mayra foundations and you are the person who had paid for his medication.

Aryan responded, we're the only ones who know that there is no Mayra foundation, but for them, it's a glimmer of hope because his salary can't cover the medical expenses. "I won't be a part of your lies," she said, "this is your fault, and you have to face the consequences alone."

While leaving, Aryan asked her, "Just a moment ago, you asked, what if that old man was unable to rescue your daughter, what would have happened then?"

Aryan continued speaking, unsure if she was still listening, "I don't know if you'll come or not, but I believe you won't miss anything when it's about Mayra, so I'll be waiting for you."

18

Chapter Eighteen

Aryan, who had a secret plan for the party, asked Akash and Yogesh for support. However, they had already left to get things ready, leaving Aryan waiting. Urvashi's appearance in a beautiful dress transforms his demeanor from flirty to gentlemanly, and he takes her to a site already adorned for a grand celebration. The simple yet massive decorations impressed Urvashi, who was the chief guest. The local praised her for her support, and then the party began.

When Aryan dropped Urvashi home, she exclaimed, "It's been a long time since I had such a great night." Aryan gave her a packet of handmade sweets for Mayra and asked for her name; she replied as Urvashi Malhotra and left with a smile.

Meanwhile, Yogesh, who is helping Akash and others clear the area, accidentally bumps into the same girl and she immediately starts arguing again without hesitation. Aryan reaches the site and intervenes, soon Akash arrives and takes his sister away. This surprises both Yogesh and Aryan. To clear up any confusion and be a good friend, Aryan arranges a get-together.

Akash introduces his two younger sisters, Anshika and Ankita, who are dressed in a new style that intrigues Aryan. Akash responds by saying that they recently graduated from fashion school and are now searching for an opportunity.

Yogesh, who nearly got into a fight with Anshika, finally apologizes. Shreya, the daughter of an old man who studies business, appears to be incredibly talented and has impressed everyone. When they saw Akash and his sisters booking a cab and it got late, Aryan gave his car keys to Yogesh and said, "Take them home and then meet me near the airport."

He picked up Aryan from the airport, and they are now heading to the set location. When they silently entered the restricted zone, the police stopped them. However, upon seeing Yogesh, their senior officer, they were released. When Aryan reached the site, he noticed a large amount of imported weed, which was not easily available and highly restricted. Yogesh asked, "How did you manage to get this?"

"Resources easily manage everything," replied Aryan.

While taking stock, Yogesh noticed the DIVINE logo on the boxes, triggering memories of his insult and giving him a clue to bring down the CEO. They went to the bar, feeling happy and got drunk. It was there that Yogesh finally confessed his feelings for Anshika, someone he had liked since their first meeting. Afterward, they left for Yogesh's home.

While gently placing Yogesh on the bed, Aryan prepared to depart, but his mother's request to stay, reminding him it was his house too, made him change his mind. Aryan rushed to work the next day, grabbing the files he had been working on in a hurry. Upon arriving at the office, he noticed everyone engrossed in the latest headlines, buzzing about the party from the previous night and the Mayra foundation's support.

Aryan appeared shocked, angering Urvashi, who he followed, but she refused to listen. He confronted her, but it's just a small thing that will be forgotten easily. She cautioned him, saying they would be in trouble if Tanisha discovered the truth, and that she was also caught up in the drama because of his lie.

As she panics, he holds her hand and reassures her, "Don't worry, I'll protect you from any questioning. It's my duty and I'll handle it alone." Yashmita arrived suddenly, causing Urvashi to leave quietly. However, when she saw Aryan with another girl, she appeared annoyed and was about to leave. Aryan wants to clarify things after seeing Yashmita leave with doubt, but he drops his files in a hurry.

While collecting papers, he discovers one that he had left in a hurry. Upon seeing Urvashi leaving, he asks her for a ride. Arriving at the hospital, Aryan heads towards the ward, with Urvashi following him. They both witness Yogesh's mother leaving after consulting with the doctor. Aryan suddenly hugs Urvashi to hide himself, surprising her. After his aunt departs, Aryan enters the doctor's cabin and asks for information, but the doctor ignored his request. In an attempt to get the details, he offers one lakh rupees.

The doctor revealed her health condition, disclosing that she's in the final stage of cancer and hasn't informed her son or sought treatment.

"While examining the reports," Aryan inquired if there was any chance to save her or prolong her life.

The doctor said we need official consent and advance payment for advanced treatment, but there's no guarantee of saving her.

Aryan confirmed, "I'll pay the full amount, so proceed with the treatment."

Urvashi and the doctor exchanged shocked glances as they listened. Urvashi interrupted him, asking, "What are you doing? Official consent is required, and you're not even her son."

Aryan replied with anger, saying, "but she's like my mother. I never experienced the love of a mother, but if there's a chance to feel it, I see no boundaries."

After signing the consent form, he proceeded to pay the full amount.

He informed the doctor, "This is a secret between us. If anything is needed, contact me and share nothing with my mother or his son. Just follow the usual procedure."

Urvashi returned Aryan to the office and Aryan entrusted her with his mother's details for safekeeping, while Yogesh, who had discovered the CEO's illegal activities, revisited the site with his crew but found nothing, leaving him frustrated. Now, he seeks a new clue that only Aryan can provide.

Aryan finds Akash upset at work and asks him what's wrong. Akash explains he wants to help his sisters with a new startup, but it's difficult because of other financial responsibilities.

Aryan advised, "Take it from me, and feel free to return whenever you're ready. There's no deadline."

Calmly, Akash expresses, "It's a great feeling to achieve something rather than receiving a gift, but you asking means a lot to me."

Aryan proposed to Akash to choose an insurance plan to cover a wide range of things, and Akash agreed, bringing the day to a close. Yashmita, who was still angry with him, was leaving. He quickly grabbed a rose from the garden and dropped it in her car. They shared a passionate kiss to make up for his sudden departure. As she left, she handed a small gift to Aryan.

19
Chapter Nineteen

Aryan, upon leaving, found an empty office and searched Tanisha's room for evidence she had against him. Suddenly, the lights were turned off, causing Aryan to feel scared. He quickly tried to turn them back on, but she stopped him, pulling him closer. He realized her presence was not what he expected. They shared a long, passionate kiss, and she confessed, "I missed you so much."

He saw his angel complain, but he still fulfilled all her desires. Upon waking, he realizes he is alone and has one hour before everyone visits the office, so he opens Tanisha's system. Realizing that all his video clips were encrypted and synced, he immediately called Anshika, an IT specialist, and Yogesh, who has extensive network access in the city, seeking their help to decrypt the files. While collaborating over a call, he inserts a drive to fetch Tanisha's IP address and infrastructure details, but suddenly Tanisha steps in.

She saw Aryan changing the insurance details. She glanced at him as he handed her the modified points and was about to leave quietly. Suddenly, she spoke up, "I like your antique recorder, its rare."

Aryan replied happily, saying it's the most precious gift he's ever received. Tanisha called Yashmita about the modified points and realized it was time to make the changes.

At noon, Aryan meets Yogesh and Anshika at a café, but soon notices that Yogesh is upset. Yogesh asks, "What are you trying to accomplish? Decoding the secure domain is not a game. If it's breached, everyone will suffer because of your foolishness."

Aryan stated, "I need those crucial details of mine, no matter what."

Yogesh's annoyance, and Aryan's rigid stance, caught Anshika's attention. She stepped in and proposed, "Why don't we decode it within the company? That way, no one can track us."

Yogesh still didn't agree as Anshika pressed on, her words filled with confidence. "Even if Aryan tries to distract her, I have my brother Akash who can get me into the company and allow me to decode her system effortlessly." Seeing Anshika confidently, Yogesh agreed with a nod.

Aryan, having submitted the modified points, worked on Yashmita's project with Akash. Akash provided ideas and support, which he often transformed into profitable points, ultimately leading to the near-completion of the project.

During his spare time, Aryan frequently visits Yogesh's home, immersing himself in the warm atmosphere of his family. It is during these visits that Aryan learns about his aunt's dreams and desires, which she gradually unveils to him. Of all her aspirations, two stand out as top priorities. Firstly, she longs to witness Yogesh's marriage, or if possible, an engagement would suffice. Secondly, she hopes to allocate some time and property to Yogesh.

She accidentally reveals that she has little time left, which Aryan ignores, "Your wish will soon come true as he has developed feelings for a girl we will meet soon."

Aryan went to Akash's home, where Yogesh and Anshika are decoding, while Aryan was amazed by his sweet home. Akash happily shows Aryan, indirectly revealing his loan on the house, which prevented him from supporting his sister's start-up. Aryan learns about Akash's weak finances. Then, he glanced at Yogesh, who also ended up running out of money. In the end, he remembered the old man's situation, who barely manages to meet his needs. This thought brings him a sense of calm, knowing that he has already submitted the modified points, which, when implemented, will benefit everyone.

Akash asked Aryan, "I attempted to choose the new plan, but it doesn't cover half of the expenses."

Aryan, frustrated by the different limit set in the insurance plan, storms into the CEO's cabin demanding an explanation. "I noticed that there are different limits set in the insurance plan, but they hardly make any difference."

Tanisha replied, "Your plan didn't seem profitable, so I incorporated my suggestions into it."

Aryan, feeling hopeless, shared his thoughts with Angel, who suggested that a trusted firm like DIVINE could modify the plan easily. Aryan discovered a clue about a modified policy that hasn't been released yet, so he asked Akash for a temporary access card in his name, which Akash quickly gave him. Now Aryan waits.

During the release of new insurance points, Tanisha visits to present the changed plan while Aryan, aware that no one is in the building, disables all cameras and alarm systems. Handing over his temporary card to Anshika, he watched as Anshika entered TRUST and started the process of installing the exception drive in the server room, connecting it solely to Tanisha's system.

During the meeting, Tanisha logged into her account, completely unaware that Anshika was meticulously copying the IP address of her system to ensure there would be no evidence of external login during her attempt to hack into Tanisha's system. Upon entering, she bided her time, anticipating Tanisha's imminent plan release. However, Anshika swiftly overturned all of Tanisha's predetermined limits and replaced them with Aryan's preferred boundaries.

Tanisha released her plan and noticed the overexcitement of the surrounding people, causing her to turn and look. However, she realized that the situation had changed beyond her expectations, so she immediately contacted her PA. Unfortunately, her PA was also clueless about what was happening. Aryan music played in the background, captivating him and drawing others to join. The music vibes took over the crowd, leaving her unable to do anything else.

With anger in her eyes, Tanisha stormed into TRUST and began searching for Aryan, who was shamelessly kissing Yashmita. Witnessing the scene, Tanisha quietly walked away. Feeling a sense of immense gratitude, Aryan wrapped his arms around Yashmita, the weight of the day lifting off his shoulders as he whispered, "You saved me today."

Yashmita stops him abruptly, making Aryan uncomfortable with her apparent interest in him. He feels trapped until Akash shows up, announcing his investment in the plan.

Witnessing Aryan in a messy situation, Akash wanted to leave. Aryan stopped him and said, "I'm happy you can now invest in your sister's start-up."

Akash replied, "I wish everything would fall into place just as planned."

Yashmita went to the CEO, expressing her frustration, "You don't understand how much he uplifts my spirits, and then you came and ruined my mood. Anyway, I'm leaving."

Tanisha said, "Being physical differs completely from being romantic. I swear he never proposed to you or even gave you a chance to express your feelings for him." listening to which Yashmita seems angry and left silently.

20
Chapter Twenty

Aryan leaves for a restaurant to meet Akash and Yogesh's family. After a small celebration, Akash surprises his sisters by offering to invest in their start-up. Everyone blesses him, but his sisters decline the help, stating that they will find a different solution this time as Akash has already done so much for them.

Anshika leaves for fresh air, followed by Yogesh who is disturbed. This time, Anshika talks about her dreams while Yogesh listens silently.

One day, Yogesh offers Anshika a lift from the fashion workshop, and later shows her a promising place for her startup. As she struggled to come up with a response, he unexpectedly presented her with 5 lakhs rupees, explaining that it was a gift from his mother.

Anshika expressed her amazement as she hugged him, and he reciprocated the embrace. Anshika proposed a fair division of the money between the sister, mother, and herself before accepting it, and Yogesh agreed, leading to the booking of the spot.

Tanisha is searching for the person, reviewing each recording as who changed the policy limit. She discovered that the recording stopped during a specific time when her account was accessed. Upon seeing this, she was confused as the newly set limits were also different from the Aryan's proposed points. Angel angrily approaches Aryan and asks if he changed the policy limit.

Seeing her angry, Aryan turns off the lights and reveals the gift he prepared, leaving her speechless as she kisses him instead of asking a question. By giving her a gift, Aryan managed to avoid her anger and kept the truth hidden.

The next day, Anshika was busy preparing the blueprint and stock list for her startup when Aryan walked in and asked why she changed the set limit from his.

She casually replied that if we released your set limit, anyone can easily blame you for this mess, since you've already revealed your plan. However, Tanisha won't approve it because she's jealous of you. Aryan, who appeared happy and on the verge of hugging her, abruptly stops upon thinking about Yogesh. He was about to leave when she asked, "How did you find out about this place? I never told anyone."

Aryan was thinking for answer when Anshika suggested, "Yogesh, he might have informed you, but either way, please take this file and ask him to locate the vendor and sponsor for this project." Aryan silently accepted the file and was about to leave when she made one request: "Aryan, please keep this a secret, even from my brother, until I have everything prepared."

Aryan noticed Yashmita rushing and not allowing him to get out of the car, asking for a ride to her workplace, which Aryan couldn't refuse. Upon arriving at the site, he immediately began working while Yashmita discreetly examined his belongings. She stumbled upon Anshika's diary and became envious, assuming he was involved with other girls.

Filled with anger, she was about to leave when she noticed Aryan looking lost and he, out of the blue, asked her to join him for lunch. While at the restaurant, she notices his unusual smile and eventually asks why he is so happy.

Aryan replied, expressing how Anshika gave him a precious feeling today, something he had never experienced before. listening which Yashmita seems angry until he revealed, "she made me feel what having a sister feels like and when she asked me for a little thing then I feel like she was asking from her brother. With gentle care, he held her hand and asked, Will you help me in giving her a surprise?"

Upon hearing Aryan's wish, Yashmita, who was previously going to throw away Anshika's diary, decides to keep it and they both leave for work. While alone, Yashmita deeply examines her work and is astonished by her fashion crafts. She seeks Tanisha's help to book a large stock and waits.

While working on site, Aryan noticed a loaded truck arrive. Upon seeing the stocks, he realized the wrong item had been delivered. Just as he was about to leave, he noticed Yashmita handing Anshika's diary. Surprised to see the same stock, Aryan held her tightly and said, "You've truly made my wish come true."

He kissed her forehead before leaving to shift the stocks, leaving Yashmita shocked as she had never felt his care before, which proved Tanisha's prediction wrong for him.

Aryan is aware that Anshika won't easily accept the stocks, so he must find a solution. While contemplating, he notices a news headline about his music going viral on the internet, which he had composed for an old man's celebration. Since he didn't know how to stop it, he asked Yogesh to find a way.

Panicked, he waits for it to stop while Yogesh just left, and Urvashi angrily walks towards him. Before she could say anything, he receives a text from a secret friend - it's stopped. He immediately switches on the news after reading and sees nothing. Urvashi took the remote and changed channels, but found no news about that night. Aryan affirmed, "I promised you I wouldn't involve your name."

While she was calm and about to apologize, he suddenly took her hand and said, "I need your help with something. Please don't refuse." She couldn't refuse him when she looked into his eyes, but at the storage center, while inspecting the stocks she had to deliver, Urvashi stated, "I need to see a sample of her work first before I can proceed."

He hurriedly left, heading to a meeting with Anshika. He tasked her with preparing three dresses for her first assignment, and she agreed.

A few days later, Aryan contacted Urvashi to meet in secret. When Urvashi arrived at the location, she saw Aryan searching for Mayra, but couldn't locate her. Aryan asked, "I want Mayra." Upon seeing his seriousness, she directed the staff to bring her. Aryan handed Mayra a package when she arrived and told her to get ready. A while later, Urvashi walks out in a well-wishing dress and Aryan can't take his eyes off her. Without hesitation, he pulls her close and admires her from head to toe, leaving Urvashi unable to resist.

Aryan suddenly approaches Mayra, who appears angelic, and they share a joyful moment together. While taking a picture of Mayra and Aryan, Urvashi appeared emotional. Aryan lovingly comforted her, wiping away her tears and embracing her. They both cherished the special moment they shared. He played his recorded composition, and they enjoyed it. When departing, Urvashi mentioned her plans to meet Anshika and finalize the agreement.

Aryan, who still has a package remaining, waits for Yashmita to arrive. He had also handed her the package, asking her to get ready. She sees herself in a well-wishing dress and predicts that Aryan might propose to her. She moves out, and upon seeing her, Aryan holds her. He says it's a small gift for supporting his sister, and she prepared it specifically for her. She loses all hope, and with a fake smile, she leaves.

When Aryan was leaving, he noticed one remaining package. The last dress in the package was completely distinct from the others. He called someone to meet him and dimmed all the lights while waiting. At last, his angel arrived and he took her straight to the dressing room. When they were alone, he wanted to kiss her, but she refused.

Aryan, seeing her ignorance, appears wild as he unzips her dress from behind while holding both her hands. Eventually, Aryan pulled out the last dress and made her put it on, then he ignited a lighter and observed her from toe to head. Unable to control himself, he pressed his lips against hers in the darkness. But when he was about to make love to her, she suddenly stops him and slips away without a word. In anger, Aryan exits the spot.

Tanisha goes straight to the shower after reaching the palace, and as she comes out, she sits still, reminiscing the moment she was leaving and saw Angel leaving in a hurry. Tanisha appears suspicious and abruptly assigned her a task to complete. While being busy, Angel left her phone open and Tanisha came across Aryan's text about a meeting.

Upon arriving, she appears to be trapped with him in a intimate moment, but the marks won't impact her; instead, she seems shocked, suspecting that Angel could be the one who aided Aryan and leaked the policy. She thought she was going crazy until she saw Mayra wearing a lovely dress, which reassured her and allowed her to fall asleep.

21

Chapter Twenty One

The following day, Tanisha, suspicious, revoked all access to Angel's account, even for her personal assistant. Aryan, being disturbed, noticed Angel in front of him, but he ignored her and focus on his work. He works all day without looking at his Angel, so she pulls him into a dark room.

Aryan prevents her from taking any action and asks why she left him alone last night. She apologized, saying she couldn't come last day because of being stuck with some work. Aryan seems shocked and silently leaves, wondering who he unknowingly gifted the dress to. He tried to remember her, but stopped when he realized she was his secret girl.

Tanisha spotted Aryan and left, seemingly annoyed. Urvashi, who had promised, arrived with Mayra at Anshika's workshop, where Mayra was still wearing her dress. Mayra received care from Anshika, and Urvashi asked if Anshika had prepared a dress for her daughter.

She replied, yes!

Urvashi calmly states her demands, saying, "I liked your work, so I chose to invest in it. You need to get ready an enormous collection of dresses. I'll handle the expenses and we'll split the profit 50-50."

Not knowing anything about the business deal, she called Yogesh, who read the agreement and agreed since it was profitable for all. But Urvashi deny signing the deal. Upon seeing Urvashi's refusal to sign the deal, Yogesh directly asked, "If you won't sign, how can we trust you?"

She instructed workers to unload the stocks, stating that she would give them workshop stock in advance and sign the contract on release day, when the product will also be launched.

Until then, we'll execute an alternative consent agreement. "I, Urvashi, agreed to work with you, willingly investing all my money in production that will not be sold until a treaty is signed between the two parties."

The Urvashi sign was already present, and now it only needs the consent of two girls. After seeing the deal and the stock in the workshop, both girls finally signed their first deal.

Yogesh then departs, carrying evidence of the transaction, and asks Aryan, "I don't know how long you can evade this, but one day she will find out that everything was your doing. What will you do then?"

Aryan responded nonchalantly, saying, "By that time, she will be wealthy enough to provide for her family. Meanwhile, we'll have another project to focus on - your love story. I don't want my aunt to wait any longer to meet her future daughter-in-law."

Yogesh smiles and says, "We'll definitely do it, but let's finish this work first."

Aryan arrived at the office and witnessed everyone in a state of panic because of the policy that benefits citizens but burdens the company financially. Aryan reviewed the list of those in need that the TRUST covers, including the elderly, uneducated youth, infants, malnourished individuals, and more. However, the company has limited stock remaining, so someone must distribute carefully it to avoid tarnishing their reputation.

Aryan witnesses an emergency where nobody attempts to help, so he quietly drives the heavy truck. Despite everyone's attempts to stop him, he refuses to listen and drives recklessly. As he arrived, he noticed numerous individuals waiting in front, and he distributed his limited stock until it ran out. Upon seeing the remaining crowd, he smiled and expressed gratitude for his ability to fulfill people's needs.

More loaded trucks arrived with abundant stock. Even after the delivery, there is still more stock left. He decided not to stop there and is now leading a convoy of trucks to rural areas covered by the TRUST. Aryan alone is delivering 6 months' worth of stock in just one day, later assisted by TRUST employees and the police force.

Finally, everyone goes back to the office where Tanisha and the seniors were waiting, except for Aryan. Annoyed, Tanisha asks Angel and Yashmita to find his location. She drives the car herself and eventually stops, seeing Aryan having dinner with a homeless person. Tanisha appeared lost amidst everyone's smiles and excitement until a little girl handed her a package, saying it's both delicious and plentiful, something they had never experienced before.

While she opened the package and saw the fine-grained food, she became emotional. She couldn't believe she had done something like this before. The little girl then took her to where Aryan was, and when Tanisha saw him, he brought her in front of the crowd, saying, "Finally, we have our organizer who silently manages everything, but today she's joined us all."

Upon his greeting, everyone paid homage to her for her supportive actions. Tanisha appears relaxed as she joins everyone for dinner, seeing them happy.

While Tanisha was leaving silently after dining, Aryan stops her and gives her a package with a smile, saying it's for Mayra from him. Upon seeing his smile, she questioned the ease of him giving away credit to someone like her.

Aryan responded by saying that being rich is insufficient without having a compassionate heart. He then held her hand and added that the experience he had today was priceless, surpassing any amount of money or pleasure. One of his friends had asked him if having a big company like DIVINE made anything possible, which he now realizes is true based on his recent encounter. When he addressed Angel's suggestion, Tanisha appeared annoyed, withdrew her hand, and left, while Aryan had not yet finished his composition after dinner.

22
Chapter Twenty Two

The next day, TRUST support dominated all news outlets, breaking a record. Everyone remains silent until Aryan steps in, then they all hug him at once. Aryan stands there silently, cherishing the feeling. Suddenly, the entire crowd clears a path for Mayra. When she reached, Tanisha took Mayra away, cautioning to stay away from her as she's still not safe near Aryan.

Despite her ruining everyone's mood, Aryan ignores her and silently heads to Yashmita's work site. He's been working all day, not going to TRUST for a few days, and staying at the work site. One day, Anshika visits the office to meet Akash, but she can't find Aryan and texts him.

After a while, Aryan calmly visits the office meeting with Anshika in the cafeteria. Suddenly, Yashmita arrives angrily and asks where he has been for the past few days, stating that she has been waiting for him.

Disregarding what she said, he welcomed Anshika with Yashmita, mentioning that she was the first to appreciate and recommend your work to Mayra Foundation. Yashmita is amazed after finally meeting her so-called sister, and Aryan suggests she take Anshika as an intern in her project due to her untapped potential, to which Yashmita agrees and offers her temporary access.

Aryan works at both the work site and TRUST, getting along with every staff member like a friend. They often make jokes and seem joyful. Aryan also organizes parties at random places in his spare time, making it difficult for Tanisha to verify the spy who helped him. One day, Tanisha saw Anshika working alone on the Yashmita project and greeted her herself.

Upon finally meeting Tanisha, Anshika realizes she knows nothing about her and greets her formally. After that day, Tanisha notices Anshika is always busy with work and only contacts one person: Akash. Tanisha eventually discovers that Anshika is Akash's sister. Tanisha trusts Akash and offered her sister to work on their project because she finds him trustworthy. Anshika keeps her distance from Yashmita because of their history. Aryan manages Yashmita by focusing his attention on her only.

When Anshika moved to Tanisha's cabin one day, she observed Tanisha seemed anxious and was completely engrossed in her phone. When the phone rings, she refrains from picking it up, as if she's fearful. Anshika puts the call on speaker. Angrily, a man shouted, "Despite my warning not to get involved in our family matters, you still refuse to listen. Now, because of you, my daughter's marriage is in jeopardy, and you're the only one who is going to save it."

Despite Tanisha's silence, Anshika responds, "She's currently unavailable, but I'll make sure she reaches out to you once she's back."

Tanisha quietly exits, accidentally colliding with a person carrying items, who turns out to be Aryan. His tablet, files, and other belongings scatter, but he manages to save his antique recorder. In a fit of rage, he instinctively grabs the person's neck without identifying them, causing fear among onlookers. Tanisha, frozen in shock, witnesses his loss of composure over Yashmita's gift.

Aryan, upon regaining consciousness, gradually releases his grip and begins to leave, but stops when he realizes he is surrounded by her guards. He quickly turns back and apologizes without making eye contact. "You're completely out of all business from now on," she said, and then she left, mentioning her intention to start legal proceedings. Aryan, who had just become the favorite of all, suddenly turns against them, leaving him alone in the office; only Yashmita remains, holding his hand and leading him past the guards.

Aryan was silent and lost in thought, focusing on his hand, when Yashmita interrupted and asked that he usually doesn't do unusual things like what happened today.

"I don't know how it happened," Aryan replied. Since Aryan doesn't want to talk, she left him alone to calm down.

The next day, everyone arrived and saw that Aryan hadn't left and was still at his desk. Tanisha arrived and her guards surrounded him, asking him to leave. he moves closer to her and said, "I am sorry for the incident, but I'll pay you up for my act."

Aryan burst into laughter when he saw her ordering the police and lawyer to start the legal process. Despite shocking everyone, he remained fearless and declared, "I will uphold my promise and never abandon TRUST. If you doubt me, feel free to test your luck."

The legal and police authorities from the DIVINE group arrived at the scene, ready for Tanisha to begin the legal procedure. Tanisha, though defeated, refuses to retreat and confronts him by pointing a gun angrily.

Aryan reminded Tanisha to think twice before taking any action, as the law regulates everything for those working in the DIVINE group.

Yashmita and Urvashi reached the location where Urvashi calmly persuades her to lower the gun. seeing Yashmita with Aryan, Tanisha finds a way to screw him saying, "you are right, everything and everyone works for you but not in TRUST."

She instructed her lawyer to issue a legal notice to Aryan, explicitly stating, "Aryan openly threatened Tanisha, the CEO of TRUST, with his influence. If any harm befalls Tanisha, Aryan will be solely accountable."

With a pen in hand, she signed the notice and requested Anshika and Akash to do the same as witnesses. Aryan appeared frantic, while both of them displayed unease, their eyes fixed on Aryan as if they were coerced into this situation. Observing this, Aryan grabbed the papers and questioned, "Why involve innocent employees in a deal that is between you and me?"

Tanisha replied in a calm tone, "I will choose any strategy or tactic that will lead me to victory. I have learned this important lesson directly from the CEO of the DIVINE group."

Aryan was on the verge of tearing the papers, exclaiming, "This isn't fair, and I won't allow you to do this." Tanisha, cold-hearted, responded, "It's your choice, either them or you. But think carefully before acting." Repeating her words, Tanisha waited for Aryan, who contemplated Akash's financial situation and Anshika's dream project. Finally, he smiled and remarked, "Being wealthy isn't sufficient if you lack compassion." With a smile, he signed the deal and handed it to Tanisha.

Out of nowhere, Yashmita snatched the papers, declaring they were unnecessary. She turned to Tanisha and said, "It's time to make the changes."

Tanisha halts the procedure, and then both Yashmita and Tanisha enter the meeting room. Yashmita walked out after a while and told everyone to leave because she convinced Tanisha not to pursue any legal action against him, causing both parties' legal representatives to leave.

Aryan wanted to congratulate Akash, but Akash angrily pushed him away, saying, "I don't want to be your friend anymore. Your presence only brings destruction and I have too many responsibilities that I can't be your friend." Before Akash could say anything more, Aryan said, "Farewell, brother. I will end this friendship myself" and walked away.

23

Chapter Twenty Three

Aryan won't come back to TRUST since that day until one day when employees arrived at the office and discovered a long line of young people registering for fixed and guaranteed scholarships. They all check the databases where drive information is posted at midnight to see if it's officially launched, then they get to work. After a while, Tanisha was shocked to find that 30% of the registrations had already been completed when she reached the office. She logged into the system and realized that she had only posted the details at midnight. Faced with no other option, she had to call Aryan back to the office.

Upon reaching the office, Aryan is greeted by a large crowd, who warmly welcomes him. He then takes the stage and announces an assured scholarship, backed by an official government notice, which will be conducted by the TRUST. Following this, many DIVINE staff members begin to work with the TRUST staff until everything was completed.

Along with his staff, he enters TRUST and notices everyone's annoyance. He greets them with a smile and praises their great plan, expressing his pride in being part of TRUST. No one agrees with him as he hasn't started the work, but Tanisha eventually accepts it before leaving without a word. Seeing her silent, he becomes curious about her strange behavior and visits a spot where Urvashi was already waiting, only to be yelled at by her, "Why did you call me here? What have you done to expose us?"

Aryan replied, "our work isn't completed yet, on which we agreed."

She replied, "I am not going to be a part of anything after this. or else with you, I also have to face the consequences."

As she was leaving, Aryan asked, "What if I can turn a lie into truth?"

Aryan asked if he launches the Mayra foundation and offers her a maximum share. Would she help him gather some details?

She agrees, but adds, "Even with all the details I've given you, you won't be able to solve the problem."

He listens without responding and then leaves, while Tanisha has already left to visit her uncle in her hometown. She found herself trapped in a palace after reaching a certain place, where all the wedding preparations were complete, but they couldn't proceed with the ceremony until Tanisha settled a large sum of money.

Tanisha, who was kept hostage by her uncle Gajendra, greeted her, "Welcome, now we have you. My daughter Nia's marriage can be fulfilled easily. Make yourself at home as you have to work a lot in your cousins' wedding."

He left her alone with other family members who despised her for past incidents. With no other option, she sought solace in Nia, who stood out from the rest. As soon as Nia saw her cousin, she welcomed her with open arms, bringing a glimmer of happiness. Together, they immersed themselves in the remaining tasks of the marriage ceremony.

As the groom's family arrived at the palace to discuss the requested price after the marriage, their expressions turned sour upon spotting Tanisha. To diffuse the situation, her uncle assured them she was present because of a promise made by his late father. He urged everyone to remain calm, emphasizing that they had all gathered there to find a resolution.

In the living room, where both families of the bride and groom were present, Tanisha made a decision. She said, "As my father promised, I will take full responsibility for the loss in his first business and will repay the invested amount to all of you."

Akhilesh, the groom's uncle, raised a minor concern by asking about the interest. He kept speaking despite the shock on everyone's faces, saying, "If we had put it in the bank, we would have earned interest. So, why not do the same?"

Despite many being convinced by his view, some remain loyal to their morals. This advice could potentially damage the relationship between the groom's family. Groom's father, Sanjay, rejected his brother's advice, stating, "We're not here to make a business deal. Your late father was our friend, so we won't be unjust in his absence. We only want the invested amount."

Akhilesh reluctantly agreed to his brother's words, and for a moment, it seemed like everything was settled. However, Tanisha's voice cut through the tension, saying, "I am ready to settle the full amount, but I don't have it all."

Sanjay's ears perked up as he asked, "What does it mean?"

Tanisha explained that she only had half of the amount in hand, promising to provide the rest after marriage once she received her profits from the investment. Upon hearing this, Akhilesh couldn't agree to her terms and retorted, "We demand the complete sum, or else there will be no wedding ceremony here."

Sanjay looked into Tanisha's eyes as he spoke, his voice filled with a mixture of trust and warning. "I can trust you because of my late friend," he said, "but if the full amount isn't settled, I will end this marriage on the day of the ceremony."

Akhilesh seemed annoyed as he cut off his elder brother, his voice sharp and impatient. "You're responsible for your share," he said, "but I'm not ready for it. It's either all or nothing."

Sanjay asked him to leave, which made him angry. He warned everyone not to let the marriage happen and then left. Afterward, both families agreed to Tanisha's terms and finalized a wedding date in 12 days. Before that, all the rituals and ceremonies will be carried out with the support of both families.

The ceremony was going smoothly until both families and a large crowd were trapped in the bride's palace because of Akhilesh's intervention. Sanjay and Gajendra joined forces to stop him, but Akhilesh has the backing of local leaders and hooligans, who nearly killed all the guards.

Witnessing the situation worsen, Tanisha finally gave up the TRUST for the sake of her late father's promise and prepared to leave the palace. Suddenly, a door swings open and armed guards, all of whom are Akhilesh's men, enter with gifts and decorations. Aryan follows, greeting everyone, and just as everyone asks questions, Akhilesh enters.

Sanjay at once points the gun at Aryan, who was standing before Akhilesh, saying, "one bullet and both of you down."

Aryan replied calmly, his voice resonating with assurance, "Uncle, we arrived here to commemorate, not to engage in conflict. I have also convinced my friend Akhilesh, who has come to surrender and will no longer disrupt the festivities."

Akhilesh admitted, "My greediness caused us significant loss and resulted in the deaths of the guards." Aryan broke the silence and proposed, "What if he compensates for all the losses?"

Sanjay observed every family that lost their men and asked for his shares, to which Aryan agreed on behalf of Akhilesh, surprising everyone. While handing over the shares, Aryan said, "Now, you will forgive and allow him to take part in the celebration as part of the family."

Sanjay asked Aryan how he managed to convince him.

Aryan cracks a joke, and everyone welcomes him except for Tanisha, who quietly leaves. Aryan, witnessing an Indian wedding for the first time, asks Sanjay if he can join them, to which everyone agrees. Aryan manages and learns Hindu rituals, often joking and spending time with his family, who now treats him like one of their own. One day, Aryan meets Nia, whom he admires.

Tanisha suddenly appears and whisks her away, questioning, "What were you doing there?" Nia responded, "We just countered and nothing happened."

Tanisha angrily replied that anything could happen because he's not good with girls and only exploits them, so it's better to keep your distance from him. Nia asked when she was leaving, saying, "He came here only for you."

Nia left Tanisha to ponder as she said, "Everyone knows he can't take his eyes off you, except for you."

On the day of the wedding, Aryan arranged a lavish celebration and gave each family member a pair of clothes as a gift. However, Tanisha refused the gift. At night, everyone gathered for a marriage ceremony, including local leaders and hooligans. Akhilesh became suspicious of them, but Aryan ignored his warning and enjoyed the ceremony.

A hooligan points gun at the marriage procession and on bride where local leader Manoj asked family, "you all enjoying celebration but I won't let it happen until I get revenge on you all."

Akhilesh asked, "What is this and what revenge are you talking about?"

Manoj's face turned red with anger as he exclaimed, "I paid a hefty sum and even lost my own men defending you, only for you to team up with this young man who offered you double what he asked for in exchange for his shares. I invested in those shares too, but now it's not about the money anymore. It's about trust. And I will take everything from all of you for betraying me."

Just as he was about to order to fire, more armed forces appeared and surrounded the entire palace. In the midst of it all, Aryan stepped forward and calmly asked, "Brother, I'm not sure about your expenses or revenge plans, but today, this marriage will take place. Whoever is present here must bless the couple and leave silently, as I have already promised everyone. However, my brother, you are spoiling the celebration now."

Manoj boldly aims his gun at him and declares, "You may be wealthy and able to purchase anything you desire, but you cannot stop me."

Aryan asked, "Who said I will?"

State ministers and the DM arrive and tell Manoj to hand over the weapon or else the CEO will be informed, resulting in dire consequences for all. Manoj drops his gun, after which Minister pleaded before Aryan saying, he knew nothing about you or about the DIVINE group. Hope you will end this here or everyone has to pay for his unforgivable sin.

Aryan's soothing voice brings a sense of calm as he says, "I don't enjoy trouble either, so please take your men and depart." Sanjay suddenly slapped Akhilesh and told him to leave and never come back, saying he wasn't invited anymore.

Then he approaches Aryan and asks, "Even though you're not part of our family, why do you support us?"

Aryan responded, "Because of Tanisha, she never abandons her employees or anyone in need. She also supports the DIVINE group when necessary. But when she needs help, who is there for her? So, I'm here to support her as instructed by the CEO of the DIVINE group."

Sanjay and Gajendra both say to Aryan, "You are like a son to us, and our family will never forget all that you have done for us." Aryan invites everyone to a marriage ceremony where he notices Tanisha in traditional attire for the first time. Aryan finally approaches her and compliments her, saying "you look well-wishing." He takes her picture without permission and then departs.

Tanisha, in the marriage ceremony, searched for her uncle Gajendra, who was engrossed in a conversation with Aryan. They were later joined by Sanjay, and all of them hurriedly left for the backside room. Tanisha left to see, but Nia asked her to stay with her. Eventually, Tanisha managed to reach the room and opened it.

Aryan was seen discussing documents with both uncles, but when Tanisha appeared, he quickly hid them. Tanisha invited everyone to join the ceremony, which is about to conclude, and both uncles left. Aryan was leaving when she closed the door, insisting that he was keeping something from her that she needed to know. She takes hold of the document concealed in his coat. Unexpectedly, he embraces her tightly and confesses, "You don't enjoy my touch, but it happens, and that's what I love the most." He takes the document and departs.

Following marriage, Tanisha is required to surrender the trust she had given to Gajendra, but Sanjay intervenes, claiming that Aryan has resolved everything between the families, rendering it unnecessary.

She recalls the moment when all three entered the room to discuss something, and that's when Aryan said, "Everything has already been sorted out in a secret meeting, just like you did with Yashmita."

In the backseat of the car,

Tanisha remembered of the meeting with Yashmita, where she angrily demanded an end to all deals with her and threatened to sue Aryan for his mistake. Yashmita responded, "I can increase the share from 50% to 70% if you protect Aryan from any legal action."

Tanisha agrees to the terms, acknowledging, "I can agree to your condition, but this will be the final opportunity. If this fails, I'll terminate the deal, and his career." She realizes and sees Aryan still holding her hand while resting. She attempts to free herself from his grip but then notices his peaceful sleep, which she couldn't disturb, so she lets him rest.

24
Chapter Twenty Four

Tanisha reaches the villa and immediately goes to her room to change. Then she heads to the hall area where she finds Aryan still there, playing with Mayra. She was about to yell at him until Urvashi showed up and asked Aryan how he got there.

Aryan responded, there is still one document I need to give to Tanisha as its TRU… Tanisha hesitantly mentioned that we need to submit the TRUST balance sheet for ITR, and she took the document to her room for safekeeping. When she turned, she noticed Aryan in her room and saw him admiring her.

Just as she was about to yell at him, he interrupts her by placing his hand on her lips "Let's keep quiet about where we've been.

He gently withdrew his hand while Urvashi intervened, saying, "Aryan, it will take some time to prepare food. It's best if you stay and join us for dinner." Aryan agreed and departed.

Tanisha's angry gaze was fixed on Aryan as he happily assisted Urvashi in placing dinner at the dining table with Mayra. Eventually, Aryan made a dessert, and they all sat down for dinner, but Tanisha made sure Aryan didn't go near Mayra. And also, she had made arrangements for her own meal. Urvashi attempted to persuade her by saying, "It's delicious, give it a try."

Tanisha responded, "I want nothing that he has done." With Mayra, she left the dining table, leaving Aryan and Urvashi. Aryan always ignores her rude behavior with a smile, which Urvashi notices and blesses him, saying, "She doesn't know what you've done for her, yet you still handle all her hatred with a smile."

He responded calmly, saying, "It doesn't matter until I have you and Mayra." After kissing her cheeks, he suddenly stopped and asked hesitantly, "I didn't mean to." Urvashi added, "Since it's typical for you to flirt with girls, you couldn't control yourself."

Urvashi holds his hand, grateful that he saved not only trust but also Mayra's future and indirectly Tanisha's life, as trust is her soul. Holding her hand, he declares that no one will ever come near her or Mayra as long as he's around. About to kiss her, he hesitated and pulled away, muttering, "I have a terrible track record with beautiful girls. We should keep our distance, or else Tanisha will surely have our heads."

Tanisha walks to the kitchen later at night, carrying a plate of sweets, and calmly sits with Mayra. Urvashi noticed Mayra enjoyed eating Aryan's sweets the most and remarked, "Maybe Aryan loves Mayra even more than us." Tanisha appeared annoyed while listening, but she stayed silent until she fed Mayra.

Urvashi attempted to take Mayra from Tanisha, who refused and stated, "Being in love is simple, but carrying its responsibilities is not." Urvashi was irritated by Tanisha's taunting about her marriage and Mayra's upbringing, making her contemplate revenge. Tanisha never approved of Urvashi being both his brother's girlfriend and wife.

When Tanisha arrived at the office the next day, she searched for Aryan, who hadn't come to the office but had instead gone to Yashmita's work site for a few days to avoid meeting Tanisha. One day, Aryan visited the office in the evening, took a few files, and was about to leave when he noticed Tanisha waiting for him.

She took the files to examine them and stated, "You must be in the office to access the details and work on any project."

"Did you miss me?" he playfully asked.

Seeing this, he stayed close and carried on, making her annoyed. "Are you jealous when I spend time with Yashmita instead of you?" She hands him back the details, saying not to come to TRUST anymore because everything he needs will be provided at the worksite.

Her departure brings him a sense of calm as she effortlessly falls into his trap. He walked directly to her cabin, reinserted the drive, and silently left when he finished decoding her new credentials. He waits outside the office every day, learning Tanisha's routine and knowing when and where she leaves for work, making it easier for him to execute his plan. However, one day Tanisha seems late for submitting her ITR. While being in the car, she notices that her car turns in the wrong direction and asks the driver to turn, but he ignores her.

Seeing Aryan, the driver, she looked deeply and angrily yelled, asking if he thought it was funny to turn, as it needed to be submitted today. Aryan turned up the speaker and sped away to escape her yelling. Out of nowhere, she yanked the emergency breaker, bringing the car to a halt, and hopped out to catch public transportation. Shortly after her, Aryan also sat beside her in the taxi, heading back to the office where they were stuck in traffic.

Aryan played his composition through a taxi speaker, and as people listened, they started to recognize the music that had been randomly released on the internet. This led to more and more people gathering to enjoy the music, even when the traffic signal turned green. She steps out and finds every road blocked by a large crowd enjoying music, while Aryan watches, amazed at others enjoying his music. He holds her hand, making her forget her stress.

She appeared lost when she witnessed his joy in others' happiness. As she was about to reach for his hand, a bullet was fired and missed. Aryan instantly grabbed Tanisha's hand, and they ran together. The bullets continued to be fired until they found a hiding spot. Seeing Tanisha's fear, he made her look into his eyes and said, "Don't fear. No matter what happens, stay hopeful. I'll protect you from any harm." saying this, he called for help.

Aryan's car suddenly arrived at their location. When they arrived, they saw Angel, who came to help, driving recklessly to get them out of the line of fire. She saved them and brings them directly to TRUST. Tanisha reached there and received a link from the stranger once more. Upon opening it, she saw a live view of a massive firing taking place at FAITH. She tries to leave in a hurry, but Aryan stops her even though she doesn't listen.

She was leaving for FAITH when she saw Aryan standing in her way, whom she ignored and accidentally bumped into, injuring him badly. Just as she was about to leave, DIVINE's force blocked her path. However, she continued and collided forcefully with their vehicle, causing damage to her car. Despite being injured, she still wants to leave, but Aryan stops her by bleeding hand. Tanisha yelled at him as her FAITH was destroyed, then she fell unconscious.

25

Chapter Twenty Five

Two days later, Tanisha wakes up suddenly, hearing a melodic tune playing from a nearby recorder. She examined the location, which wasn't a hospital or her villa. She felt strange and decided to leave. When she stepped out of her room, she was surprised to see a massive palace with an army of servants, guards, and doctors all prepared to serve one person, Tanisha. Rushing towards her, they all saw her awake, and she angrily stopped them, asking, "First, tell me where I am right now?"

"Daughter, you are currently in the CEO palace," one of the senior staff members told her. She appeared shocked and wanted to leave, but he insisted, "You can't go until we receive orders from Aryan." He instructed the doctor to administer another tranquilizer, causing her to fall asleep once more until her medication continued.

After finding out she was in the CEO palace, Tanisha couldn't handle it and attempted to leave again, but was stopped by a servant. One day, she hears the same melody and glances at Aryan's antique recorder, about to angrily throw it. Without warning, Aryan grasps her hand and takes a seat beside her, leaving her in silence and he departs.

Tanisha steps out at night to find Aryan waiting at the dining table. When she sits in front of him, it reminds him of the destruction of the FAITH, which throws everything into anger and makes her want to leave. Aryan tells her, "You're not going anywhere until I say so."

She yelled, her voice filled with frustration, "Why are you doing this? I am not your puppet to be controlled at your will."

Aryan held her hand gently, his voice soothing as he whispered, "You're a wounded princess, and I want to heal you."

Guiding her back to her room, he helped her lie down and positioned himself nearby. His phone suddenly rang, and he promptly picked it up. It was Urvashi, and he reassured her that she was fine and resting.

"Does she also know about my status?" Tanisha asked as she listened to their conversation. Aryan replied, "I haven't told her until now, as I informed her that we left for dealing with a big project."

"So," she asked, "how much longer do you plan to confine me in this cage?" Aryan replied, his voice filled with concern, "until you seem alright."

She seemed annoyed as she listened, her voice tinged with frustration as she asked, "Why do you insist on caring for me so much? I don't want any of your care or support." Listening this, Aryan departs in silence.

In the late night, while everyone slept, Tanisha suddenly woke up and took a walk around the palace. She stopped at a certain point and gazed at a portrait of a beautiful lady. She appears lost, only to hear the familiar melody emerge from the darkness. When she turns, she finds Aryan high on drugs, asking emotionally, "Doesn't she look pretty?"

I can't remember what she looks like anymore. Despite trying to walk, he kept going, saying, "She abandoned me to bear this suffering alone."

He fell and discovered that Tanisha supports him, so they end up in the same room. As she is about to leave, she notices his pain, and despite her intention to leave, she can't bring herself to go.

She finds herself in his arms as Aryan, feeling sleepy, gradually pulls her closer to him. Whispers filled the air as he held her gently, pleading, "Please don't abandon me in the darkness." She kissed

Aryan's forehead, assuring him that she was there. Aryan, awakened by a phone ring, immediately departs, having already granted all the servants the day off, making it clear for Tanisha to also leave.

As Aryan reached the investigation spot, he found Yogesh reviewing his car, which had been subjected to gunfire. Aryan questioned, "This is not what I had requested?" Witnessing Aryan's anger, he retorted, "I never made it to the location, confirming that the gunfire and devastation were all genuine, just as we intended to intimidate Tanisha."

Aryan's shocked expression revealed his disbelief as he exclaimed, "So you're saying we could have lost our lives if we hadn't run from that spot?" Yogesh replied, "yes"

Aryan left the spot in shock, his mind filled with thoughts of what could have happened to Tanisha on that day.

As Aryan reached the palace, he noticed Tanisha sitting alone on the front steps, patiently waiting for him. He approached her and asked, "Why didn't you leave, even when there was no one to stop you?"

"I never liked royal treatment," she replied calmly, her voice steady and composed. "But everything changed this morning, and now I find myself unwilling to leave. I'm still waiting for you to treat me with kindness."

Saying this, she leaves, and Aryan follows, entering a room where she sits calmly before a grand piano, patiently waiting. As she saw Aryan for the first time, he played a tune before her. Entranced by the melody, she seemed to be consumed by his pain, unable to bear it any longer. She had the urge to leave, but Aryan stopped her and asked for a dance.

As Tanisha danced to his tune, she caught a glimpse of his apologetic eyes, silently begging for forgiveness. She could easily read his eyes and said, "No need to regret anything from the past, just hope for the best."

She gently kissed his forehead, evoking strong emotions in him as he tightly held her, pleading, "Don't go today." When Tanisha hears his first wish, she feels loved. Aryan took her back to the room and, lying next to her, said, "I apologize for everything. Please forgive me," before falling asleep.

Tanisha watched as he apologized repeatedly, noticing his bandaged heart, a gesture reserved only for her. She felt guilty and wanted to apologize for everything she had done to him, prompting him to hold her tightly while she stayed close to his heart. Meanwhile, Yogesh, who was still investigating, discovered an unusual bullet. He immediately ordered a review of the nearby building's recordings and anxiously awaited the results.

Anshika hurriedly visited the spot where Yogesh was and saw Aryan's car in a terrible state. Hesitantly, she asked, "Is he okay?"

Noticing her fear, he reaches for her hand and assures her that he will track down the person who tried to seek revenge on their friend. Worried, Anshika called Aryan, and Tanisha overheard the conversation, realizing Anshika was also in contact with Aryan. She doesn't know it yet, but Aryan disconnected the call, which seemed to annoy her and make her leave Aryan's palace.

26
Chapter Twenty Six

Upon arriving at the office, everyone inquired about her health, but she ignored them and searched for Anshika, who was absent. She tracked Anshika's laptop location provided by the company and found her in a workshop filled with Yashmita company merchandise. To her surprise, she spotted Yogesh and Anshika together, leaving her confused. She left for her home without further thought.

When Aryan returned to the office after a few days, everyone seemed offended except for Yashmita, who hugged him and refused to let go for a long time. Aryan tried to calm her down as she expressed her possessiveness, yelling and cursing Tanisha for her actions.

He angrily silenced her and stormed off, demanding she stop speaking about her. He then left in anger. Upon seeing him favor Tanisha, she immediately went to her cabin and yelled, "What did you do to him that he's turning against me because of you?"

Calmly, she responded by asking why you invested heavily in a random stock that has no connection to your workplace, but rather belongs to Anshika workshop. Do you have an explanation for this?

Yashmita replied angrily, it's none of your business as I came to warn you not to remain close to Aryan or I will destroy you and your company. Upon leaving, Tanisha couldn't help but listen to her threat. However, instead of showing annoyance, she responded with a smile. "Who's about to collapse?" she asked. "You didn't realize who you were playing with."

Aryan, who left the office in anger, went straight to Yogesh's house. Upon reaching, he sat next to his aunt and remained silent. She noticed his tension and asked, "What's bothering you? This isn't like you."

Aryan admitted, "I unintentionally made a mistake, but it was never my intention." She casually replied, her voice carrying a hint of nonchalance, "If you feel you are wrong, just tell that person the truth. Let them decide what to do next. Doing so will release your stress."

Aryan hugged her tightly before preparing to depart, and she whispered, "Try to surprise her with something special; she won't be able to refuse."

Aryan purchased a small gift, its wrapper crinkling in his hand, before heading towards the TRUST office. Upon arrival, he found the office deserted, with everyone having already left for the day. Seeking solace, he quietly entered Tanisha's cabin, where he found her seated, her back turned towards him, lost in peaceful slumber.

Aryan, unable to meet her gaze, seeks solace in a place where he can confront his error. "I deeply regret everything," he confesses. "I never intended for any of this to come between us. I even contemplated the worst just to instill fear, but when it became reality, I realized I could have lost you. I apologize and am willing to do anything to make amends, even if it means you seeking revenge."

He closed his eyes, waiting for her forgiveness. Suddenly, her lips met his in a desperate kiss, surprising him. When he opened his eyes, he saw Yashmita kissing him, causing him to pull away and ask, "What are you doing here?"

She replied, "You apologize for everything and ask for anything I want, so I want you to marry me. I can't imagine my life without you." She held him tightly, leaving Aryan in shock, as he never expected this. Tense and on edge, he spotted Tanisha outside her cabin, winking at him with a mischievous smile. It was clear to him that Tanisha had orchestrated everything, leaving him trapped and unsure of how to proceed.

Yashmita caught a glimpse of Aryan in the mirror and sensed his reluctance through his silence. Meanwhile, Tanisha reached her villa and found Aryan waiting for her. He grabbed her with a furious expression, demanding, "What do you think you're doing?"

Tanisha counter questioned him, her voice filled with skepticism, "That's what I want to know, what goes through your mind when you're planning a fake threat for me that unexpectedly becomes real?" Realizing she had all the knowledge, he calmly attempted to explain, saying, "I didn't understand how it became true, but I didn't have any intention of doing it."

She replied, "I did."

Aryan seemed shocked as he let go of her hand, her grip on his collar tightening angrily. She continued, "Since the day you entered my life, everything has become worse, and you're the only one to blame. I can never forgive you as long as I live."

She gets her hand off and continued, "but somehow you proved to be profitable for me. I had already claimed insurance, which will compensate for all the losses you caused my company. After that, we are even."

He felt a pang of hurt for the first time, but then he smiled as he said, "the thought that I had wronged you tormented me, and I wanted to apologize." He handed her a gift and added, "You fooled me with your kindness, but little did I know my princess had no heart capable of feeling, not even a simple apology."

As he stood among the rustling leaves, his phone buzzed with an urgent text from Anshika, "its urgent."

He turns towards her workshop, his curiosity piqued. As he reached the entrance, he noticed the furrowed lines on her forehead and inquired, "Why do you seem so tense?"

Without uttering a word, Anshika silently handed him the hard drive, a triumphant smile on her face. He quickly checked to see if all his videos were there.

Continuing, she explained, "Every sight before you is the last remaining copy; everything else has been erased." Aryan, consumed by thoughts of revenge, was leaving silently until he abruptly halted and inquired, "How is Akash? Is he alright?"

She replied, "yes!"

Gratefully, he expressed, "I am truly thankful for everything you have done for me; this will forever be etched in my memory."

She holds him tight, her voice filled with concern, asking, "Are you okay?"

Aryan's eyes widened in amazement as he calmly uttered, "Yes!"

Yogesh arrived suddenly, feeling a sense of discomfort as he observed them being close. Aryan gets off her, exclaiming, "Finally, she made it!"

During the conversation, they departed for the bar, leaving Anshika alone. She seemed unsettled upon seeing Aryan irritated for the very first time.

Aryan, at the bar with Yogesh, disclosed that Tanisha orchestrated the actual firing on herself.

Yogesh appears shocked when he heard this. Aryan asks to halt the investigation and declares, "Anshika is my sister and always will be—I won't interfere in your love." With that said, he departs, leaving Yogesh to contemplate his promise, which seems to bring calm from Aryan's perspective.

Aryan finally visited Angel's house, immediately embracing her tightly. When he regained his composure, he said, "I trust you and only you." He then handed her the drive and said, "I trust you with this drive, and I'll only ask for it back when I really need it."

Urvashi received a sudden text from Aryan and was about to leave for a meeting when Tanisha stopped her, asking, "Where are you going this late?"

Urvashi reassured, "It's important, but don't worry, I'll come soon."

Tanisha, suspicious, checked Urvashi's mirrored phone that she had already mirrored. Tanisha appears irritated with the text while Urvashi, upon arriving, witnessed Aryan's employees dispatching the merchandise. She urgently asked everyone to stop when she saw Aryan didn't care, and she yelled, "You promised me you would actually bring the Mayra foundation to existance!"

Aryan stated that it's time for you to take over Mayra foundation since everything is already in place, but there's one thing he's waiting for that could hurt Tanisha the most. Urvashi finally had the opportunity to seek revenge and replied, "on Tanisha's birthday!"

Aryan provided significant manpower to Anshika for timely stock preparation, while Yogesh bypassed TRUST's firewall and security to redirect her site to the Mayra foundation portal. Shreya handles billing and shares studies with Tanisha regarding investments. Aryan then assisted the rest of the crew to complete the work ahead of schedule.

Tanisha spent time with Mayra, who later asked Urvashi about her meeting with Aryan.

Urvashi calmly responded, "As I mentioned before, he's the one who loves Mayra even more than us."

Excitedly, she shows Tanisha the gift; a pendant that Aryan had given to Mayra. Just as Tanisha was about to throw it, Urvashi stepped in, asserting, "You can't decide what's good or bad for my daughter."

Tanisha opposed when she saw her about to take Mayra, saying, "I always knew your love was for my brother's money, and today you've proven it."

Saying this, she takes Mayra along with her, leaving Urvashi annoyed. She muttered to herself, "If not today, then tomorrow. But one day, I will bring you down."

27
Chapter Twenty Seven

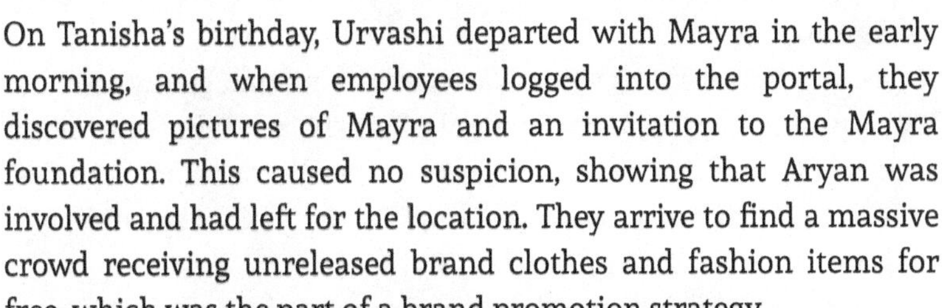

On Tanisha's birthday, Urvashi departed with Mayra in the early morning, and when employees logged into the portal, they discovered pictures of Mayra and an invitation to the Mayra foundation. This caused no suspicion, showing that Aryan was involved and had left for the location. They arrive to find a massive crowd receiving unreleased brand clothes and fashion items for free, which was the part of a brand promotion strategy.

People admired the high-quality fabric suitable for all ages. Everyone must wear new clothes for the cover page. Upon reaching the spot, Akash discovers that Urvashi has invested in the project, for which he expresses his gratitude.

She disclosed that Aryan was the one who persuaded her to invest in Anshika start-up, with Yashmita covering the stock expenses. Akash, after discovering this, thanked Aryan for his support and asked for an apology. Finding out which TRUST employees also said sorry to Aryan. Finally, the entire community and office staff appear prepared for the live broadcast.

It surprised Tanisha to find no one in the villa and try calling Urvashi, who doesn't answer. She angrily arrives at the office, only to find it empty. Out of nowhere, Yashmita collided with her, resulting in coffee spilling all over her. Before she could say anything, she swiftly offered her a spare dress to change into. When she comes back, she realizes she has also gone. Tanisha discovers

Mayra's foundation card on the desk and searches for it online, leading her to her own company portal page, which shocks her and prompts her to leave.

Upon arrival, she discovered that a complete fashion setup had been organized, with participation from every staff member, employee, and people from the local community. Upon seeing Mayra, she quickly took her and was about to leave, but the press stopped her, seeing her they thought her as a model.

Whenever she encounters different lighting, her dress color shifts because of the neon fabric. Suddenly, the light dimmed, casting a myriad of colors across the crowded space, where Aryan began dancing with each person to his music playing in the background.

As Mayra walked closer, Aryan reached out and gently took her hand, urging her to dance. Suddenly, Tanisha appeared and Aryan locked both her hands behind her back. They began dancing to a set tune that Aryan had prepared, saying, "Finally, you accepted my gift, making you look like a princess."

He sticks closer and stands still, mesmerized by her beauty while everyone captures her in their photographs. Suddenly, a blackout occurred, and when the lights came back on, all eyes were drawn to Tanisha's dress, which had transformed into a more exotic design.

when light drop off again, they were at back stage where Aryan suddenly turns Tanisha sticking to wall and kissed her back desperately, licking her all the way from back. he turns to her front and when she's about to slap him curtain opens. While on stage, she feels a sharp pain in her back, as if someone has cut her with a blade, bringing back memories of Aryan cutting her dress during the Lazor show, which now leaves a cut on her skin.

Finally, she saw the Mayra Foundation logo featuring Mayra's face as the company's emblem. Aryan heads to the piano to play a dedicated tune he prepared for the Mayra foundation, and as he plays, the projector displays an image of Mayra and the company's success. Tanisha seems lost and eventually wants to hold Mayra, but instead of Tanisha, Mayra walks towards Aryan, whom he holds with care.

She scanned the area and noticed that all the staff, office employees, locals, as well as Yashmita, Angel, Akash, and Yogesh's families, were present to support Aryan. Witnessing Aryan's revenge, she expressed her pain and openly declared, "Today, you took everything from me. I promise to gift you the same, where you'll have no one's support, just like you gifted me today."

Aryan ignores her words as he regains everyone's trust and finally blesses Tanisha, who always ends up gifting precious feelings that bring happiness to everyone. Yashmita kissed Aryan and pulled him into a dark room where they got intimate. Anshika saw them in a messy situation and stopped Angel and Urvashi from passing by.

Angel hears a strange voice and walks in to find Aryan getting close to Yashmita. She quietly leaves. Aryan notices her leaving and chases after her, but can't catch her. Urvashi, seeing him stressed, admires him and softly touches him, saying, "You always find yourself in interesting situations, which excites me even more."

Aryan, feeling tense, holds her by the waist and asks, "Do you know what I do when I get angry?"

He grabs her waist even harder, Urvashi who feels excited widens her neck whom he was about to kiss but stops seeing Mayra. He held Mayra and took her away. Urvashi, who was leaving with mixed feelings, was interrupted by Yashmita, who inquired, "Aren't you showing too much interest in him lately?"

While listening, Urvashi smiled and left without making a sound. Despite numerous attempts, Aryan couldn't reach Angel, so he entered Tanisha's cabin and searched her system for Angel's address before leaving.

Witnessing everything, Tanisha calls and warns, "he's coming, be prepared."

Aryan reached Angel's home, shrouded in darkness, causing him hesitation before finally entering. Out of nowhere, Tanisha, who was disguised as Angel, unexpectedly grabs him in the darkness, but he manages to hold her back and suddenly the lights come on, revealing the police who were there all along, making him glance at

Tanisha. Aryan tried to escape from Tanisha, who was holding him forcefully, but the police quickly apprehended him and separated him from her.

Aryan attempted to contact Yogesh, but Tanisha confiscated his phone and instructed to isolate him from all matters until she succeeds. As she was leaving, Aryan pleaded with her, "I have a responsibility to fulfill, and if you do this, it will have a ripple effect on many lives. I beg you, don't be the cause of anyone's destruction."

However, she refuses to listen to anything before he was taken away, where he finally said, "Keep my phone on, you will soon realize I am telling the truth" and he was taken away. Aryan's phone rings, and he sees Urvashi calling, but Tanisha switches off the phone and leaves.

28

Chapter Twenty Eight

Aryan has been missing for 3 days while Tanisha makes policy changes, ultimately reducing staff salaries and bonuses to compensate for the losses caused by Aryan. She caught sight of Urvashi leaving the villa in a rush, leading her to the hospital where she overheard a conversation between Urvashi and the doctor, where the doctor demanded more money for treatment.

Upon hearing this, she immediately blocked all of Urvashi's accounts. However, when attempting to make a payment, it failed. She contacted the bank, who informed her it was a technical issue that would be resolved soon. However, Urvashi persisted and approached Yashmita for help, but Yashmita disregarded her and began to walk away. Urvashi said, "I asked for this money because Aryan needs it urgently, and when he's not around, you're refusing to help. I'm warning you not to do anything that could harm him even more."

Yashmita's words were filled with anger as she demanded, "I'll give you whatever you want, but I need Aryan back first."

Tanisha noticed Urvashi's excessive worry and searched her belongings, where she discovered patient details that Urvashi had set aside along with Mayra foundation information. She delved deeper into the investigation and found out that Anshika, Ankita, and Sulochana were partners, but the remaining 50% was still a mystery. She instructed the legal officer to uncover the truth.

Meanwhile, an unknown notification appeared on the CEO's phone. Upon seeing a video of Aryan playing music and a link to his recent video and music releases, the CEO angrily broke the phone, halting all ongoing treatments in the USA. Aditya stopped him while he was leaving, but the CEO asked, "Where is my son?"

Aditya had no response, so the CEO commanded a search for his son's whereabouts.

A group of officers and a legal prosecutor abruptly enter TRUST and rush over to Tanisha. They inform her, "Keeping him away won't be easy anymore. We found out the CEO is looking for Aryan and is about to return to India."

Tanisha smiled and said, "Once this CEO takes over, my work will be complete. Release him." She posted a few more Aryan links and tagged the CEO in the newly created channel, waiting. Tanisha discovers Urvashi, who angrily breaks things and yells, "You intentionally trapped him, blocked my account, and did everything possible to hinder Aryan. Why?"

Tanisha replied calmly, her voice tinged with a hint of sadness, "He did blunders to me and to my company, but I remained passive until he attempted to take Mayra away from me, something I cannot tolerate even for a moment. And it's not just him; if anyone tries to take Mayra from me, I will sever all ties, regardless of who they are, even if it's you. No one will be spared."

Finally released from the trap, Aryan opened his eyes to find himself in an unfamiliar part of the city, isolated, with no means of communication or escape. He sought help from the people nearby and attempted to contact Yogesh, but his phone was switched off. Then he dialed Akash, but received no response. As he tried to call Yashmita, he realized he had forgotten her number. Before he could take any action, he noticed his staff had arrived and were bringing him back to the city.

Upon reaching the city, he goes directly to TRUST. Upon arrival, he sees Tanisha waiting, but before he can reach her, he is struck from behind. When he turns around, he realizes it's Akash. Akash was taken down by Aryan's staff just as Aryan was about to reach

Tanisha. Akash yelled from behind, calling Aryan a coward and a loser with no morals, accusing him of only thinking about himself. Aryan turned and ordered his men to step back, allowing Akash to be freed. Akash blindly attacked Aryan, who tried to stop him, until Anshika came between them to protect Aryan. Aryan hit Akash back, causing him to retreat.

Spiting out blood, Aryan said, "I will not see you as a friend anymore if you tried to protect Tanisha"

Akash disregarded warnings and made another attempt to assault Aryan. Uninterested in fighting, Aryan commanded his staff to subdue Akash, resulting in a rapid takedown. Seeing this, Anshika intervened by shoving Aryan away and going back to her brother.

Tanisha walked over to Aryan, displaying the recording of Anshika stealing information from her system. Finally, she handed him a copy of the FIR that Akash signed against Aryan, in order to safeguard Anshika from the fraud case. Aryan turned his gaze towards Anshika, who, while trying to help him, inadvertently damaged his brother's pride, leaving him in a state of confusion.

In a hurry, Urvashi arrived at the spot and, upon seeing Aryan, she exclaimed, "Yogesh!"

Yogesh, who was drunk, steps in along with the police force. Yogesh angrily hurled a wine bottle at Aryan, causing him to bleed profusely. Aryan struggled to regain his balance.

Yogesh shouted, "You called me brother, but brothers don't hide or lie." He then threw the medication papers at Aryan and questioned his authority to sign the consent form for his mother's treatment.

Aryan replied, "she's my mother as well."

While yelling, "she was my mother, and she had only one son," Yogesh hit him hard.

Aryan interrupts abruptly, asking in shock, "What do you mean?"

Aryan, filled with tension, glanced at Urvashi who remained silent. Eventually, Yogesh disclosed, "She's gone because of you. You paid for her expensive treatment, but they refused to continue without the remaining amount. When my mother last asked to see you, you weren't there." With these words, Yogesh aimed his gun at Aryan, who bravely redirected the gun from his head to his heart, challenging, "Go ahead, brother. Perhaps I can finally be free from this burden."

Yogesh walked away after skipping his gun, saying, "I can't punish you, but I hope you feel the same pain I'm going through." Aryan stayed silent and walked to a corner of the office like a lifeless body. After a moment of silence, he saw Urvashi and questioned, "I didn't do anything wrong, so how did all of this happen?"

She embraces Aryan, assuring him that everything will pass slowly. Aryan held her tightly, shedding tears for the very first time. Seeing Aryan with Urvashi, Yashmita's insecurities rise, and she finally makes a desperate call, declaring, "I must have Aryan, no matter what."

Tanisha suddenly grabbed her phone and asked, "What did you do?"

Yashmita responded, saying, "he's mine and mine alone."

Yashmita gave an unopened gift, saying, "Give this to Urvashi, as it will be her last gift from Aryan."

Tanisha finds Aryan lost in pain and suddenly recalls his last words echoing in her mind, "I plead with you, don't do this, don't be the cause of anyone's destruction."

Tanisha was leaving, but she couldn't shake his words from her mind, "keep my phone switched on, soon you will learn I am not a liar." Desperate to escape his hurtful words, she sprinted away, seeking solace in her secluded villa.

29
Chapter Twenty Nine

Urvashi, who empathized with Aryan's pain, finally kissed his forehead gently before departing in silence. As she left, she made a conscious effort not to glance back, determined to move forward. When she reached the villa, she locked herself inside and let her tears flow freely. Finally, when she reunited with Aryan, she seemed fixated on his touch, more concerned about his pain than her own. She then turned her gaze to her late husband's portrait, murmuring, "Living alone isn't easy; it takes courage, just as you left me all alone."

Tanisha sits alone, her mind filled with Aryan's words that weigh heavily on her conscience, reminding her of her role in Yogesh's mother's demise. Despite the warnings and pleas, she remained deaf to advice, leading to a catastrophic mistake as she sought revenge on Aryan, who, even in his own predicament, prioritized the lives of others. Tanisha's eyes begin to tear up as she ponders, with Mayra attempting to halt it. Tanisha held Mayra close and cried a lot.

Yogesh, sitting alone, asked his mother's portrait, "You promised you wouldn't leave until you saw your grandchildren. Why did you leave so soon?"

In the midst of his rage, he started breaking things, upset that he never got to introduce you to his favorite person. Anshika prevents him from breaking every portrait by holding him tightly. Yogesh holds her tightly, overwhelmed by her care, and finally breaks down crying. Anshika kissed Yogesh's lips to comfort him and took him to the room where he held onto her to ease his pain until he fell asleep.

During the funeral, Aryan was left behind as everyone gathered. Yogesh, remembering their bond as brothers, expressed his emotions and stormed off angrily. In the cabin, Tanisha witnessed Aryan holding a bouquet and saying, "This is the last gift I wanted to give my aunt on her final day, but I couldn't." He approached Tanisha and added, "I tried to warn you not to be the cause of someone's downfall."

She slapped him suddenly, and Aryan held her tightly, making eye contact. He asked, "You knew exactly what you did, and I will make sure to take everything from you."

"Even as you leave," she said, "I still have a hold on your nerves."

"I've already got my freedom," Aryan stated, smiling.

she replied, "you are wrong."

Aryan turns and hears Angel's voice saying, "you are wrong." saying this, she handed drive to Tanisha. Aryan's eyes widened in shock as he remembered his father's words, "The new CEO has many secrets, including one about her mysterious personal assistant that nobody knows about yet."

Aryan continued, "I always referred to you as an Angel, but I don't know your name."

she replied, "I am Cassandra."

With a smile, Aryan confessed, "I never realized I was flirting with Tanisha's secret PA." Tanisha and Cassandra both appear shocked by how he found out about this.

He approached Cassandra and said, "No one has hurt me as much as you have." As he spoke, he presented a gift and explained, "I went to your house to apologize, but you and your accomplice conspired against me, causing me to lose my aunt and my brother forever."

Cassandra still hasn't accepted the gift that he left on the desk and left, despite Tanisha saying, "you played well."

"Cassandra questioned, 'Do I meet your loyalty standards now that I have my feelings in check?'"

Tanisha replied, "You did."

Tanisha stopped her and reminded her, "You forgot your gift." She handed it to her and Cassandra left.

Despite Aryan's broken state and loss of support, Tanisha patiently waits for her special gift she planned for his birthday. Aryan, who is now alone and has nowhere to go, finally goes to Yashmita. Witnessing his brokenness and restlessness, she immediately led him to the room where he lay down and held her close until he fell asleep.

Yashmita stayed by his side until the day before his birthday and planned a special dinner for two where she indirectly proposed to him. However, Aryan, still lost, didn't understand her intention and thanked her for supporting him, which offended her. Despite this, she didn't react and silently wished him a happy birthday before leaving. Despite seeing her leave, Aryan knowingly ignores the marriage proposal, which leaves him feeling remorseful as he questions whether or not his actions were justified.

After thinking all night, Aryan decided to calmly make Yashmita understand and left for work. Upon arriving, he discovered she was leaving for TRUST, which he pursued. Upon arriving at the office, he discovers it adorned for a party, but no one is in sight. Suddenly, everyone appears, showering him with birthday wishes. Despite this, he continues to search for Yashmita, who eventually shows up and declares, "Finally, it's time to make you mine."

As he tried to explain, the CEO of CNH Limited suddenly appeared and said, "Son, you have impressed my daughter so much that it has compelled me to meet you and discuss future plans." Everyone remained silent as Aryan asked in shock, "Future planning?"

Yashmita steps in to explain "our marriage."

Seeing Aryan tense, the CEO calmly asked him, "Son, you seem pale. Did you not like what you heard?" Without warning, he grabbed Aryan by the neck from behind, his voice low and threatening. "Young man, think twice before you utter a word and consider who you're pleading to."

He asked this, quickly retracting his hand, and continued, "By the way, I found out it's your birthday today, and I've already promised her you'll get married." Aryan finally spoke, his voice filled with hesitation, "but I can't do it."

Asking which CEO laughed and said, "I named my daughter Yashmita, meaning always success, and after she was born, I never experienced failure." Unexpectedly, armed guards emerged from the crowd and surrounded Aryan. Upon seeing the guards and their logo, the CEO cautiously asked, "Son, you never mentioned your background?"

Just as Aryan was about to speak, armed forces intervene, witnessing the warm greeting between the CEO of DIVINE group and CNH CEO, who says, "old friend, it's been a while since we last met."

The CEO mentioned receiving a formal invitation to his nephew's wedding from Yashmita and expressed a desire to meet her.

Learning that Aryan is the CEO's nephew, he appears astonished and gestures for his daughter to come forward. The CEO complimented his daughter, saying she is beautiful and caring, someone anyone would want to marry, but his nephew Aryan cannot do so without his permission.

Her father inquired, "So, what's your decision?"

"I refuse it," the CEO replied.

The CNH CEO confronted the DIVINE CEO, asking if they were aware that their decision could lead to mistakes for their company.

The CEO calmly responded, "I don't believe anyone can accomplish that."

The CEO of CNH responded, "Hasn't your nephew already done it?" The CEO appears clueless while saying, "Your nephew has made false promises to my daughter, jeopardizing our partnership. To rectify the situation, you must agree to a marriage proposal, or else face the consequences."

I don't think doing this will benefit you, the CEO said while listening.

The CEO of CNH was perplexed with Yashmita's new project details, which showed that 70% is with TRUST and only 30% is with CNH limited. He appears irritated with Yashmita for making a pointless decision without consulting him. The CEO insisted, "We're at a stalemate. Either you end your partnership with DIVINE, causing us significant loss, which I will compensate through your daughter's new project, or we can put an end to everything here, with no one benefiting except for resentment and loss."

The CNH CEO agreed and said, "Goodbye, brother, but before we go, I want Aryan to apologize to my daughter." Aryan apologizes as Yashmita expresses anger, saying she wanted him but didn't expect him to be spineless and reliant on the opinions of others for life decisions. What kind of life does he lead?

CNH CEO takes Yashmita's hand and says, "We're leaving now" due to Aryan's silence and the potentially worsening situation.

Aryan thanks his father soon after they left, and the CEO stops showing him the list of payments made via projector-

- Shreya's education costs 10 lakhs, while the old man's family has a PF of 50 lakhs.
- TRUST has a relief stock of 1 CR and a fund of 10 CR.
- A policy initially valued at 25 CR increases to 100 CR.
- Medical treatment 75 lakhs,
- Mayra foundation has a budget of 3 CR.
- Nia will receive 3 CR cash and 0.01% of the partnership in DIVINE as written consent.

The CEO guards forcefully brought Yogesh and Akash's sister, along with his damaged car hidden in Yogesh's workshop. Aryan looked at his father, who held his blood-stained shirt, and said, "Son, your mistakes have consequences for everyone."

Aryan defends himself to the CEO, stating, "I only wanted to help and did nothing wrong."

The CEO shouted, "You can't make any decisions until you earn it. All you do is misuse my resources, name, and power, and I won't forgive you for this."

The CEO took his tablet, furrowing his brows as he reversed all the changes. Aryan, noticing this, asked, "What are you doing?"

The CEO responded, saying that I am taking back everything you gifted.

Aryan, who seems thoughtful of others, said, "I'll give up everything and do as you say, but please don't do this."

The CEO stops, instructing his staff to take everything from Aryan. Aryan gave everything he had, but when the CEO saw his belongings, he approached and took his antique recorder, saying, "Son, you've destroyed my trust and now you'll have to face the consequences."

The CEO's guards detained Aryan, who had angrily yelled at the CEO for breaking his recorder. The CEO stated it was payback for betraying his trust, and that Aryan had six months to repay the invested amount or face severe consequences.

30
Chapter Thirty

Finally, Tanisha arrived and discovered only the revealed information, realizing Nia was the DIVINE shareholder. Also, the promised amount was paid to the groom's family, seeing which she seems shocked thinking why he involves in her family matter?

She stumbled upon Aryan. As she saw his tear-filled eyes, she stood frozen. Hesitantly, he handed her the broken recorder. "Finally, you've won," he said, "as you've taken the last thing left of my late mother." He left Tanisha, who eventually discovered that the gift was from his mother, not Yashmita. She feels guilty about planning the worst birthday gift for Aryan, and her guilt led her to leave.

Urvashi attempted to call Aryan to wish him, but couldn't reach him. When Tanisha reached at the villa, Urvashi tried asking about Aryan, but Tanisha silently retreated to her room and locked herself in. Observing her distress, Urvashi gathered that something happened at the office, causing her to stop calling Aryan and wait.

The following day at the office, everyone arrived to find a massive cake in the hall area, and Aryan greeted them with a smile, inviting them to join his birthday celebration. They all appeared surprised and frequently asked about his health, but he ignored them. Finally, Aryan reached the CEO cabin where Urvashi was reviewing files. He gave her a fake smile, handed her a cake, and was about to leave in a rush when she asked, "You didn't let Mayra wish you?"

Aryan suddenly stops as Mayra hands him a gift, which he opens to find a recorder. He couldn't contain himself and tightly hugged Mayra for a moment. Urvashi appears emotional upon seeing this, and quietly leaves when Tanisha walks in. This time, Tanisha remains silent and calmly focuses on work while seeing Aryan close to Mayra.

Urvashi, witnessing Tanisha's coldness, expressed, "Maybe I am selfish, but I can at least empathize with someone's pain, which you disregard." Urvashi then left Mayra with Tanisha and departed, to which Tanisha showed no response.

It has been a few days since Aryan stopped getting along with people and enjoying himself. Cassandra attempted to approach but couldn't when she saw his cold-heartedness. Aryan, who always departs early and arrives late at night, finally made his way to the palace. On this particular day, Aditya awaited his arrival at the dinner table, and Aryan quietly joined him. Aditya noted the length of time since their last conversation, stating, "Son, it's been a long time since we talked."

Aryan and Aditya sit together in the hall, engaging in casual conversation. Eventually, Aditya presents a card from his wallet, expressing, "I may not be as wealthy as your father, but this is everything I have from the bottom of my heart. Please don't refuse." Aryan immediately hugs him.

When the CEO arrived, he found Aryan peacefully sleeping on the couch on Aditya's lap, which made him want to see his son, but Aditya stopped him and he left quietly. The CEO, sitting alone in the study hall, noticed Aditya looking upset and asked what was bothering him. Aditya responded, "Since childhood, I always saw Akash with a smile, but after that day, I haven't seen that smile again, and you're the reason for it."

With bated breath, he cautions the CEO, "Though I may not be his biological father, he is my son. If you harm him again, I will depart from this palace and from your life."

"Did you give him the new card?" the CEO asked."

Aditya replied, yes! and leaves angrily.

While Cassandra, who had been at Aryan's desk, searched through his belongings and discovered Tanisha's unpublished roadmap, she found herself torn between Tanisha's loyalty and Aryan's care. Ultimately, she decided to take the entire document and leave.

Everything was going well until Tanisha showed up one day. She had a scheme to unveil, but it didn't go as planned and she left the event disappointed. It has become a regular occurrence for her not to attract many attendees or investors for her project, yet she still holds out hope for the big project her team has been working on.

Cassandra went to the CEO's cabin to show that the project has been taken over by a random startup company. Tanisha appeared silent upon hearing this and later discovered that more projects had been taken over by various random startup companies. She appears suspicious because her team's project was the only one taken over. Cassandra logs into the DIVINE portal and discovers that they are all connected to each other, with DIVINE making a massive donation. Upon reviewing the recordings, it was discovered that Aryan often stays up late at night.

31

Chapter Thirty One

The next day, Aryan arrives at the office and discovers that all his access has been revoked and his work details are missing. He approaches the CEO and asks why his access was suddenly ceased.

Cassandra responded, "You've been moved to site work."

She silently handed over the project details and left. Tanisha initiates a significant project with 3 steps, exclusively assigning loyal employees. Cassandra, who wasn't included, questions Tanisha's doubts about her loyalty.

Tanisha gives her charge of the project, saying "Your duty is to protect my projects, which I can't risk after he found out who you are and what you mean to me, but he won't take any action until you divert his attention." Until then, I will assert my big project, which is most needed by TRUST.

Upon hearing this, Cassandra agrees to her project while Tanisha demands her loyalty one last time, stating "I want this project at any cost."

Cassandra monitors Aryan as he silently works and spends free time with the workers. Despite Cassandra's repeated efforts to approach him, he consistently ignores her as if she means nothing to him. One day, a loaded truck loses control and heads towards a worker. Cassandra stops it by closing the entrance gate. Out of nowhere, several vehicles suddenly trespassed and bumped into the blocked vehicle, causing it to move again. Aryan was about to get hurt, but Cassandra pushed him out of the way and got badly injured.

When Cassandra wakes up hours later, she realizes she is in the hospital. Aryan prevents her from getting up, saying, "You need rest. Please stay put."

She held his hand tightly as she saw him getting closer, whispering, "Please don't go until I fall asleep." He stayed by her side, patiently waiting for her to drift off. Eventually, she fell asleep, and Aryan, hoping to find specific files, quietly tried to unlock her phone but failed. Finally, he entered "Angel" and unlocked the files. Aryan searched for data but found nothing except their first meeting picture till now. He looks lost, then finds her saved notes, saying, "I listen to Aryan music that makes everyone feel special, but I want his special feeling that's only for me. Maybe not today, but one day my wish will come true." Reading which Aryan kept her phone aside and leaves silently.

Cassandra woke up one day to the sound of a familiar melody. She peeked out the window and saw musicians playing the tune just for her. She hears the entire staff and locals enjoying music as she leaves, and when she reaches the work site, a worker greets her and wishes her a speedy recovery. Then she walks to the back, where she finds Aryan teaching music notes to some young people, and a few musicians notice Cassandra, greet her, and then leave. Aryan was leaving too when she said, "You still care about me, even if you act like you don't." He left right after hearing that.

Aryan, being at work, remembers about the day Cassandra got hurt and started walking in a hurry to the neighborhood, looking for someone. He couldn't find him, so he stayed there until he does. Aryan continues searching for that person until one day, when the missing person's parents become seriously ill, whom Aryan takes to the hospital, but still he doesn't appear.

Tanisha's men secretly visit the hospital one day to see the patient and discuss their fees. Aryan, who was secretly following them, ultimately discovers Sonu as the culprit. Sonu is an undergraduate student whose fees are covered by the recently implemented policy. Aryan found him and grabbed his collar, taking him straight to TRUST and then to the CEO cabin. He asked Tanisha, "It took time, but I finally discovered that you were behind Cassandra's accident."

Tanisha calmly replied, "It wasn't intentional, but it happened." "Did you do it intentionally?" Cassandra asked from behind Aryan. Tanisha seems silent as Cassandra says, "I did everything to make you believe I am loyal, but you don't care for anyone."

Aryan clenched his fist around Sonu's neck, his voice filled with betrayal. "I supported you at every step, and this is how you repay me?" Tanisha responded, "It's because of your actions that someone else has to suffer."

Aryan appeared clueless when she finally confessed, "when you disappeared out of nowhere, he crossed the boundaries of the TRUST, and my men caught him and were handing him over to the police. However, he pleaded to meet you for his parent's treatment. Fortunately, you weren't present, so I covered his parent's medical expenses. In return, he agreed to do my work, but Cassandra rescued you that day. Otherwise, you could have been hospitalized."

Aryan told Sonu to leave and then accused Tanisha, "you possess no morals."

Tanisha tightly grips his collar, her voice filled with anger, "There's so much more I have planned, I'm far from finished." He angrily pulls her closer, ready to say something even worse, but abruptly halts, uttering, "Do your best to seek revenge, but in the end, you'll be the one defeated." Challenging her openly, he walks away.

Aryan noticed a strange shift in everyone's behavior as he left. Earlier, when he entered, they were working and appeared tense. Now, they were doing nothing and seemed oddly calm, but Aryan chose to ignore it and continued on his way. A few days later, when Aryan decided to leave the area, he discovered some documents on his desk that left him shocked.

Sonu asked, "is it helpful for you?"

Aryan stormed off angrily after seeing him, but Sonu pleaded, "If you're angry, direct it at me. I swear, I didn't do anything knowingly."

Aryan stopped and Sonu picked up the story, admitting, "I wasn't prepared for this job when my parents were kidnapped out of nowhere. They weren't sure about the job, so they injected me with drugs, leaving me completely powerless. When I discovered my mistake later, I approached Tanisha who betrayed me, but her associates prevented me from approaching her. On my way out, I managed to grab the documents she's been hiding from you. They have everything set up to make you stay away from TRUST so that they can easily execute their plan, which I won't allow."

Aryan responded, "After this, I'll see what needs to be done."

Despite knowing Tanisha's master plan, Aryan doesn't go against her. Until the project release day, everyone continues working. However, Tanisha once again fails to receive a positive response, leading to TRUST reviewing the backlogs. In the first stage, they implement worker input and strategies, but in the second stage, Tanisha's output worsens.

While Tanisha was thinking about her project, she received a notification on Aryan's open channel. A new playlist had been uploaded, which started trending. Tanisha, feeling annoyed, made a decision. Aryan arrives at the worksite only to discover the project has abruptly shut down, leaving the workers jobless and unpaid.

He walked straight to the CEO's cabin and asked, "What are you up to?"

Tanisha ignores as Aryan reviews the details; suddenly, he looks at it and hands it back, saying, "make changes to point 3, 4, and 9 or it won't be like the past 2 cases."

Tanisha ignored his suggestion and crushed the details, throwing them away. Tanisha appears stressed about the project after Aryan's departure and works tirelessly until the third stage release.

The grand event organized by Tanisha, attended by top businessmen, took a surprising turn when the DIVINE shareholder and a few start-up CEOs arrived. Instead of releasing the TRUST project, they launched DIVINE business strategies.

Tanisha was shocked to see that it was exactly the same as what she was yet to release, when suddenly a huge crowd arrived to present Mayra Foundation's new collection while performing to Aryan's playlist. The project, modified by TRUST, was presented and grabbed everyone's attention, even though she knew nothing about it, and investors ignored DIVINE strategies to invest in TRUST.

32

Chapter Thirty Two

Finally, Aryan arrived with Urvashi, who invested in his plan. Tanisha was leaving angrily when the CEO crew intervened. She quickly turns away, avoiding eye contact with the angry CEO who heads straight towards Aryan. Everyone had already invested in TRUST, but when Urvashi and Aryan distracted them with music, Tanisha quietly left while everyone focused on the CEO.

The CEO said, "You're a disappointment. I treated you like a son, but not anymore. My real son would do anything to make me win, unlike you. You betrayed my trust and gave my success to the TRUST without my approval."

Tanisha, who was on her way out, stops. The CEO asserted, "You may believe you took the success from DIVINE, but let me remind you that every step, every expense, and every investment you made all belongs to me." In anger, the CEO grabbed Aryan's collar while Aryan held Urvashi's hand, filled with fear. The CEO declared, "I will spare you today so you can see firsthand the collapse of everything you established. Make the most of your life until then."

The CEO and his crew departed, and then Tanisha took Urvashi's hand and brought her along. Aryan was left alone, only having locals who always supported him when he asked for help.

"Who gave you permission to get involved in the matter of TRUST?" Tanisha shouted at Urvashi.

She retorted, "Nobody talks to me in such a manner. And remember, if I hadn't intervened, you might have lost this project, all because of Aryan, who even defied the CEO for the sake of TRUST."

Tanisha's voice grew stern as she saw her taking the side of Aryan. "You won't be allowed to leave this villa," she declared. Upon the guard's arrival, Urvashi accused, "You're only doing this because your brother isn't here. If he were, you would never dare to treat me like this." Tanisha took Mayra away from her, saying, "He's always by my side, which you couldn't see."

Akash was about to leave TRUST when Aryan, holding him by the collar, angrily asks, "How could you do this?"

Akash retaliates by hitting Aryan, but this time Aryan refuses to back down and engages in a serious fight. Aryan, witnessing Akash's injury, decides to leave the fight. Akash confesses, "I did all this to seek revenge on you. I shared every TRUST-related detail under your name with Tanisha, who has already planned to harm you when she returns to TRUST. Finally, your story concludes here."

Akash cursed him and left, while Aryan, who is badly injured, walks to the CEO's cabin. He checks the recording details and discovers that Cassandra took all his information, which he had deleted along with the fighting incident. As he was leaving, he saw Tanisha in front, feeling dizzy. He held Tanisha for support and then passed out.

Aryan wakes up later and sees Tanisha's blood-stained dress. He starts to leave silently, but she says, "We have a lot to discuss." Upon hearing this, he turns around. She asked, "Who should I fire this time, you or Cassandra, for sharing details with DIVINE?"

Aryan responded, "I did it because you withheld everyone's salary, but in the end, you got what you wanted, so no one is leaving since you have no evidence."

Tanisha approached and cautioned, "I will take legal action against anyone who assisted you. It's best if you leave voluntarily, or I will press fraud charges against the entire team, including Urvashi. I won't back down."

Aryan, who couldn't risk anyone's job nor leave the organization, finally spoke after she handed in his resignation letter. He said, "I never wanted to be here, but somehow, I got along with the team, the needy people, and the company culture. Overall, I never liked you, but when I saw you stressed for the first time because of this project, I did what felt right."

While saying this, he tore the letter and continued, "I made a mistake, but I also saved TRUST, which provides food to people in need who are in danger because of me. The CEO won't stop until he recovers my investment, so I won't leave TRUST."

"You only prioritize yourself, so what is holding you back from abandoning TRUST?" Tanisha replied.

Aryan declared, "I'll stay until I discover my missing girl." Help me in finding her, or else I won't leave empty-handed.

Tanisha vividly recalls that night when she held Aryan closer, feeling his warmth against her. Tanisha deleted the saved video of Akash and Cassandra, which Aryan saved.

Aryan runs into Ankita while leaving, who dropped off Akash. He attempts to indirectly assist but is abruptly stopped by Anshika. She drags him aside and reminds him of the harm he has caused to those who have tried to help him, specifically mentioning Urvashi and Akash. Upon hearing this, Aryan returns to the CEO's cabin, only to find that Urvashi has already left. Subsequently, he heads towards her villa.

Upon arrival, he discovers Urvashi sitting calmly. Noticing Aryan's blood-stained shirt, she asks if everything is okay. Aryan paid no attention to what she said and asked if she was okay. Urvashi said "yes."

He quietly leaves, closing the door. Urvashi confirms to Tanisha that he has left without a doubt.

Tanisha, who was in a meeting, observed Akash's injury and easily deduced that he had been in a sudden accident. Tanisha asked him to take a break and remove his name from all projects. He tried to explain, but she ignored him and passed the responsibility to Cassandra for the new DIVINE project.

Despite Aryan's deteriorating relationships and emotional distress from past events, she assigned him most of the trusted and important work. Without seeing, he took the file from Cassandra and left.

Aryan tirelessly works day and night on the blueprints for the new project, yet still finds some missing points he tries to address by reviewing old files and the work of TRUST. In the record room, when Tanisha was already there, the lights suddenly went out, causing him to tightly hold her hand to prevent her from leaving. Tanisha, who takes pleasure in hurting him, refuses to leave even though she knows he's afraid of the dark, leading her to turn on a flashlight.

As he gets closer, he focuses solely on her. When the lights come back, Aryan quietly leaves while Tanisha examines her hand, which bears a painful mark that she ignores as she admires his work. Upon seeing it nearly finished, she departs, while Aryan, who works late at night, locks the file with the sole key and heads to the restaurant where he works part-time to pass the time. Aryan has made new friends who are all struggling to make a living, and through them, he learns about the problems and sacrifices of the middle class.

Aryan, who hasn't shared the blueprint yet, thoroughly examines it, adds a few more points, and then shares the details with the CEO before going to a restaurant. While working, Aryan notices his colleague Tejas pursuing his dream of writing lyrics in his free time, which reminds Aryan of his own past life where he could freely follow his music. However, those days are gone and Aryan quietly walks away.

When Tejas resumed his writing, he came across a pile of lyrics. He tried to find out who helped him but couldn't, so he went back to work. A few days have passed since Aryan noticed Tejas working on lyrics. They sat together and talked about their health. During their conversation, Tejas shared his wishes and responsibilities. He mentioned that he had to choose between pursuing his dreams or supporting his family. Aryan remained silent, unsure of what advice to give him.

Aryan, working at TRUST, glances at the calendar and realizes time is running out. He quickly starts preparing and eventually calls Anshika for some last-minute help, to which she agrees. Aryan then approaches the restaurant owner, seeking a grand celebration that will attract a lot of attention. However, the owner doesn't have sufficient funds to organize the event. Aryan comes up with a solution by offering Aditya's debit card to cover the expenses.

Finally, Aryan made his way to Tejas, eagerly asking for a chance to showcase his lyrics. The restaurant spread the word about a masquerade party through brochures and social media, drawing into a large crowd. Tejas warmly welcomed everyone, singing along with the talented music band that Aryan had organized to support him.

Aryan waits for a special guest in a growing crowd, finally spotting Anshika and Yogesh entering the party. Suddenly, the party transforms into a romantic theme, and Tejas sings Aryan's lyrics as everyone dances. Yogesh, who was focused on Anshika, abruptly stops dancing when he hears Aryan's music. Anshika notices and draws closer to him, while Aryan continues playing the tune from the background. Gradually, everyone clears the spot for the loving couple, who dance gracefully.

After finishing the dance, Anshika revealed a look of surprise on her face and exclaimed, "Happy birthday, Yogesh!" As Yogesh watched the preparation, a pang of emotion washed over him, reminding him of his mother who always took care of it for him. Anshika held his hand tightly, her gaze locked with his as she whispered, "I will always be there for you when you need me the most."

A large cake was soon brought out to celebrate, where everyone blessed Yogesh for a successful life and good health. Then, calmly sitting with Anshika, he found everything prepared to his liking as dinner was served.

He tasted the food, stopped the waiter, turned his side, and took off his mask. Upon seeing Aryan, he was about to yell but Anshika's hold stopped him. Calmly, he asked, "You played well organizing the best celebration. Everything was to my liking, and I had Anshika beside me whom I always loved. Until now, I believed it was all her doing and was really happy. But when I learned it was all your doing." He let go of Anshika's hand and said, "All I see is a liar who deceitfully took my mother, who was all I had."

Yogesh, in anger, destroyed everything that was prepared and then threw his cake at Aryan. Aryan was silently leaving, bearing all the insults, while Yogesh continued without stopping. Then, he turned to Anshika and expressed his feelings of being hurt by her taking Aryan's side over his own. He concluded by saying that she was not the girl he had always loved, and he could not accept that.

Anshika tried to stop him from leaving, but he angrily pushed her away. Aryan supported her and said to Yogesh, "You can't be a son or a lover." Yogesh takes off his coat when he hears this and notices Aryan standing beside Anshika. Before anyone can react, they engage in a serious fight. Aryan eventually stops, but Yogesh continues until he points a gun at Aryan, who manages to disarm him using a trick.

Yogesh pulls out another gun as Anshika steps in between, becoming a target for both. Yogesh refuses to lower his gun while Anshika pleads with Aryan to stop, and he agrees. Yogesh loads the gun upon seeing him leave, preparing to shoot. However, upon noticing Anshika standing in front of Aryan for protection, he cannot bring himself to do it. Frustrated, he angrily fires at the restaurant ceiling until his gun is empty.

Anshika, intending to surprise Yogesh, ends up hurting him badly. Tejas, who followed Aryan, and discovers him sitting alone outside. Tejas asks him, "Your lyrics are amazing, so why did you give them to me instead of doing it yourself and making more money?"

Aryan sat calmly until a crowd and press appeared at the restaurant. Finally, Tejas' old mother arrived, whom Aryan had invited to the party. Ignoring everything, Aryan looked at his mother and said, "Money isn't everything for someone like me." With a gun hidden on his back, he faces Tejas in the front, giving all the credit for the party night, and then departs.

33

Chapter Thirty Three

Aryan, who is injured, still comes to TRUST to work on DIVINE's project. Suddenly, Akash hits him from behind after finding out that last night's incident went viral. Aryan finds Akash drunk and disoriented, unable to think or act wisely. Aryan starts walking far away from Akash who is following him, yelling and throwing company stuff, but he ignores it all until Cassandra suddenly intervenes. Aryan covers her, but Tanisha gets hit. Aryan quickly pulls Akash away from the scene, while Akash was cursing him for being worthless.

Aryan disregards everything and restrains him in one location before exiting. He encounters the entire DIVINE crew waiting for him, including the CEO who angrily throws project details at Aryan. He claims they were all copied, resulting in a 2 crore fine. In order to cover this news, DIVINE must purchase a small firm, which holds no value to DIVINE but to cover the mess created by Aryan.

Aryan remained silent, knowing nothing, as the CEO continued. "Son, I hoped you would learn from your past mistakes, but it seems you are still the same worthless person who only cares about his own comfort. Experience earning with dignity once and you'll understand the true value of the sacrifices we make daily, while you spend it freely on anyone. You have nothing, not even a trustworthy friend or colleague, and no supportive relatives. Prove your worth before showing your face to me."

The CEO, before leaving, mentions, "And the amount I paid today is already included in your list." The CEO departs with his team. Aryan, with no place to go, goes back to work with a first aid box. He went straight to the CEO's cabin and without hesitation, he held Tanisha's hand to bandage it. As he was leaving silently, she asked him, "Don't you want to know who leaked your work?"

Upon hearing this, Aryan remarked how glad he was that someone had done it, causing the CEO to reconnect with his nephew, whom he had nearly forgotten. However, today I had a close encounter with him, someone who spoke to me after a long time, and I wholeheartedly bless that person who leaked my work.

Aryan called Anshika to pick up his brother, but everyone had already left. He found Akash unconscious and untied him, but Akash suddenly stabbed him in anger. Aryan tried to stop him but couldn't. Anshika arrived and Aryan hid his blood, holding Akash who seemed lost and ready to attack. When Akash saw Anshika, he stopped and left.

Aryan saw the blade that had been stabbed into him shortly after they left. It hurt when it touched him. Tanisha held him tightly and asked him to look at her, then suddenly removed the blade. Aryan, hurt and bleeding, holds her tightly. Tanisha desperately tried to stop the bleeding. However, it is too late, and he loses consciousness, leaving a final message: "Don't judge anyone before knowing their full story."

Tanisha, facing this situation for the second time, is at a loss for what to do. Finally, she chose to bring him to her villa to avoid the police and CEO, which she doesn't desire. Upon arriving at villa Urvashi was shocked to see Aryan and Tanisha covered in blood. She helped Tanisha take him to the guest room, but now they are both unsure of what to do.

Tanisha's driver's wife and a nurse arrived with medication, starting his treatment without asking anything. Aryan yelled frequently in the treatment, causing Tanisha to close the door. Mayra was in front of her, whom she embraced before leaving. Urvashi stayed until they were done, but before leaving, they said,

"Too much bleeding done already which will take time to heal."

Urvashi offered a large sum to keep them quiet, but they refused, saying they did everything for their son and walked away.

Urvashi, unable to bear Aryan's condition, holds his hand and takes care of him. Aryan finally wakes up and finds Urvashi close to him, kissing his forehead to bless him with good health. Then, the doctor and nurse enter to check on him. Upon leaving the room, Urvashi discovers Tanisha peacefully sitting with Mayra, whom she informed of his recovery. Tanisha interrupts, saying we need to keep the CEO isolated until he fully recovers, otherwise everything could be ruined.

One day, Mayra walks into Aryan's room and silently lies down next to him as she sees him resting. Despite being hurt, Aryan holds her with care. Both girls enter, searching for Mayra, and find her with Aryan. Tanisha appears irritated and prepares to intervene, but Urvashi intervenes, saying, "He hasn't been sleeping well since he arrived at this villa. Let him rest tonight."

The next day, when Aryan woke up, he discovered that Mayra was gone. Upon noticing, he realized that he was bleeding heavily, which Urvashi witnessed. Unable to wait any longer, she removed his clothing to clean his wound and began discussing Mayra as she bandaged him, eventually inquiring about his family. He tightly gripped her hand, wincing in pain. Observing his anger for the first time, Urvashi silently exits the room.

Urvashi expressed her concern to Tanisha about Aryan's family, questioning why the CEO didn't visit him or acknowledge his son's longing for his presence.

Tanisha responded by saying, "he's not someone anyone could love."

Urvashi interrupts, stating that perhaps he's the most despised person she's ever encountered, but no one else could love Mayra as he does. Mayra unknowingly hurt him while sleeping next to him, but he still held her with care as he bled all night. She explained, "I am now envious of him who has nobody to take care of, but everyone he helped treats him like family, something we can never achieve no matter how hard we try. We will always be strangers living under the same roof."

Urvashi left Tanisha to reflect on Aryan's behavior from the very beginning till now, where he selflessly thinks about others and lacks support, even from the CEO, when he's in pain. She appears calm as she is the one who systematically dismantles every support Aryan once challenged her on, leaving him in pain. Aryan, who had been alone in the room for a long time, finally emerges despite the servants' attempts to stop him. He sees Tanisha, who smiles and says, "It looks like we're even now."

This reminds him of the time he ruled Tanisha in his palace, and now it's her turn. Without panicking, he smiled and replied, "You may view my palace as a trap, but to me, your villa is a magical place where I have my princess and a loving queen taking care of me." With that, he returned to his room, leaving Tanisha trapped in her own game. The CEO, who had already taken everything from Aryan, ordered everyone to find him, but he remained untraceable.

34
Chapter Thirty Four

Aryan, who is still healing, notices Urvashi receiving constant calls and answers one for her. After the phone calls, Aryan inquired of Urvashi, "How long have you been hiding this from me?"

Aryan, noticing Urvashi's silence, decided to dress up, but Urvashi intervened. "Please help me, otherwise I'll never be able to forgive myself," Aryan said. She takes Aryan straight to the hospital, only to find police there. Before she can react, Aryan emerges with the help of an old man's wife, fearing the police might detain him.

Urvashi accidentally crashed the car, prompting police and locals to rush to her rescue, while Aryan went to see what happened, and she instructed her men to bring another car as everyone continued to care for her. Aryan enters the room to find Anshika sitting next to an unconscious Yogesh, who overdosed on drugs.

Aryan, sensing fear of losing him, confessed, "I'm sorry for everything. I should have told you about the treatment, but I didn't want to stress you out. However, I kept my promise and introduced her to Anshika, and she accepted her wholeheartedly."

"I won't die," Yogesh replied, "until I get my revenge on you."

Aryan tightly holds him, while Urvashi suddenly steps in, saying, "We need to leave now."

Aryan, before departing, said goodbye and promised to wait for him.

They all exit from the backside and arrive at the villa where Tanisha was already waiting. She yelled at Urvashi, "You knew that we could all get in trouble, yet you still took him out."

Aryan suddenly steps forward and confesses, "I asked her, so if you have anything to say, say it to me."

Tanisha forcefully pulled Urvashi's hand, shouting, "Stay out of my family affairs!" She then turned to Urvashi and said, "We'll deal with our issues once this matter is resolved."

Filled with uncertainty, Aryan asked, "What secrets are you all keeping from me?" Tanisha ignores the comment and leaves with Urvashi.

In an attempt to locate his son, the CEO resorted to enlisting local thugs and drug dealers, while Aryan remained oblivious and spent quality time with Mayra. One day, while searching for Aryan, the CEO's staff found a restored deleted recording of a fight between Akash and Aryan, leading to Akash being taken into custody. The CEO's men held TRUST hostage, while Tanisha, unable to intervene, witnessed it unfold. They eventually found Aryan in the record room and informed the CEO, ready to depart. Suddenly, Aditya arrived, gathering all the details, and proclaimed, "I will handle everything."

Spotting Aditya, everyone departs. Upon seeing Aryan after a long time, he tightly embraces him, asking, "Kid, where have you been?"

Aryan replied, I just wanted some time alone to clear my thoughts. Aryan received a small gift from Aditya, and upon opening it, he appeared emotional and asked, "Did the CEO have knowledge of this?"

Aryan attempted to give back the gift upon noticing Aditya's silence; I refuse anything without the CEO's permission or awareness. Aditya stopped him, his voice filled with conviction, "It always belongs to you."

Aryan agreed to accept it on the condition that he give him everything he collected from TRUST. Aditya gave the details to Aryan and walked away. Aryan remained standing until Aditya left and suddenly fell. Cassandra supported him, but he ignored her and went inside. He handed all the details to Tanisha and said, "Burn it all." Once her men had burned everything, she proclaimed, "Now, it's time to make a decision about Aryan and Akash's fate."

Akash appears clueless while Tanisha continues to speak, "you were once a trustworthy employee. However, your recent actions have caused a loss of TRUST. I have tried to hide this every day, but now you must face the consequences."

She gave him the resignation letter and told him he was fired. She made it clear that he was solely responsible for his actions and that TRUST had no connection to him or his behavior.

Akash asked with a tone of disbelief, "You can't do this to me, I've always been loyal to TRUST."

Tanisha replied firmly, "If I save you, it will put TRUST in jeopardy, and I will always prioritize TRUST over anyone else." She coerced him into signing the resignation, but Akash, who refuses to accept it, defends his actions. Tanisha was about to expose his true intentions, but Aryan intervenes, saying, "I take full responsibility, don't involve others."

Akash angrily hits Aryan, prompting the guards to take him down, causing Tanisha to yell at him for creating a mess that she has to fix.

Her men forced him to sign the letter when she asked, then they handed the signed letter to Tanisha. Aryan suddenly took it and tore it in front of everyone. Tanisha yelled, "You are the most selfish person I've ever seen who only cares about himself."

Aryan remained silent and she said, "To save him, someone needs to take the blame for everything." Aryan then grabbed pen and paper and wrote, "He is responsible for everything."

Tanisha informs Akash that he will be spared now, all thanks to a fellow colleague. However, he will no longer be part of any significant projects. Tanisha will reassign him to a regular employee role, where he must prove his worth once more. If Akash finds this reasonable than its fine, if not, he is still free to resign. Witnessing his loyalty being questioned, Akash angrily cursed everyone and walked away. Tanisha then inquired Aryan, who was also leaving, about the feeling of being cursed for one's actions.

Aryan doesn't respond and holds Tanisha's hand for support as they walk to her car. They then leave for the villa, while Aditya, upon returning to the palace, discovers blood on his hand, which reminds him that it's Aryan's blood. Out of nowhere, the CEO asked, "Have you had the chance to meet my son?"

Aditya, concealing his hand, responded that he's fine and I gave both the phone and your gift. As he was leaving, the CEO asked him, "Where are all the files you took?"

Aditya replied, I burned it all.

The CEO responded, saying that you always defend Aryan, but it won't be long before I bring him down for betraying my trust, and no one will be able to save him. Aditya informed the CEO, "he's living in your daughter's villa."

The CEO paused, a smile playing on his lips as he said, "I'm glad you're keeping a close watch on him. Also, make sure to keep an eye on both of my children. I don't want anyone to harm them." After he left, Aditya, visibly anxious after witnessing Aryan's injury, instructed his men to monitor Aryan's activities and the people he interacted with. He emphasized the importance of his son's safety, giving them permission to take down anyone suspicious without hesitation.

35

Chapter Thirty Five

Akash, with no destination in sight, made the bold choice to betray TRUST and venture into DIVINE, where he ultimately encounters the CEO. The CEO angrily grabbed Akash by the neck, making it hard for him to breathe. Suddenly, he let go and said, "I would have killed you for touching my nephew, but I have one task for you. If you do it, I will grant you double what you've lost."

Akash asked, "Tell me the order for me?"

The CEO replied with a stern tone, "Go back to TRUST and demand an apology from both my children." Akash seems irritated after the CEO mentioned, "Save your anger and guts for the future, where you'll have a chance to seek revenge. But for now, do as I say."

Akash came back to TRUST, while the CEO, who felt betrayed, demanded, "gather every minute detail about Aryan immediately." He got Aryan's investment plans to seek revenge on TRUST.

Anshika, who has never received gratitude from Yogesh, saw him lost and cold. Before leaving, she expressed, "Since the beginning, I have liked you and always was by your side. When you become jealous or overprotective, I feel love for you. But now, it hurts me to see you cold and lost, where you don't allow me to heal you." Before leaving, she finally expressed, "If not me, then no one will care for you like I do."

Yogesh holds her hand and asks, "Can you love me as I am?"

Anshika responded, I wish you could witness my love for you, but your mind and heart are consumed by revenge, impenetrable even by my care. Yogesh led her to the room, laid her on the bed, and said, "I need you to heal my wounds today."

Anshika kissed him with desperation, and they had a passionate encounter. Yogesh holds Anshika in his arms, finally calm. Aryan's words echo in her mind at the hospital, "Only you could save my brother and bring him back to life, or else I could never forgive myself." With a kiss on Yogesh's forehead, she promised, "I'll never leave you, not now."

Aryan contemplates Tanisha's statement about saving everyone to prevent the CEO from destroying TRUST once he learns what happened here.

Aryan asked Urvashi if the CEO knew of his current location. Aryan was about to leave when he saw Tanisha in front of him, asking, "Where do you think you're going?" Aryan replied, "do nothing that could make the CEO mad."

"I have to go immediately," Aryan said. he was leaving whom Tanisha stopped, "you can't leave not until I ask you to."

However, Aryan refuses to listen to her when he suddenly gets injected with a tranquilizer dose from behind by Tanisha.

He fell and her guards took him back to the room. "You're doing it wrong," Urvashi said. Tanisha warns, "Make sure he doesn't leave this time or I won't be nice to you." Tanisha is afraid the CEO won't show up until Aryan recovers, but in the end, the doctor informs her that Aryan's injury is healed, but there are still some complications to be dealt with.

She ignored everything and gave the order to set him free. Aryan headed directly to his palace in search of his father, who did not meet with him, and then went to his room to rest. In the night, Aditya finds Aryan in his room with healing stitches and marks. Aditya covered Aryan, but when he turned around, he saw the CEO uncovering the sheet and witnessing his son in a terrible condition. The CEO left quietly, and Aditya tried to defend himself when the CEO asked, "My son used to share everything about his life, but now he's hiding things from me. Look at the state he's in!"

He angrily grabs Aditya's collar for the first time, yelling, "You knew my son was hurt and still hid it. I trusted you to take care of him, but not anymore." The CEO vowed to spare no one responsible for harming his son, but Aditya revealed, "It's your daughter."

The CEO stopped and Aditya explained, "I kept it hidden because both are your children and you shouldn't make any hasty decisions. We need to think calmly before taking any action." The CEO interrupted, his voice filled with a chilling determination. "Maybe I can't do anything worse to either of my children, but I can certainly bring harm to their loved ones."

Aditya's eyes widened in shock as he warned, "You're making a big mistake that will hurt everyone." The CEO's reply was filled with anger and determination. "Even though she knows he's my son, she still lets it happen. She has to learn a lesson," he said. "I will destroy everything she has created until now."

Aryan, while reaching TRUST, discovers a new crew for a big project that he needs to lead. Suddenly, he notices Akash, who appears quiet but eager to talk. Aryan asks him, "Do you still want my apology?"

Akash suddenly grabs Aryan and apologizes, admitting his mistake, but clarifying that he never intended to act that way, as it was an overreaction regarding his sister. Witnessing Akash's heartfelt apology, Aryan forgives him, declaring, "She is my sister too, and I will stand by her till the end." Aryan asked Akash to join in the project, but Cassandra vehemently opposed, saying, "I can't trust this person anymore."

"No one will talk about trust and responsibility," Aryan replied, "until you don't know how to earn it."

"I run this project," Cassandra replied firmly, "and when I say no, it means no." Aryan expressed his anger, saying, "Do whatever you want, but I'll do what I feel like."

She immediately gave him the paper, saying, "Write down what you can do and do as you please." Aryan complied and left with his crew and Akash to work.

Aryan collaborates effectively with his crew and is delighted to have his friend back, while Cassandra remains skeptical of both Akash and Tanisha, who unexpectedly show kindness towards Aryan, a difficult feat that she closely monitors. Aryan shares his ideas and strategies with Akash and the crew, ensuring everyone knows what to do and when to do it, resulting in efficient work before the deadline.

Akash frequently invites Aryan to smoke weed despite knowing it will worsen his wounds, intentionally doing so until Aryan unexpectedly collapsed at work. The doctor informs Cassandra that his smoking is hindering wound healing and weakening his immune system. Aryan, who once again takes it lightly, leaves to smoke, angering Cassandra, who exclaims, "You can't do anything without consulting me."

Aryan is leaving, but is surprised to see armed guards surrounding him, who are all Tanisha's men. He asked, "Why do they obediently follow your orders?"

"You knew exactly who I am to Tanisha," Cassandra replied. In her absence, she gave me exclusive special force and access. Hearing this, Aryan handed her the weed and continued working under the observation of the guards.

36

Chapter Thirty Six

Akash was leaving one day when he abruptly halted by Tanisha's guards. He spotted Cassandra silently taking drugs from his pocket, which he had been secretly giving to Aryan. She appears annoyed and silently leaves, while Aryan searches for Akash and finds him injured. Aryan immediately takes him to the hospital, where they inform him that Akash is badly injured and will take time to regain consciousness.

With no other option, he dialed Yogesh's number. When Anshika noticed, she grabbed his hand and said, "He might be in trouble, don't reject his call." Upon hearing Aryan's deep voice, Yogesh heads to the hospital.

Upon arrival, he discovers Akash in a terrible condition and, without glancing at Aryan, asks, "Who is responsible for this?" Aryan warned him not to tell anything to his sisters or they would panic.

Yogesh informed Anshika at her home that it was Akash who called from Aryan's phone, as they were leaving urgently for a new project and would be back in a few days. Anshika holds a composed Yogesh after a long time, mentioning, "I missed this Yogesh who supports his friends when they need him."

Yogesh said, "I'll stay here until Akash comes back," which they all agreed upon. Akash finally woke up after 2 days, but Aryan and Yogesh couldn't figure out who did it because he couldn't speak.

Aryan's absence from work and the palace has raised concerns for Tanisha. She has asked Cassandra to track Aryan's phone, which she does instantly. However, when Cassandra sees the hospital location, she remains silent and heads there.

Upon arrival, she searches for Aryan, hoping he's safe, and eventually finds him seated beside Akash. Quietly, she joins Aryan, holding his hand, while he remains unresponsive to his friend's deteriorating condition. He pleads, "Please assist me in finding the perpetrator, examine the TRUST recordings, and inform me." Cassandra agreed.

During their rest at night, Cassandra informed Tanisha about the need to take Akash to the hospital because of his serious condition. She didn't respond to Akash's news, but she insisted on being updated about Aryan regularly.

Cassandra seems suspicious when she heard this, so she searched for the TRUST recording. She discovered Tanisha was the last person to meet with Akash before he went to this state. She appears tense, contemplating what she will say to Aryan when he requests the recording.

Aryan, sitting alone, received a text from a stranger saying that what he's looking for is saved in a TRUST recording. He finds Tanisha sitting at her desk and asks, "Do you mind if I see the recording?" She granted permission, but he discovered nothing and was about to depart. "Did you ask the CEO?" Tanisha inquired.

Aryan replied, "my uncle, don't hurt other people."

Tanisha replied, "He's much worse than what you already know about him. He shows no mercy to anyone, not even his own nephew."

Aryan responded calmly, stating, "He's not what you think."

Tanisha responded by saying that maybe not today, but someday you will find out about him, and then you'll hate him just like I do.

Out of nowhere, he pulls Tanisha close and declares, "He's all alone, only has me. Watch your words or you'll see a different side of me." She questions, "What about you? Don't you feel hurt and disrespected when he humiliates you?"

With a smile, Aryan replied, "He may act like he hates me, but deep down he loves me the most and would never harm the people I care about," and then he walked away.

Few days later, while Tanisha was working, she received a text from a stranger that terrified her. Hesitantly, she opened the text, only to learn that he was still alive; 'Your wishes are about to come true, as you will soon receive a visit from many important guests. Finally, all your loved ones will gather in one place to welcome me.'

Aryan, unaware of everything, witnessed the old man entering the ICU room. Aryan noticed his tension and asked about his concern. He replied, "Everything is sinking quickly." Aryan, who seems clueless, is taken straight to his locality by the old man, only to find the CEO's men seizing their land with the help of local thugs.

Aryan, visibly shocked, called Anshika, urging her not to leave Yogesh alone. Upon arriving at TRUST, he discovers investors and buyers obstructing the gate, demanding reimbursement because of substantial losses from her recent project and sudden policy devaluation.

Aryan broke all barriers and entered the TRUST boundaries by ordering the old man to keep driving without stopping, regardless of what happened. He rescued Tanisha and Cassandra before calling Aditya and asking for backup.

Urvashi called Aryan to inform him about rival intrusion at Mayra foundation before rushing to the spot. Upon arrival, he discovers Urvashi and a worker trapped in a dense crowd. The CEO's staff were aiding criminals in clearing the studio while the CEO himself remained composed at DIVINE. He receives a mysterious text threatening his son's life and is sent a link that reveals a live feed of the situation. Aditya and his crew arrive just in time to assist in Urvashi's rescue.

Tanisha noticed a stranger wearing the same mask in the crowd, approaching her directly. She grabbed a gun from the guards and began walking towards him without hesitation. Aryan, who rescued Urvashi, discovers a masked man aiming a gun at Tanisha, causing everyone to close their eyes in fear as the masked man fires. Finally, everyone discovers that Aryan took a bullet for himself, smiling at Tanisha before losing consciousness.

Tanisha got another text saying, "Hope you like your birthday gift." She glanced at a stranger who vanished into the crowd, and before anyone could react, the CEO arrived with his security team. Witnessing Aryan getting shot, the CEO quietly carried him away.

37
Chapter Thirty Seven

The entire city was on high alert and shut down by the CEO's silence, who sits beside his son as doctors treat him. In the meantime, Yogesh discovers Aryan was shot and sets aside his hatred to focus entirely on finding the culprit. Urvashi, who no longer speaks, leaves behind some pictures of Aryan. Tanisha, sitting silently in the hall, sees Mayra approaching and holds her with care. Mayra holds the same picture that Urvashi left, which reminds Tanisha of his last words, "he's just an old man who has no one but me."

The CEO, who avoids meetings and isolates himself, remains unresponsive and even forgets his own identity. Aditya was hesitant to disturb him, but he was informed about a guest. As the CEO's daughter walks in, everyone clears a path for her. She discovers Aryan lying unconscious and recalls his words, "he never says it, but he loves me the most."

As she held back her tears, she noticed the CEO approaching anxiously. When she turned to face him, he handed her his immune booster and asked her to save his son before collapsing unconscious. Tanisha, who finally has the opportunity to seek revenge on the CEO, is confronted by Aryan when she points a gun at him, having been informed by Cassandra that "everything was set up by the CEO to take revenge for hurting Aryan."

After 3 days, Yogesh finally found the link to the culprit, who used to be a DIVINE shareholder. Upon arriving at the scene, he discovers the culprit kneeling before the CEO, surrounded by armed police forces. Before anyone can comprehend the situation, the furious CEO begins firing bullets until his weapon is empty, while the dying culprit is set ablaze by the CEO.

Witnessing this brutal assassination, everyone is left terrified, except for the calm CEO who turns to Yogesh, the informant, and asks, "I want this kid to be promoted as he will be responsible for all my legal matters." With that, he departed to TRUST. Tanisha, aware of the CEO's arrival, angrily aims a gun, but the fearless CEO taunts, "You should have pulled the trigger while you had the chance."

While she lowered her gun, the CEO continued, "I knew you were seeking revenge." Tanisha exclaimed in shock, "It was never about TRUST, you just want to manipulate me into coming to you by creating false misery to gain TRUST, right?"

Tanisha was devastated and ready to leave when the CEO mentioned, "he's adopted," causing her to pause. The CEO explained, "He was my late wife's final wish, as she cared for him like her own son. But to me, he is the spitting image of myself, something my own son could never be. One day, I will make him into what I am today."

Tanisha angrily removed the curtain upon hearing this. The CEO appeared shocked as he gazed at the large crowd eagerly awaiting Aryan. Tanisha remarked that Aryan, unlike the CEO's son, had earned their support and trust despite not being born into wealth. Tanisha admitted to hating Aryan even more than the CEO's son, as Aryan had taken everything she had earned. However, she couldn't hate him because he possessed a loving heart and caring feelings that the CEO could never have.

The CEO requested, "assist him in achieving success if you wish to avoid his resemblance to me." Upon witnessing the CEO's selfishness, Tanisha responded, "considering his utmost trust in you, what if he discovers everything?"

The CEO responded calmly, saying, "You would never do that, as you are too emotionally invested and don't want to be the reason for our separation." Tanisha remained silent upon hearing this, and the CEO asked, "Now, tell me, where did you hide Aryan?" Tanisha responded, "You won't see him unless I allow it."

The CEO becomes angry and says, "You can't always save him. One day, he will come back to me, and I will mold him into what I desire the most." Tanisha said to the CEO, who was leaving, "Aryan almost makes me want to call you father. He always asked me if you loved him the most." listening to which CEO turns.

Witnessing Tanisha's anguish, the CEO kissed her forehead and entrusted him to her, instructing her to care for both of his children. Tanisha received another text from a stranger mentioning; 'The CEO's mistaken in thinking he eliminated me. One of my pawns was taken instead. Your secret is secure while I'm still breathing.'

After reading, Tanisha appears terrified and leaves. Upon arriving at the villa, she locked herself in, recalling the moment she was about to shoot the CEO. Suddenly, out of fear, Aryan held her hand, reminding her of Mayra, who held Aryan's picture and spoke for the first time, seeking his help to relieve her niece's suffering. Aryan, too, relied on the CEO as his only hope. Contemplating this, she lowered the gun, held his hand gently, and kissed his forehead, seeking forgiveness. Aryan suddenly wakes up to find himself alone and silently departs.

He enters the dark house and goes straight to the bedroom. He lies next to Cassandra, cushioning her. When she feels Aryan's touch, she holds him even closer. Tanisha knows where Aryan has been and lies to the CEO, saying he is with her to protect Cassandra's identity. She wanted to keep him secure until he heals, but above all, she's concerned about a stranger whose primary target is Aryan, which she can't inform the CEO about.

Cassandra and Aryan were together, but something had changed between them. Aryan finally decided to confront the issue, "what is it that is keeping us apart?" The moment he asked this, she clung to him even tighter. Aryan noticed her guilt and sorrow, leading her to the bedroom and urging her to lie down. He approached her to offer comfort, but she couldn't bring herself to meet his gaze. Aryan spoke softly, "I need your care to navigate this deceitful world."

Despite Cassandra hurting Aryan badly, he still longs for her affection. She reluctantly kissed Aryan and gradually lost herself to satisfy his every desire, while Aryan struggled to overcome his sorrow, which Cassandra revealed, "I feel like I die every day thinking I lost you that day."

Holding him tightly, she pleads, "Promise you won't leave me alone after this." In response, she pulls Aryan closer, wanting to be intimate with him. Aryan kisses her eyes and fulfills her desire.

38

Chapter Thirty Eight

The next day, when Aryan goes to TRUST, everyone acts strangely and nonchalantly, which he tries to understand, but no one wants to talk about it. He discovers Tanisha hasn't been to TRUST since that day. He then decided to visit her. When he reached the villa, Urvashi saw Aryan and immediately embraced him tightly. After exchanging greetings, he walked directly to Tanisha's room. Inside, he found her standing in the dark, gazing at her late mother's portrait. She whispered, "I still can't accept that she's gone. To me, she's still alive."

Aryan completed, "so do I."

Seeing Aryan acting nonchalantly as usual, she refrains from reacting and begins to walk away. However, Aryan's words compel her to turn and look at him, even though Tanisha had refused. "I am desperate to see the eyes that despise me the most," Aryan stated.

Aryan daringly kissed Tanisha's tear-filled eyes, his touch filled with tenderness, saying, "at least you are transparent about your feelings." Before leaving, he reassured her, saying, "Even though you may feel lost now, remember there are many who still believe in you."

Tanisha asked, "what about you?" To which Aryan smiled and left.

The next day, everyone visiting TRUST discovers a grand celebration underway. Everyone initially believed it was Aryan, but he's not responsible. Then Tanisha walks directly towards him and says, "I'm not going anywhere until I receive my answer." Aryan appeared happy when he saw Tanisha at work, but then he quickly turned around to hide her from the CEO, who commented, "Glad to see you back at work."

Aryan tried to greet his father, but the CEO ignored him and went straight to Tanisha, saying, "we have some business to do." He then headed to the meeting room with his staff, followed by Tanisha. Aryan waits in the meeting room as the CEO ignores him and abruptly leaves when the meeting ends.

Upon hearing a loud noise, everyone enters the meeting room to find Tanisha visibly annoyed, causing no one to approach her. Meanwhile, Aryan, who had witnessed her smiling moments earlier, is disheartened by his father's actions and leaves quietly. Tanisha, under a time limit, must resolve everything or face the consequences of the CEO. Aryan, longing for answers about the past, encounters Cassandra, waiting to bring him home. Aryan questioned Cassandra about the events that occurred during his absence in the past few days.

She tightly grips his collar in fear and anger, but releases it by counter-questioning him, "I still feel incomplete, love me more," which Aryan fulfills. The next day, instead of going to TRUST, Aryan goes to the villa and asks Urvashi the same thing, but she ignores him. He then tries to check with Aditya, who also refuses to share anything. He has no choice but to return to Cassandra, who supports him despite his confusion, but he can't stop thinking about Tanisha, who seemed frightened after the CEO's last visit.

Aryan made multiple attempts to meet Tanisha, but he faced restrictions. Yogesh is still searching for the main culprit, as the person they had earlier was just a pawn and was easily traced. Yogesh comforted the restless Anshika, assuring her that Aryan has recovered and is back to work as usual.

Despite her lack of response, Yogesh continued speaking, "I will keep Akash occupied so you can meet him quickly." Reaching TRUST, she walks straight to Aryan and clings to him, holding on desperately. She whispers, "I was so scared." Aryan cautiously holds her back, reassuring, "I'm okay now," as he sees her terrified. Cassandra walks in and sees Anshika too close, which makes her feel uncomfortable. Aryan gently separates them, introducing Cassandra as the person helping him with new projects.

Cassandra decided not to stay, and upon leaving, she said, "Please continue, I'll join another day." Aryan turned to Anshika after she left and pleaded, "I need your help to uncover what happened in the past few days. You're the only one who can bridge the gap between both parties, so please find the truth before it's too late."

After Anshika left, Aryan followed Cassandra into the meeting room and quickly locked it, only to realize that Tanisha was there. Finally, he had the opportunity to confront her, but she interrupted him with a stern warning, "Don't you dare spout nonsense or try to persuade me about the CEO, or I will walk away."

Aryan agreed, pausing briefly before casually inquiring about her desires, while she initially brushed off his question, she gradually began to disclose them, until he eventually posed the question, "What is your deepest longing in life?" As she listened to this specific question, a look of confusion crossed her face before she responded, "If I had the opportunity, I would restore FAITH to its previous glory." Soon she said this. Cassandra steps in, her voice filled with concern, asking, "where were you? I was looking for you everywhere."

Cassandra immediately left upon seeing Aryan locked with her, prompting Tanisha to taunt, "Looks like you're not taking good care of my PA." She then left. Aryan remains, gazing at the camera, patiently waiting for everyone to leave. Aryan enters the CEO's cabin quietly, searching for the recording of what the CEO specifically asked her in the meeting. In the middle of his checking, Cassandra steps in and questions when he'll stop playing around with Tanisha.

Holding his hand, she led him home, but they didn't sleep together as usual. At night, Aryan walks to the hall to escort Cassandra to their room. As they lie down together, Aryan embraces her and reassures her, "I won't do anything you're uncomfortable with." Cassandra responds by holding him even closer.

39

Chapter Thirty Nine

During weekends, Anshika would ask Akash about his new project, which he would explain well but then abruptly stop. Anshika casually suggests checking with Aryan, since he was also working on the same project. Why not get the details from the records room?

Akash stated that there is no other copy of the project and clarified that Aryan was not involved due to being shot. Anshika checked one point and then visited Yogesh for more details. She asked Yogesh about his investigation and he suddenly became annoyed and revealed that the CEO had killed the main witness in front of everyone, who was just a puppet, as the main culprit is inside TRUST, which he will find soon. Hearing this, she was shocked and was leaving in a hurry. Yogesh stopped her and asked, "Aren't you staying tonight?"

Aryan, oblivious to everything, attempted to reconcile with Cassandra when he suddenly got a call and hastily left. While driving, Aryan received a call from Aditya who warned, "hurry up and drive fast before it's too late."

Aryan arrived at the site and saw Tanisha surrounded by CEO guards. He jumped into the crowd and shielded Tanisha on his back until the CEO arrived. The CEO drove the car recklessly and aimed at Tanisha, but Aryan refused to back down. The CEO's car crashed as he turned it, and despite being badly injured, he walked towards Tanisha. He pulled out a gun and pointed it at her, but Aryan shielded her by taking the gun's aim on himself.

The CEO shouted that Tanisha, who wanted to kill you, is the main culprit while Aryan defended her.

Aryan's reply, "I knew already," left the CEO in shock. He responded, "Your lies won't protect her. She must pay for destroying my trust. I trusted her more than anyone."

"You also trusted me, so I should be the first one to be punished," Aryan replied.

The CEO appeared irritated and attempted to bypass Aryan to reach Tanisha, but was halted by Aryan's hand on his chest. Aryan remarked, "You once referred to her as your daughter, and now you wish to harm her."

Perhaps you'll never forgive me for insulting you, but if I can prevent you from making a grave error, I'm willing to try.

When the CEO saw Aryan standing against him, his grip on the gun loosened, and he locked eyes with his son. In that moment, he no longer saw him as a beloved son, but as someone who opposed him because of a girl. He spoke, saying, "You chose her over me, but let me warn you, once she's done with you, she'll kick you out of her life, and then you'll be left with no one."

Aryan had planned to explain to him, but the CEO abruptly turned around. Witnessing his father's enraged face, Aryan tightly held Tanisha's hand in fear. The CEO's voice boomed with anger as he shouted, "You are no longer my son! And as for the one you betrayed me for, I will make sure to strip you of everything before you hand her over to me." With those words, the CEO stormed off.

As Aryan loses Tanisha's hand and starts to leave, Tanisha's voice trembles as she asks, "Do you also believe that I wanted to kill you?"

Aryan responds, "I don't care about what's going on between you two anymore, nothing matters to me after you took the last thing from me. I am perplexed why both the company and individuals place such immense trust in you despite their unawareness of your willingness to jeopardize both your pride and their lives for a small profit, as you did to me. However, I am unlike you, as I have finally obtained something I have been lacking for years, and find solace in the society where numerous underprivileged individuals look to me with hope.

I won't back down, even if I have to fight with the CEO. I won't betray their trust. If you try to ruin that trust, remember that I have nothing to lose, but you have much to lose, so think twice before deciding anything.

40
Chapter Forty

Following that day, the CEO began to strip Tanisha of everything, including her clients, rights, and shares in DIVINE. They put all her projects on hold, yet Tanisha refused to be defeated. Finally, the CEO ordered two teams, one led by Yogesh to take control of the locality and the other led by the senior general to seize TRUST by force. Anshika was aware of Yogesh's hatred for Aryan, so she warned Aryan about a partial threat at TRUST to ensure his safety, causing Aryan to rush to the site.

Upon his visit to the site, the general commanded his armed forces to annihilate everything. The mess began, but stopped when Aditya stood at their protest. However, the general persisted and commanded the firing to commence, igniting a bloody war between his forces and Aditya's army, transforming the entire office into a battlefield soaked in blood. The CEO instructed the general to step back upon learning that Aditya was at the site. Aditya, his hand covered in blood, called Aryan and said, "son, TRUST is secure."

Aditya, while on the call, heard nothing from Aryan except for the sound of a large vehicle, gunshots, troops shouting for help, and asked, "son, where are you?"

Aryan responded, "I will do whatever it takes to protect my family." Aditya hastily departs with his armed forces, urging his son to flee the scene while he takes care of things, but Aryan responds, "It's too late now."

Aryan witnessed a large group of police and hooligans causing destruction, and joined a local youth group to fight against them. Finally, Yogesh opens fire to halt everyone, as the entire neighborhood is held at gunpoint by the police and the armed forces. Aryan offers, "Cease all activities, and I will depart without causing a scene."

Yet, Yogesh instructed his men to evacuate the premises and they set houses ablaze. Witnessing Yogesh's misconduct, Aryan fights back and a scuffle ensues. After a while, despite being covered in blood, Yogesh continued without stopping, while Aryan witnessed the destruction of his people and their burning homes. Aryan finally accepted his defeat, giving Yogesh the opportunity to seek revenge, stating, "As long as you endure the pain, your people will be safe. But if you resist, I will reduce everything to ashes." Aryan agreed to these terms.

Yogesh launches a full-scale attack on Aryan, who endures it all. Even when he couldn't bear it anymore, Yogesh persisted in hurting Aryan. Aditya and his armed force suddenly invade, indiscriminately firing at everyone - local troops, CEO armed forces, and the police. Yogesh, who was here to carry out his orders, commanded his men to return fire. Aryan attempted to intervene, but Yogesh paid no attention. However, before Yogesh could take any action, Aditya used Anshika as a hostage, causing Yogesh to order his team to stop.

Aryan asked Aditya to release Anshika when he saw her at the site, but Aditya declined. However, when Aryan commanded him like a master instead of requesting, he allowed her to leave. When Yogesh catches Anshika, he deceives everyone and commands to shoot at Aditya's troops.

Additional police forces arrived at the site and assisted in vacating the area while Aditya attempted to flee from Aryan, who was shot near the shoulder by Yogesh. Witnessing his uncle being shot, Aryan grabs Aditya's gun and they both aim at each other, ready to shoot. To intervene, Anshika steps in between them. Aryan lowers his gun upon seeing her, but Yogesh, consumed by hatred, seeks revenge and fires a bullet at Aryan. Fortunately, a young man from the neighborhood jumps in and takes the bullet for Aryan, saving his life.

Aryan witnessed the deaths of young men and shouted before the police force launched an attack on the troops, destroying everything as instructed. After completing their task, Yogesh ordered the force to retreat.

Later that evening,

Aditya, covered in blood, angrily walks to the CEO's cabin where Yogesh and high officials are present. Aditya indiscriminately begins shooting at the officials, fatally injuring them, and just as he is about to shoot at Yogesh, the CEO emerges and commands him to lower his weapon. Aditya confronted the CEO, yelling, "I warned you before, if anyone touches my grandson, I won't spare anyone, not even you." He shot at the CEO staff, killing everyone present, but remained uncalm and declared, "For one injury to my son, I will take the lives of ten of your men. Pray that nothing happens to him, or I will kill this person. My son means everything to me."

Once Aditya had gone, the CEO inquired of Yogesh, "Why didn't you inform me about what took place at the site?"

Yogesh replied with a firm tone, "What matters is that you wanted the land vacant, and I followed your orders." The CEO locked eyes with Yogesh, his gaze filled with a warning. "If you dare to cross Aryan again, I'll ensure you meet your demise before anyone else. Consider this your first and final warning."

At the hospital, Aditya, with his freshly bandaged wounds, made his way to Aryan's room where he was admitted, and patiently stayed by his side until he woke up. Aditya held Aryan tight, feeling his son's warmth and hearing his voice filled with relief. "How's everyone? Did you save everyone?" Aryan asked.

Aditya lied effortlessly, meeting his gaze as he assured, "The CEO has already given the order for the force to retreat, so everything is taken care of." This statement brought a sense of calm to Aryan, who then inquired, "Once I'm discharged, can I meet everyone?"

Aditya insisted, "You've spent enough time with everyone. Now I want my son's time, and you're not leaving until you're healed."

Aditya remained silent, his tense expression revealing his inability to fulfill his proposal, and he abruptly turned to leave. Aryan, yearning for the carefree days of their childhood, asked, "Do you remember when you used to take me to the farmhouse outside the city? Can we go there? I can't bear to stay here any longer." Aditya noticed Aryan's pain from the CEO's decision and gently held his hand, assuring him, "Nothing has changed since you left. Nobody, not even the CEO, is allowed to enter there. You're safe."

Aditya led Aryan to a secluded spot, far away from prying eyes, while the CEO ruthlessly dismantled TRUST asset, with both hooligans and police aiding him without question. When Yogesh left for work, he caught a glimpse of Anshika standing there, but ignored her. As he walked away, she couldn't help but ask, "Is your hatred more significant than our love?"

As Yogesh remained silent, Anshika continued, her voice filled with disappointment, "Our love story could have been more enchanting, but I never anticipated that it would end like this." With a heavy heart, she retrieved the ring locket she had been clutching, placed it on his desk, and silently departed. Instead of leaving for his next target, Yogesh took the locket and chose to say no to the CEO task, locking himself in his house.

41
Chapter Forty One

After few weeks,

TRUST, unable to hold on any longer, finally collapsed when the last remaining project disappeared. To salvage the situation, Tanisha called for an emergency meeting and offered 6 months' salary in advance to all employees, urging them to leave TRUST and seek better opportunities. She delivered the remaining stock to the small NGO's who were aiding the nomads who lost everything, with TRUST.

Tanisha, after doing everything she could for everyone, finally isolates herself from everyone's reach. Urvashi, seeing everything lost, decided to leave as promised. Tanisha won't stop her this time and will let her go easily. Tanisha, who previously did everything to win over Mayra, now appears to be heartless.

Aryan, who was close to recovery, received a text that made him glance at his mini-MP3 player from Mayra and prepared to meet her, only to be halted by Aditya saying, "you're not going anywhere."

Aryan mentioned that it has been a while since meeting with the family. Aditya was leading him back to the cottage, holding his hand. Aryan pulled his hand away and questioned, "Are you hiding something from me?"

Aditya has finally disclosed that the CEO took everything as promised, leaving nothing but ashes. Aryan was leaving without asking anything further, prompting Aditya to try and stop him. Aryan then expressed disappointment, saying, "I trusted you to handle everything, but now it's all gone."

Aditya said, "You were dying and my son meant everything to me, so I chose you over anyone else." Aryan grabs his hand and says, "You care about me more than my dad. I know you'll be there for me if I'm in trouble. As long as I have you, no one can harm me. But now, let me go and fix the mess my dad made." Then he leaves.

Urvashi, who was leaving the palace later that night, was surprised to see TRUST staff and employees gathered with presents and decorations to celebrate Mayra's birthday, so she allowed them inside. As a gesture of appreciation for Tanisha's dedication, they celebrated Mayra's birthday as a family. While they were having a good time, they all gave many gifts to Mayra. Eventually, Aryan showed up at the party, and everyone seemed frightened when they saw his scars.

Aryan kneels down and offers a handmade cake. Aryan gives Urvashi the legal papers as a birthday gift, expressing that it's the only thing he has left after losing everything. Urvashi examined the legal papers belonging to the Mayra Foundation, as she was its caretaker until Mayra turned 18. Urvashi stated that the CEO would go after the company and not stop until it's destroyed.

Aryan stated that he was not present for his people in the past, but now he is determined to protect Mayra at all costs, even if it means facing the worst of the CEO. He holds Urvashi's hand and says, "I want you to take over the business again. I promise the CEO won't pursue us this time. He has issues with me and the TRUST owner, but they aren't involved here. And if he still comes, I will be there to stop him. Despite being cruel to the world, he loves me the most. So, there will be no misery this time."

Urvashi examined the contract and remarked, "It won't be easy since we have to restart everything from scratch and there are no workers remaining."

Aryan extended his hand to the TRUST employee and said, "You already have the team, all they need is a project and guidance. Just give it a try and I'm confident we can regain what we lost in the past few days, slowly and easily." Urvashi gazed at Tanisha, her eyes filled with admiration for her unwavering trust and loyalty towards the organization. She held Tanisha's hand tightly and whispered, "Without you, TRUST is incomplete. Mayra foundation owes its success to you. Please help us regain what we have lost, and I assure you, we will stand united as a family, no matter what you decide."

Tanisha, who had lost everything, found hope in Aryan. He not only helped her revive her company but also made Urvashi's presence meaningful. Tanisha's eyes were filled with tears as Urvashi held her close, whispering, "Finally, we have you back. I promise, I'll never ask you to leave again. We are a family, and family stays together, no matter what." Soon, everyone gathered around, holding hands and making Tanisha feel like she had a big, loving family. She looked at Aryan, who quietly left, leaving her with the best gift.

After a few days, Urvashi and the employees began the process of setting things up, and Shreya joined in to assist. Seeing that only Anshika and Ankita were left, Aryan asked Anshika to meet him. Anshika finally visits the site and upon seeing his scars, she is reminded of that day and doesn't know how to apologize. Aryan asks, "Are you okay?"

Aryan carefully held Anshika in his arms when she hugged him. After a while, when she appears calm, Aryan proceeded by expressing his happiness that she didn't object to his request and came to assist in rebuilding TRUST. This company is more than just a business to me, it's a family that thrives when everyone is united. My biggest fear is failing.

Anshika holds his hand, her touch providing reassurance as she says, "With you by our side, everything will be alright." When Anshika returned, Aryan appeared calm, but when she left for work, he asked, "How's your love life going?" Anshika paused and smiled, answering, "I'm confident he'll be fine without me because his revenge means everything to him."

Aditya, who appeared tense, returned to the palace. The CEO inquired about his day at the farm, asking if he had enjoyed himself. Aditya responded, "Being at home and spending time with my son was far more enjoyable than living in this palace with lifeless individuals." Aditya's cold attitude made it clear that he was still upset.

Urvashi made progress with the help of staff and employees under guidance, and within a month, Mayra foundation started growing in the fashion industry. However, the CEO was still impatient as Tanisha remained free, despite shutting down TRUST. Despite blocking all her assets, he was still unsure why she didn't show up and who was assisting her.

In his state of confusion, he came across news about Mayra foundation's upcoming product release, which piqued the CEO's curiosity and reminded him of Aryan's investment in the company, bringing clarity to everything. The CEO discovers Tanisha's new source of income, initially considering taking action against the company, but decides to instead plan a surprise gift for his children and patiently waits for the perfect moment.

Without knowledge of the CEO's intentions, everyone dedicated themselves to the product and its imminent launch. Just before the launch, Aryan received a phone call from Aditya, who informed him of his serious health condition. Urvashi appeared tense as she was about to be left alone, but Aryan reassured her, saying, "You're in charge here. If anything goes wrong, just call me." and left.

42

Chapter Forty Two

Aryan arrived at the hospital and was guided to the ICU room, but upon entering, he discovered that all the doors were locked, trapping him in a CEO's scheme. He called for help, but no one came. When he tried to call, there was no signal. Despite his efforts, he couldn't escape and now sits, waiting for rescue.

At midnight, all doors opened and Aryan rushed to the site, shocked to see Mayra foundation on fire with many injured visitors and staff. Witnessing destruction all around, Aryan's hope vanished as he watched the CEO restore what was lost in the war. Suddenly, Urvashi, with bloodied hands, approached Aryan and questioned, "Where were you when they attacked us? You should be here to witness that we have lost everything, leaving only ashes behind." After Urvashi left, Aryan noticed Mayra standing alone in the crowd, her face filled with shock.

Aditya appeared with the rescue team, their footsteps echoing through the chaos as they helped the injured people. Meanwhile, Aditya frantically searched for Aryan, but he was nowhere to be found. Being tensed, he furiously commanded his men to search for him in every corner, while Aryan anxiously waited outside the ICU room. After some time, the doctor arrived and conveyed, "They are no longer in immediate danger, but their condition remains critical. We are closely monitoring them, but if there is no improvement, surgery may be necessary."

Aryan walks to Tanisha's palace after leaving the hospital and discovers Tanisha lying motionless in the hall, holding a gun. Aryan, upon seeing this, resigns himself and prepares to face his fate.

What Tanisha had left with her seems to be dying, and she has lost everything finally. Her family, her community, the Mayra foundation - all lost or destroyed. All these things broke her, and in the absence of anyone around, she clung to Aryan, dropped the gun, and cried for the first time, confessing, "He took everything from me. Please ask the CEO to stop, as my family is all I have left. If I lose them, I will die."

Aryan held Tanisha gently as he wiped away her tears, promising to resolve the situation, but pleading for her to prioritize her well-being and the well-being of her people.

Tanisha appears confused about how she will face everyone after what happened. Aryan comforts her, saying, "You are not just the owner of TRUST, but also the face of the company who always supports the needy. This time, they need you. They don't see you as a person, but as a source of hope. And so do I." Tanisha, seeing Aryan's blind trust in her, agreed to his terms and Aryan departed.

At the CEO palace,

Aryan called the CEO for a meeting, and he agreed. After a while, Aryan reached the CEO's palace, where the entire DIVINE group had gathered, and amidst them all, the CEO sat calmly, observing Aryan's miserable state. His torn and blood-stained dress showed his defeat as the CEO handed him a shocking contract, surrounded by high officials, shareholders, and business partners. Aryan disregards everyone and gazes at his father, who understood that signing this deal was impossible for him. However, at that moment, Aryan saw not a father, but a businessman, determined to close the deal at any expense.

The CEO asked, his voice filled with a mix of anticipation and warning, "Once you sign this deal, your life will undergo a transformation. You'll need to suppress the very essence of your character until the deal concludes. Only when you achieve the set goals then only you can regain your former life. But failure means losing not just your character, but your entire past. So, I ask you, do you possess the courage to put pen to paper?"

Aryan hesitated, reluctant to sign the contract and turned to leave. The CEO's voice grew cold as he warned, "Once you walk away, there's no going back. Think carefully, because if I don't get what I want, everything you hold dear will crumble. This all falls on you, so make your decision wisely."

Aryan, having lost all hope, finally took the pen, but before signing, he asked, "Will everyone regain what they lost if I sign this?"

The CEO's response was, "everything will be restored to how it was before."

Finally, Aryan signed the deal and wanted to say many things to his father but stayed silent. He then handed over his phone, cards, and everything one by one, given by the CEO. The CEO requested the last item, stating, "I want your MP3 player as well, it's part of our agreement." Aryan, feeling emotional, reluctantly surrendered his second most valuable possession, while still having one item remaining - his mother's gold chain. As he was about to give it up, the CEO intervened, stating, "The deal doesn't apply to emotions, so you can keep that."

Aryan, disappointed, left empty-handed and bid farewell to his father, "It was a pleasure doing business with you, Mr. Rajnish Kumar Mishra."

The CEO looked at his son's signature, appearing perplexed. The shareholders are annoyed because Aryan signed the wrong deal instead of the main company papers, pressuring the CEO to have him sign the correct one. The CEO's armed forces halted them while the CEO, holding ordinary deal papers, appeared content as he finalized his first successful deal with his son and, before departing, declared, "I achieved my goal."

Aryan gazes at the palace's main gate one final time before departing forever, with no place to call home. Unable to find any other option, he finally departed for the only remaining place available to him, while Tanisha received a text from the CEO. Upon opening it, the text stated, "You have one final opportunity to demonstrate your value. Make Aryan successful as I envisioned, and I will reward you tenfold for your past earnings and losses. If you accept my terms, you may resume your position at TRUST, as everything has been arranged as before. The decision is now yours."

She calmly replied with the word "agreed" and watched as the CEO and high authorities swiftly restored everything overnight. The local residents were given financial aid and food for six months until their temporary homes were built. A senior surgeon visited the hospital to perform surgeries on Urvashi and Mayra. The Mayra foundation, which had been destroyed, began rebuilding its architecture. Finally, Aryan reopened the previously closed TRUST organization.

43

Chapter Forty Three

Next day,

Everyone gathered at the office. Tanisha arrived at the site later and instructed everyone to resume work. She then walked to every corner until she finally discovered Aryan taking a break in the record room. While working on the new project, she quietly added a few points and left. Aryan woke up and gave the project details to Cassandra to include in the new project list before going back to work. Aryan was the only one left working on new projects in the evening for three consecutive days.

Tanisha reaching palace thinks about Aryan weird attitude. Suddenly, an unusual thought struck her mind and she hurried to the company. When she arrived, she found Aryan standing alone in the rain. As she stepped out of her car, Aryan asked, "Why did you come?"

Tanisha replied, "Not only have you not changed your clothes in the last 3 days, but you also don't have any expensive belongings."

Aryan gently grasped her hand, their fingers intertwined around the handle of the umbrella, as they walked leisurely through the rain. "Isn't the rain soothing?" she said, as if it had the power to wash away all stress, anxiety, and pain.

Aryan held her closer, his grip filled with anger, while Tanisha disregarded his actions and locked eyes with him, seeing the pain he couldn't accept or express. Tanisha asked, her voice filled with concern, "If you don't want to share it, then there's no need. But at least let me help you, like you did when I needed it the most." She extended her hand towards Aryan, offering him the house keys, which he accepted before departing.

Now, Aryan lives in the servant quarter behind Tanisha's palace. Slowly, he turns back to life, his world brightened by the presence of Mayra, whose health improves greatly under Aryan's attentive care, bringing happiness to Urvashi, who knows that Mayra is the one thing Aryan handles with utmost care.

Tanisha appeared composed, taking in the orderly surroundings, until the day Cassandra arrived at her palace. Cassandra handed her the new project details and a note from the CEO before abruptly leaving. Just then, Cassandra caught sight of Aryan and Mayra in the back garden. Cassandra was going to see Aryan, but Tanisha intervened, saying that Aryan wanted to be alone with Mayra. Cassandra steps back and leaves silently upon hearing that, "he will call when he wants to, until then exclude Aryan from every project as I don't want them disturbed." by Tanisha.

Later that night, Aryan went to the palace and placed Mayra on her bed before noticing new project details. However, before he could look at them, Urvashi approached Aryan and invited him to join her for dinner, which he declined before leaving. Tanisha showed up and asked the same question, which Aryan couldn't ignore and joined them. Urvashi, sitting at the dining table, turned to Tanisha and inquired, "Have you looked through the files that Cassandra left today?" Aryan exhibited surprise upon learning this, yet stayed silent.

Aryan saw Tanisha standing in front of him when leaving the palace at night. He quietly walked past her as she asked, "You didn't consider Mayra even once? Despite knowing that she likes you and her health improves when she's with you, you still want to leave?"

Aryan assured, "I'll come back before Mayra wakes up."

As he was about to leave, Tanisha's guards swiftly closed the door, trapping him inside. Aryan turned towards Tanisha, who had a strange yet caring attitude, as she extended her hand towards him and said, "You're not going anywhere until I say so." He gently held her hand and followed her to Mayra's room, where he sat on a chair in front of them, observing their peaceful rest.

Aryan has been silent for a few days and is not allowed to leave or get any details about TRUST. One day, when there was nobody around, he contacted Urvashi and requested her assistance in escaping from the palace, which she managed to do. While in the car, she asked where they should go. Aryan quietly redirects the vehicle towards TRUST, causing Urvashi to caution, "You're making a mistake, and if she finds out I aided you, we'll be in trouble." Aryan disregards her and heads straight to the CEO cabin.

When Aryan entered the cabin, he caught Tanisha in a secret virtual meeting, but she quickly ended it and asked, "Who released you despite my instructions to stay in the palace?" Aryan disregards Tanisha's anger and insists on getting the details she refuses. Aryan forcibly holds her with one hand and obtains the details. Despite appearing calm, he keeps the details and silently departs, prompting Tanisha to ask, "Didn't you find what you were looking for?"

Aryan appears confused and stops, she asked again, "Didn't you come to check the details sent by the CEO at the palace?" Aryan replied, "Yes, but it's the ordinary paper, not the one which CEO sent, that you're hiding. However, I will quickly find a solution, and until I do, I refuse to leave. Instead, I will continue coming to the office regularly, and you will no longer have control over me." Tanisha calmly asked, "Did you even read the words written on that paper?"

Aryan seemed silent, his eyes avoiding Tanisha's gaze. Tanisha took a deep breath, her voice tinged with hurt, as she handed him the details. "You're right, I can't control you. But your words cut deeper than your actions this time, making it clear how you truly see me."

Aryan wanted to confront Tanisha, but she didn't allow him. Instead, she continued, "You wanted to be free. Fine, consider yourself liberated. From this moment forward, you are free to do as you please, but please allow me to convey one crucial message: our paths must diverge. We cannot coexist in the same location, and this time, my resolve is unwavering. No amount of words or actions can alter this truth."

After saying this, she left Aryan alone, who then examined the details. He was shocked by the new project that aligns with his thoughts, a project he was supposed to lead, only to discover it was a surprise project that he accidentally ruined. While Aryan was leaving and keeping the details at the desk, Tanisha's driver suddenly stopped by. Aryan greeted him, asking about his well-being and if everything was fine since they hadn't seen each other in a while. Instead of greeting Aryan, Uncle immediately sensed something was amiss and asked, "What's wrong? What's making my son so unhappy?"

Aryan seemed surprised as he listened, and before he could inquire, his uncle disclosed, "Son, you've never asked about my health. Instead, you always give me a hug and joke around. But today, I see a gentleman who genuinely cares for his uncle, something we're not accustomed to." Noticing Aryan's tension, he proceeded, "If you're free, come over and let's chat."

44
Chapter Forty Four

Aryan walks straight to Uncle's house, seeming uncomfortable and avoiding eye contact, after seeing the CEO temporarily established at Uncle's new locality. Aryan's aunt embraced him tightly as he entered the house, bringing him a sense of calm after a long time apart. The entire community gathered to welcome Aryan, despite the CEO causing trouble. They still love him, and Aryan appears calm witnessing their caring gesture.

After Aryan left the area, he waited for Tanisha to arrive at her palace. After a while, she arrived and completely ignored Aryan, as if he meant nothing to her. Aryan appears tense upon seeing Tanisha's cold demeanor, and Urvashi attempts to address him, but he refuses to listen and states, "I may have made mistakes, but what she's doing is wrong. However, I will fix everything I've messed up, and until then, I won't be around."

Aryan vanished for a few weeks until, one day, Tanisha spotted breaking news about the Mayra Foundation's top-secret product release during a meeting. Tanisha was amazed and began investigating all account and partner details to find out who subsidised the Mayra foundation and organized a great event with world-famous designers. She searched for a long time but couldn't find anything, and in the end, she left for the event.

Upon arrival, she observed the presence of everyone at the event, including TRUST partners, employees, locals, and their workforce.

The big task was completed quickly by them, while she couldn't understand anything as the show continued showcasing the latest design. Finally, Mayra appeared on stage wearing a lovely dress. She approached the shy girl, who normally feared meeting strangers, but today she boldly stood before the enormous crowd and walked towards Mayra. Suddenly, Aryan appears on stage dressed just like Mayra, followed by Urvashi. They perfectly represent a complete family, which was the event's final design and theme i.e., family.

Aryan approached Tanisha to reveal the truth behind the event's success, but the CEO and his legal team showed up. Everyone stood at the back of Aryan, terrified by the destruction he caused previously. The CEO praised Aryan, saying, "The profit is impressive, which will benefit DIVINE as now the Mayra foundation becomes a new franchise offered by Tanisha at an interesting rate."

While Aryan appeared shocked, the CEO proceeded, "I hope she informed you all that she has transferred all rights of the Mayra foundation to me in exchange for TRUST." Before Aryan could comprehend the situation, the CEO's men began seizing all assets, but Aryan intervened by pushing one of them angrily. Just as the men were about to reach Mayra, Aryan angrily pushed them aside. The CEO stated, "I didn't come here for theatrics. I want my money. This company was built on my funds, and money is everything to a businessman. When you have it, you can take your company back. But until then, this company is mine, whether or not you like it."

Aryan once again found himself helpless as he failed to secure Mayra foundation, which was Mayra's gift. Aryan, seeing people seizing everything, appeared broken and was leaving. The CEO asked, "Without your surname, you are nothing but an ordinary man. Yet, I am treating you and your people calmly. Take this mercy and never stand before me, or I will forget our agreed deal."

Urvashi angrily questioned Tanisha, "who gave you the right to transfer the Mayra foundation rights to the CEO?" since she is the rightful owner.

Tanisha corrected Urvashi's words, reminding her she was just a caretaker and not a CEO. Tanisha's intention was to reclaim TRUST, and she has no regrets. Urvashi appears furious and questions why Aryan didn't give Tanisha the rights to the company, suspecting that Tanisha would act without thinking in order to regain control. Urvashi believes Tanisha's actions were wrong and cannot be justified by any words or actions.

Tanisha seems tense, her brows furrowed with guilt, as what she did weighs heavily on her conscience. As Tanisha worked late into the night, she suddenly sensed someone approaching her cabin, sending a shiver down her spine. With a sense of unease, she cautiously opened the door to find Aryan standing there, avoiding eye contact. They stood in silence for a moment, unsure of what to say.

A moment of complete silence passed before Aryan broke it by asking, "Can I have the file you prepared for me?" Tanisha silently handed the file before leaving, and asked, "Do you still want to work for TRUST?" Aryan departed without uttering a word.

Aryan's smile vanished after that day. Completing the assigned task is his top priority, even though he often faces various challenges. Luckily, Aryan's secret helper, continues to assist him in managing resources and suggesting better plans. By following the guidance, he not only achieves his goals but also gains new skills.

Aryan effortlessly achieved each project level, gradually building the TRUST and attracting numerous partnership opportunities. Aryan's business strategies make him the new face and voice of TRUST, leaving Tanisha behind. However, he denies all proposed positions and credits Tanisha, choosing to remain an employee.

While Tanisha remained silent, Aryan kept setting records and generating significant profits for TRUST. During a grand party organized by Tanisha, everyone gathered, but without Aryan's music, there were no party vibes. He sat alone, watching others revel in his success, feeling no joy, and quietly retreated to the records room. Aryan, working late at night, followed a familiar tune and arrived in a dark hallway. He discovered a recorder playing his tune, reminding him of the deal with the CEO, which he angrily destroyed.

45

Chapter Forty Five

While in a meeting, Tanisha got a text from a stranger advising her to sabotage Aryan's project. Just as she was about to ignore it, she received another text containing confidential DIVINE details. She asked everyone to leave her alone and sat in solitude, pondering the unexpected revelation shared by a stranger. Aryan continues working on the final stage of the project, unaware of what's happening behind his back, and is desperate to finish it for TRUST's profit. One day, Akash visits Aryan's site.

Aryan is amazed to see him, as it's been a long time since he met an old friend. He forgives him for past wrongdoings and they reminisce about old memories, taking a break from work. Aryan asks him, "If you change your mind, it's never too late to start over. Come to work from tomorrow." While saying this, he tossed the duplicate key to the site.

After leaving the site, Akash informs his master, in DIVINE, and reports everything about Aryan's final project to the CEO before leaving. Akash occasionally visits the site after that day, where he explains his strategies and plan of action to the CEO.

The situation continued until one day when Anshika visited Aryan's site, but was shocked to see Akash there, so she left without meeting Aryan. Later, Aryan contacted Anshika to meet and inquire about her sudden departure, but before she could explain, Akash unexpectedly appeared and was astonished to find his sister present. Aryan quickly handed Akash a crucial document that Anshika attempted to retrieve, but Akash prevented her from touching it. Observing which Aryan supports Akash, "It's crucial and I have faith in your brother to deliver it to the rightful recipients."

Aryan asked Anshika if she came to inform him about Akash before leaving quietly. Anshika turns to Aryan, who was happy to have his friend back, and chooses to stay quiet while looking into his eyes. As Aryan noticed her silence, he proceeded to discuss her health and future plans, but just as they began talking, Yogesh arrived with his friends and encircled Aryan.

Anshika, seeing this, sought refuge behind Aryan. However, before any action could be taken, Aryan cautioned Yogesh to take note of their surroundings, where they were being protected by Aditya's special guards, who had guns trained on Yogesh and his friends. Yogesh's companions step away, but he remains, extending his hand towards Anshika.

Since Yogesh came for Anshika and not Aryan, he gave Anshika's hand to Yogesh and encouraged them both to start anew. Anshika agreed to Aryan's calm demeanor, but Yogesh remained unchanged. Before leaving, he warned Aryan, "I can forgive everything except what you did to me. But for Anshika's sake, I'll endure this pain. However, if you continue to meet her, I may change my mind. It's better to keep your distance from her, as I want nothing to do with you."

While leaving, Aryan asked if he could take back the love his aunt had shared between them. Yogesh appears annoyed, but before he can react, Anshika grabs his hand. Aryan warns, "I'm only keeping quiet for my sister's sake, otherwise I would have taught you a lesson for damaging our community's place. You're safe as long as Anshika is between us."

When Aryan and his men were leaving the site later at night, a collision between cars and trucks occurred, blocking the entrance. Masked hooligans then entered the site and started destroying the product that was in the final stage. Aryan sustained severe injuries while attempting to save the product and the site. Then, Akash and Aditya arrived at the site and saved them. Despite being injured, Aryan gazed at the broken product, feeling shattered as it destroyed his hopes in an instant. Witnessing Aryan's hopelessness, Aditya tried to offer comfort, but his words fell on deaf ears and Aryan left shattered.

Aryan, feeling lonely and broken, sat near the park and called the person he loves most. After a while, Tanisha arrived. Upon seeing Aryan injured and holding the remains of the damaged product, she offers reassurance by saying, "Everything will be alright!" and holds Aryan's hand. Aryan wondered, "Why is it that every time I attempt to make things right, I end up failing?"

Cassandra rushed to the spot and found them together. As Tanisha silently takes her precious love, Cassandra seems jealous for the first time. Aryan rested with Mayra after finishing his medication. Urvashi saw them resting and seemed worried. She asked, "What happened and who did this to him?"

Tanisha casually replied, "it was a hard day for him, so let him rest." Urvashi asked, "You've changed, Tanisha. The person I knew was caring and humble, whether they were a relative or a stranger. But now, you seem heartless."

Anshika has been searching for Aryan for 3 days outside Tanisha's palace, but the guards won't let her in but she refuses to leave. Upon hearing a loud sound, Aryan went outside and saw the guards forcefully escorting Anshika away. Aryan shouted at them and was about to leave, but the guards intervened, saying, "You can't leave by yourself, it's the boss's orders." Anshika told Aryan that Akash has been missing for 3 days, and his phone is not working. Only Aryan was the last person he was with.

Aryan comforted her, saying, "Don't worry, we'll find him." A voice from behind her suddenly asked Aryan, "Did you not hear her correctly?" Aryan glanced in the opposite direction, seeing Yogesh. Yogesh then said, "She claimed you were the last person Akash contacted and was seen with. Because of this, you are our main suspect. Will you come with us willingly, or must I use force?"

Aryan glanced at Anshika, who no longer trusted him, and asked, "Did you also think I could harm Akash?" Aryan surrenders when Anshika remains silent, leading to their trip to the station. Tanisha, upon learning this, becomes tense and calls Akash to find out his hiding place. Tanisha without delay left.

<h1 align="center">46</h1>

<h1 align="center">Chapter Forty Six</h1>

She arrived at the dimly lit bungalow, entered, and found herself locked in. Inside, Akash was injured and chained, guarded by the men. This scene triggers her memory of the crooked businessman's execution by the CEO, and just as she reaches this realization, the CEO appears and says, "We have much to discuss, my dear," displaying the phone she had given to Akash.

The CEO went on, "I had assumed this individual was loyal, but he betrayed me and even attempted to sabotage Aryan's project on someone else's command. When questioned about who ordered him to do all this, he remained silent. Can you please tell me the reason behind all this and why you went against me?"

The CEO commanded to torture Akash after observing Tanisha's silence, but when she heard his cries of pain, Tanisha confessed, "Because you were going to appoint Aryan as the CEO of TRUST, a decision that all TRUST and DIVINE shareholders had already agreed upon. I won't allow you to take TRUST after taking the FAITH."

The CEO questioned, "What evidence do you have?" Tanisha revealed the confidential details to him, causing the CEO to burst into laughter and declare it as fake. He then showed her the genuine details, indicating that he intended to restore full rights to Tanisha instead of Aryan, accompanied by the CEO's exclusive DIVINE seal, absent in the fake document.

Tanisha appears shocked upon seeing this, contemplating her actions. The CEO appears devastated by her recent decision and confessed, "I treated you like my own daughter, even at the expense of my son's well-being, hoping you would help him thrive. But it seems I made a mistake."

The CEO, saying this, retracted the contract and added, "You don't deserve to be my daughter. I forgave you earlier because of Aryan, but this time you've messed up everything." In the midst of their conversation, Aryan suddenly arrived, leaving both of them shocked at how he knew about this place.

Few moments before coming to the site,

While Yogesh made a call, Aryan was arrested and reported, "As you requested, I have successfully apprehended him. Anshika also assisted me; she is innocent and believes Aryan is responsible. However, she will never know that both Akash and I work for you."

Right after he finishes the call, guards encircle the entire station. Aditya silently removes Aryan and warns Yogesh before departing.

While shooting some of his men, he reiterated his previous warning to stay away from his son. Yogesh, feeling powerless, pointed the gun at him and warned, "I spared you this time, but not next time."

Aryan was surprised to learn that both Yogesh and Akash were working for the CEO. He inquired if Aditya was already aware, but failed to give him a heads up.

Aryan asked, "what about me? Despite calling me your son, you allowed me to suffer when ordered by your master. For once, you didn't consider what I'm going through. My father's actions caused immense destruction. I worked tirelessly to correct his mistakes, but he ruined everything and crushed my last hope.

Aditya remained silent as Aryan expressed his desire to meet the CEO. Aditya handed the tracker of the site, having which Aryan asked the last thing, "I don't want you to protect me anymore and never show up even if I am dying, let me die." Listening to this,

Aditya seems broken and left.

Present time,

Aryan stood before the CEO, his voice filled with anger and determination. "Last day," he said, "you sent local hooligans to demolish my project. But it was more than just a project; it was a retaliation for the local people your ego has crushed. It was a method for me to cleanse my guilt for your actions, yet you took everything from me while I stayed quiet. You even took the Mayra foundation, a gift for a girl I consider my daughter, but you won't stop at that. Finally, you not only include Aditya but also my friends to torment me as much as possible, but you fail this time because I am emotionless and feel nothing. Money means everything to you, but for me, the trust of my people is everything. I won't let you harm anyone because I have a family now." He held Tanisha's hand and brought her to his side, saying, "I'll settle all your debts in exchange for staying away from my family."

The CEO questioned their relationship, asking, "If they are all your family, then what am I to you?"

Aryan replied, his voice dripping with disdain, "You are nothing but a money-driven businessman, consumed by your ego, obsessed with your victories, and drunk on power. You forgot about your son, who used to trust you unconditionally, but that trust is long gone. I no longer see you as my uncle because my real uncle would never hurt people and he always cares for me. However, that person tried to kill me and ruined everything I worked for. Your ego would have been satisfied if I had died in that mess, I believe."

Immediately after he spoke, the CEO delivered a hard slap to him.

Aryan smiled and stated, "Whether you accept it or not, the truth remains that you are no longer the uncle I once knew, but merely an ordinary businessman. I'm grateful that you set me free from our relationship because otherwise, I would have never met Tanisha who, despite hating me, never abandoned me. She still cares about her people, even after everything was taken from her, and moreover, she cares about me. This is the definition of a family, but you'll never comprehend. You missed the chance to have a son, and now you have lost everything - a son, his trust, Aditya, and your daughter."

The CEO remains silent, leaving Tanisha confused about why he won't reveal the truth.

Aryan declared, "I will leave with my people, and if your ego still isn't satisfied, your men can try to stop us. I am finished fighting with and for you. Everything is finished now."

He unchained Akash and left with both, leaving the CEO in silence as he watched his son depart, a reminder of the night when he took everything from Aryan. Today, Aryan took everything from him - their only remaining bond as father and son.

Aryan brought Akash to his house. Anshika tightly holds her brother and is about to apologize to Aryan, who stops her and starts leaving. Akash asks, "Won't you tell her about me?" Aryan responded, "You're fortunate to have a family. Don't destroy their trust." Then he walked away.

47

Chapter Forty Seven

At the palace, Tanisha ponders why the CEO stayed quiet. Aryan arrived late at night and quietly made his way to Mayra's room. Tanisha asked, "Where have you been?"

Calmly, Aryan responded without making eye contact, "I only wanted to see Mayra one last time, then I'll go." Tanisha stops holding his hand and asks, "Are you okay?"

Aryan turned and held her tighter, breaking Tanisha's heart. She melted and held him back, while Aryan, unable to face her, held her even tighter, seeking solace in his embrace. Once Aryan regains consciousness, he wants to leave, but Tanisha insists on guiding him to his room. She sits next to him, taking care of him while making him lie.

While resting, Aryan continues to tightly hold her hand, despite her desire to let go. Tanisha couldn't resist and lied down next to him when she saw him scared. Aryan recognized the familiar scent of his secret friend and pulled her closer, whispering, "I missed you so much, please stay with me," before softly kissing her neck. Tanisha, who was new to this feeling, desired more of his care and stayed close to him, ultimately bringing calm to Aryan as they spent the night together resting.

The next day, Aryan wakes up to find Mayra close by. He holds her gently and kisses her forehead. Mayra woke up, and he walked her to the garden, spending the whole day together undisturbed per

Tanisha's order. Urvashi's gaze at Tanisha's eyes revealed a change in her emotions towards Aryan, unlike before when she would stare at them all day. Aryan placed Mayra, who was sleeping, in her bed and went to his house behind.

The following day, Tanisha visited the CEO's palace and found him sitting on his grand chair, gazing at Aryan's portrait. When he heard the sound of heels walking, he turned and asked, "What is it this time that has brought you here? Is it about TRUST or Aryan? You can share your concern and then leave."

Tanisha responded by saying, "I came here for you."

The CEO remained silent, then she asked, "Why didn't you tell everything to Aryan when you had the chance? Why did you save me and take all the blame? You had the chance to end the war your son started and restore your relationship with Aryan. I used to want revenge on you and your son, but I can no longer use Aryan to seek revenge on you."

The CEO anxiously asked, "Is he okay?" Tanisha cuts in, her voice filled with concern, and replied, "No, he's not okay, and I can't bear to see him in pain any longer. I am tired of witnessing his struggle with the guilt and pain you bestowed upon him, so I choose to give you everything I have and disappear forever."

After giving all her shares to DIVINE and receiving no response from the CEO, Tanisha admitted defeat and prepared to leave. However, the CEO questioned why she didn't inform Aryan herself, and instead gave away everything she had. The CEO noted that the girl they knew would have fought to protect TRUST, but it seemed like she was trying to escape. "Tell me, what scare you?" asked CEO.

Tanisha tearfully admitted, "I made a mistake and ruined everything, but Aryan still supported me."

I'm afraid he'll figure out it was me, not you. I lack the courage to confront him because he has forgiven me multiple times before, but now it involves the local people I have deceived them. If this were to come out, I would not only lose Aryan but everything else as well - my people, my relationship with Urvashi, and even Mayra, who is the last connection to my late brother, not to mention the Mayra foundation which was a precious gift to her. I can't maintain eye contact, speak, or stand confidently in front of him because I lost my supportive godfather who always came to my aid.

The caring CEO gently holds his daughter's head as she cries, and she holds him tightly and cries. The CEO remains still and silent, showing neither concern nor interest. Tanisha said to him before leaving, "I wanted to meet you last time before leaving. May you always be happy and may your relationship with Aryan be resolved."

The CEO responded, "You're fortunate to have a family. Not everyone is as lucky as you. But I'm glad you've realized this before it's too late."

The next day, Tanisha and her family visited TRUST for the last time. She handed everything over to the DIVINE shareholders and was about to leave when Aryan showed up. Mayra runs towards him, holds him tightly, and refuses to let go. Tanisha pleads with Aryan, "Please make it easier for us and say goodbye to Mayra, then we'll leave peacefully."

Aryan accepted Tanisha's heartless decision and comforted Mayra by lying about going on a trip. Mayra left with her family while Aryan helplessly watched.

The CEO gazes at a portrait of Aryan while Aditya informs him that Tanisha and her family have departed for the airport. To which CEO doesn't react. Aditya stayed put after sharing the information, perplexing the CEO, who inquired, "What is causing you hesitation in sharing with me?"

Aditya grabbed the CEO's hand and turned him towards his side. He said, "You've always treated me like family, despite my position as a servant." I never had a family, but you gave me one. Now, I fear losing Aryan forever if Tanisha leaves.

The CEO took his hand off and was leaving. Aditya asked, "Can you imagine the heartbreak of losing both your children in a single day?" The CEO stops and replies, "I always wanted my children to be happy, can't I ask for that?" "There's nothing you can wish for and not get," Aditya replied, describing the CEO as a stubborn and powerful individual who consistently had proved his worth. The CEO replied in a resigned tone, "It's impossible this time."

Aditya confronted the CEO, his voice filled with determination, and said, "It's never too late until you lose hope. You're not just an ordinary person. You're the one who can bring down an entire city when a stranger hurts your son. But if you don't take action today, it's you who will hurt Aryan the worst. To prevent that, you need to stop Tanisha. Only she can bring your son back and fulfill your wish of making Aryan the successor of DIVINE."

Tanisha and her family were already left on a plane before the CEO could stop her. His men stopped everything where it was by blocking all runway and roads. The Army, police, airport guards, and everyone gathered with the airport authority head who, in a trembling voice, asked the annoyed CEO, "Why is there so much chaos?"

The CEO mentioned he wants Tanisha Malhotra and her family, who recently departed, to come back. You can do whatever you want, but I am set on having her back, no matter the expense. The airport head begged, "It will inconvenience other passengers." The CEO gripped his neck tightly and emphasized, "I won't ask twice, so comply with my instructions."

The plane took half an hour to land after deporting only Tanisha's family. Tanisha appeared surprised when she saw the entire DIVINE group and a large army force gathered at the airport, while the CEO walked past everyone towards Mayra, who was hiding behind Urvashi. He sat on his knee and pulled out the sweets that Aryan usually gives her. She took it, took a bite, and gave half to the CEO, who had it from Mayra's hand, and they held each other calmly.

The CEO's heart melted, and he expressed confidence, saying, "You are the one who can bring my son back." The CEO ignored Tanisha, making it clear he still hasn't forgiven her, saying she can't leave until she corrects the mess and returns to work.

While Aryan was still at TRUST, the company that took everything from him in just one day, he suddenly feels a gentle touch on his hand. Mayra caught his eye as he turned and he instantly hugged her with happiness. Mayra and Urvashi were present, excluding Tanisha. Aryan questioned, "Where's Tanisha?"

Urvashi said that she had been to her favorite place. She gave the address and departed. Aryan walked to the site and saw Tanisha standing at the gate of a partially demolished building. Sensing someone beside her, she looks and sees Aryan, who immediately embraces her tightly, clearly delighted by her return. Tanisha also embraces him warmly, knowing he was the reason she came back.

Tanisha responded, "We've already left, but the CEO doesn't allow it and called the plane back, so we're still here."

As Aryan was losing his hold on her, she unexpectedly admitted, "But I came back for you, not the CEO." Aryan halts, his grip slipping, as Tanisha persists, "I understand your desire to absolve yourself of guilt for what the CEO did to both the company and the local people, but until we rectify that wrongdoing, I'm not going anywhere."

Aryan kissed her forehead warmly and prepared to depart, but she stopped him by asking, "Do you remember when you asked me what I like the most? Don't you want to find out what it is?" Unlocking the door, she leads him to the building entrance and turns on the light. Aryan looks shocked when he sees the building's name and turns to her side, asking, "Are you the previous CEO of FAITH?"

Tanisha responded with calmness, saying, "no longer, it's a lengthy tale." Aryan held her hand and urged her to share everything. Witnessing his desperation, she disclosed that the CEO's son fraudulently acquired the company, and it is he who has tied us together in an unbreakable bond. I used to hate his son, whom I had never met before, but not anymore. I have you now, who is the complete opposite of him. He takes while you believe in sharing. He plays tricks while you earn with pride. Despite being the CEO's son, he could never fulfill the CEO's expectations. You will be the one to rule DIVINE, just like the CEO wanted. When that day comes, I will be the luckiest person on earth because you will set me free from this bond.

Aryan remained silent while Tanisha spoke about her favorite place. She asked him if he found it beautiful. Aryan's tear-filled eyes responded, "I feel the same way." He gently held her face, making her meet his gaze, and assured her, "I understand how much it hurts to see your business fail, but I promise I'll restore it for you."

She acknowledged Aryan's respect for her past by kissing his forehead. She expressed, "With you by our side, nothing else matters. My priority now is to prepare you for the DIVINE, just as the CEO intended. If you succeed, the bond between the CEO and you can be revived."

Aryan, while removing his hand from her, asks, "Never have dreams that can't come true." Tanisha responded, "I learned this from you and maybe one day my dream could come true." As she was leaving, she noticed Aryan staying and asked, "Aren't you coming?"

Aryan said he has to meet his uncle in the neighborhood and will leave from here. Tanisha reminds him, "Be quick, don't forget, Mayra is waiting for you," and then leaves.

After Tanisha departed, Aryan reflects on the chaos he caused in her life, affecting Urvashi and Mayra's future. Unaware of what he had done, he shouted out loud while thinking.

The CEO was informed that Aryan wants to meet him in his study room. The CEO saw Aryan outside, holding the same gift he had bought for him, and asked, "Do you know the cost of this?" "The CEO seems confused," Aryan continued, "a girl who recently lost her family and was now running the company left by her late parents. In her family, there's a widow who always helped me when I asked for it, even though she sometimes goes against Tanisha, who also has a daughter who isn't mature enough and has no father. Her future and the financial stability of her entire family hinged on the success of the company I would acquire for you, as a way to make up for never having done anything for you before. This was my plan to regain the success that was once your source of pride. I didn't realize that your pride would come at such a high price, jeopardizing an entire family's property, trust, and future for this coveted prize, which turned out to be claimed by none other than myself."

The CEO walked closer, noticing the tension in Aryan's body, and called out his real name, "Akash."

Aryan interrupted and corrected him, "Don't mention that name. It's you who concealed the truth and sent me to the same girl whose family's future I have destroyed. You already knew, I live with this guilt. I even confessed it on a phone call while you were at the hospital."

The CEO disclosed, "I was not conscious at that particular moment."

Aryan asked, "Then who answered the call?"

The CEO replied, "It was Tanisha who was looking after me." Aryan held his head and asked, "How could you? You knew she was the girl from whom I took everything, and you still sent me there to work with her. How could you?"

As he asked this, he angrily started breaking the stuff that Aditya held tightly, causing him to stop. Aryan walked closer, his voice filled with regret as he whispered, "I curse the day I took someone's peace for your pride. This hand signed the order, a great mistake of my life. How could I have been so blind?"

Uttering these words, he slams his hands onto the table with such force that his palms bleed. Without missing a beat, he turns to the CEO and adds, "Akash is dead now. Now, I identify as Aryan, determined not to be the son who destroys anyone's future for the sake of his father's pride. As the character you created, I am Aryan, and I am grateful for it. Perhaps, by being Aryan, I can correct the mistakes of both of us, something Akash could never achieve."

Aryan stopped before leaving and confessed, "I killed your son, Akash, tonight. After this, I am Aryan, an employee of TRUST, a friend of Tanisha, a caretaker of Mayra, and I will always support them when they need help. Because she means everything to me now, I will give back what I have taken from her. Until then, I won't stop."

48
Chapter Forty Eight

After Aryan's departure, the CEO appeared shattered and remained silent, consoled by Aditya who mentioned, "He's upset about what he found out today." The CEO, with tears in his eyes, laughs loudly and confesses, "Contrary to what you may think, I actually want Tanisha to be the successor, as she has all the qualities I had and Aryan lacks."

Aditya appears shocked and questions, "You always desired this outcome and never prevented Tanisha, even though you were aware of her every action and when she would act because it's all under your control, isn't it?"

The CEO shared, "The day she entered my life through business, I knew she would be Aryan's partner and the future leader of DIVINE. I created this mess in order to bring them together. And today, they will die for each other. She not only made Aryan live and fight with pride, but he also proved his worth multiple times when given the opportunity and resources. He could be the best among all businessmen, which I could never achieve. Her one lie turned my dream into reality," he says, holding his uncle Aditya tightly. "I am happy now because what I desired has finally come true."

Aditya abruptly interrupts the CEO, stating that they didn't admit their desire for each other; what they had was a sense of guilt. Once the issue is resolved, they will go their separate ways." The CEO responded, "If that's how it is, then I will create a situation where they have no choice but to fight against me. They will soon realize that they are facing a rival businessman, not a father. The decision will also determine if Tanisha is worthy of DIVINE and their relationship."

"Be cautious of your thoughts," Aditya warned the CEO, explaining that any missteps could have lasting consequences and require additional time to resolve. "I promise to unite them and do everything possible. Please pray and care for my children." said the CEO.

Aditya dismissed his words, declaring, "your conduct is not right. By following your order once, I lost my son's trust. What you're doing now might not destroy the father-son relationship, but it will shatter Aryan's trust in love and morality. Don't be so harsh with him, show him some mercy. If his mother were alive, she would have protected him." As soon as he spoke, the CEO tightly grips his neck, recalling the murder of his wife when she attempted to take Aryan from him. He strangles Aditya until he loses consciousness, declaring, "Not even death can separate us."

Following the meeting with the CEO, Aryan headed to Tanisha's palace. Instead of entering, he went to the back side of his house. Seeing him cold, Tanisha followed him. When she entered the room, she noticed his bleeding hand and reopened past wounds. Tanisha ran towards him to help, but Aryan pushed her away to avoid touching him. Tanisha persisted and asked, "We were happy a moment ago, what suddenly changed? Did you learn something about me?"

Aryan stayed quiet while Tanisha cautiously approached and gently grasped his injured hand, causing him to turn away without meeting her gaze. While gazing into her eyes, Aryan admitted, "I am not who I appear to be; perhaps one day you will discover a harsh truth about my past, and then you will despise me. Therefore, I have chosen to terminate our friendship and depart peacefully."

Tanisha questioned Aryan, "Are you brave enough to be apart from Mayra?" Aryan stayed quiet as Tanisha observed, "I noticed how lost you seemed when we left today. We are connected not because of our relation, but because of the bond you have with the local people, Mayra, our family, and especially us. We cannot sever this bond, so let it remain as it is. If any problems arise, we will solve them together, like a family."

Aryan claimed, "I have no family left; it's the guilt that keeps us bound, but once I erase it, I will leave, and nothing can hinder me." With that, he removed his hand and began bandaging himself.

Taking his hand back, Tanisha proceeded to dress the wound. She then paused and inquired, "To alleviate your guilt, you must disprove the CEO, which requires my help. If not me, no one else can help you remove the stain caused by the CEO on your character. If you want to be recognized as different and not the CEO's son, you need to think and work differently, not how the CEO wants."

When the bandage was completed, she gazed at Aryan who remained silent. Noticing this, she kept the modified file and, before departing, uttered, "If you change your mind, let me know." and left.

Next day,

Tanisha, along with a few staff and partners, visited the site for inspection, but they were unsure where to begin because of extensive damage. Tanisha decided to start over and make the project work without Aryan, so she handed site keys and project details to Cassandra. Aryan suddenly appeared and took both things from Tanisha, stating, "No need, as I am the one solely responsible for completing this project, and I will do it." Cassandra notices Tanisha's calm expression upon seeing Aryan, which unsettles her.

Tanisha mentioned we need to create a new contract for the project, and once it's ready, Cassandra will let you know. Aryan interrupted, saying, "Before we sign the contract, we need to discuss a few points."

During the meeting, Aryan proposed, "I'll take charge of the project and investor management." Tanisha appears surprised and inquired, "What makes this project so special?" Aryan fearlessly declared, "I demand 60% of the profit shares." When Aryan appeared confident, Tanisha immediately agreed, which totally shocked Cassandra. How did she agree so easily?

Aryan finished the project in 3 months with constant work, while Tanisha assisted at every step and now awaits the result. Aryan's project at the business summit surprised everyone with its high score and profit, breaking the norm in the business world. Tanisha, instead of taking the prize, gave it to Aryan. Aryan was about to grab the prize, but then he got a notification and was leaving the summit. Tanisha stops him and asks, "Why are you leaving your success party?"

Aryan showed a video where Tanisha confessed to the CEO about sabotaging Aryan's project.

Tanisha appeared shocked and remained silent as Aryan stated, "I refuse to believe this video. Just look into my eyes and deny its truth." Tanisha avoids making eye contact, Aryan questioned, "I want to trust you, tell me it's false." Tanisha's silence made Aryan feel shattered, and he expressed, "I trusted you, but you're just like the CEO who only cares about herself. I'm finished working for you. This is our final meeting, and I never want to see your face again." He stormed out in anger.

The CEO appeared out of nowhere just as she was about to throw the award. She grabbed him, crying, and pleaded, "He knows everything, he didn't let me explain. Please do something or he'll leave forever."

The CEO, moved by Tanisha's tears, gently wipes them away and asks, "Do you truly desire his return?" Tanisha pleaded with the CEO, "Give me one chance to prove my innocence. He doesn't want to see my face anymore."

The CEO stepped back and returned the award to her, saying, "Keep it safe until its rightful owner returns." Tanisha, who was previously unforgiven by the CEO, is now ready to help her immediately, forgetting everything that happened in the past.

49

Chapter Forty Nine

Upon arriving home from the success party, Cassandra is about to enter but suddenly stops. Turning around, she sees Aryan in a miserable state and without hesitation, extends her hand to him. Aryan skips her hand and tightly holds her, confessing, "I have nobody to trust but you, everyone betrays me. You're the only person I trust."

Cassandra brought him to her room and made him lie about wanting to leave. Aryan asked, "Aren't you gonna stick around?"

Cassandra hops into bed and snuggles up with Aryan, who wanted to say sorry for taking her for granted on his path to success. Cassandra, who was cold till now, saw Aryan broken and said, "Everyone might abandon you, but not me. You mean everything to me. If I lose you, I lose myself."

Immediately after she spoke, Aryan passionately kissed her and apologized. Cassandra forgave him and returned the kiss, asking, "Will you show me your affection today?" Aryan and she intimately connected, reigniting their love after a long absence.

While Aryan rested next to Cassandra the next day, she received some news headlines that made her gasp in disbelief. She hastily informed Aryan and briskly set off to locate the local people. Upon reaching the site, Aryan discovered that the CEO's legal authorities had halted all the expenses he had pledged to cover for the next six months.

As Aryan tried to process the information, another headline popped up, revealing that DIVINE planned to sell the shares of Mayra foundation to compensate for the losses caused by TRUST CEO. In response, his men hurried to the site to take control of the property. At TRUST, the atmosphere was tense with the presence of media, legal authorities, and CEO men. Tanisha was just about to sign the contract when Aryan abruptly arrived, snatching the document from her hands. With a determined look, he turned to the CEO and boldly declared, "Mayra foundation is under my ownership, and I will never allow anyone else to claim this organization. It belongs to me, now and forever."

The CEO replied, his voice filled with frustration, "This organization was built on my expense. I'm trying to cover the loss made by TRUST, but I'm not blaming them. I'm only taking Mayra's shares to prevent further damage. Consider this mercy and leave."

Aryan remains motionless and fearlessly inquired, "What is the price for Mayra's freedom?" The CEO appeared both amazed and challenged and said, "Have you ever seen this much money before, which I desire? Additionally, do you have the ability to earn that much on your own? You have 6 months to return my money, including 10 times the interest. Do you still want to buy Mayra, or will you surrender?"

Aryan remains silent for a moment, then says, "I agree."

This shocked everyone, including the CEO who couldn't accept defeat and added, "Fine, but I have a condition. You must earn all the money without any help, or I will dissolve the contract and MAYRA foundation will be mine. Do you agree?"

Aryan silently agreed and now faced an impossible task that requires TRUST's. Aryan is holding onto his resignation, waiting for the perfect moment to deliver it, and joins TRUST. Tanisha appears happy upon Aryan's return, whether willingly or forcibly. The CEO remains calm upon seeing her happiness and silently reassures himself that nothing will separate them until his dream is achieved.

Tanisha called for a meeting with the crew, but Aryan was absent, and it proceeded without him. Once the meeting was over, she searched for Aryan and discovered him in the study room, searching for a particular file. Silently, she handed the CEO's project that Aryan had previously refused. This time, he accepted it and began to walk away. Tanisha asked, "Why did you choose this project specifically? There are other projects with greater potential and profitability than this one."

Aryan responded without looking at her, "Unlike you, I'm not concerned about the profit. Furthermore, I need to demonstrate my capabilities to the CEO. If he entrusted me with this project, I am confident he has something extraordinary in mind for me, and I am determined to fulfill his vision."

While the rest of the crew chose another task, Aryan took on a standalone project with no assistance. Out of nowhere, Akash and his team appeared before Aryan and offered help. Aryan, who had already been betrayed by Akash, no longer wants to collaborate with him. Akash disclosed the Tanisha order, stating that for the CEO project, a crew will be required with him as the leader. However, if you prefer not to work with him, you have the option to leave the project since he already has experience working with the CEO and understands his work culture and style better than you do.

Aryan declined the offer and silently left, but later surprised Akash by returning with a new intern named Anshika. Akash was shocked and asked, "What are you trying to accomplish?"

Aryan confronted him, stating that he no longer trusted him and emphasized the presence of Anshika as a safeguard against deception, warning him to consider the consequences for his sister before taking any further action.

Akash told Tanisha about it, but she disregarded him, accusing him of betrayal. Despite this, she still gave him a chance because he had betrayed the CEO when she needed his help. I gave you a second chance to prevent Aryan from leaving TRUST, but since you're involved in MAYRA foundation's destruction, he will probably make a mistake seeking revenge. I desire the opportunity to control him as my servant, as you are the crucial element for me to accomplish my tasks.

Akash asked, "What if he seeks revenge on me, or if he doesn't, the CEO will. As He holds grudges against those who deceive or harm him, a fact we are both well aware of."

Tanisha remembered the past events that had upset the CEO, but he remained silent, leaving her uncertain of his intentions. However, she confidently replied, "Rest assured, as long as you follow my orders, neither the CEO nor Aryan will be able to harm you."

Before leaving, Akash expressed his concern about Aryan adding Anshika to the team, suggesting that she could be used against them. Tanisha, upon hearing this, glanced out the window and saw Aryan with Anshika, appearing calm despite her previous unease. She reassured Akash, saying, "Don't worry, I will handle it," and disregarded his request, leaving him empty-handed.

While the TRUST crew worked on various projects, Ayan and Akash's team tackled an impossible task effortlessly. During his free time, Aryan sits calmly with Anshika in the office and later leaves with Cassandra. Two months had passed since he last saw or spoke to Tanisha, until one day when Aryan visited TRUST. As he arrived, he noticed that the rest of the crew had already left for the site, leaving him waiting for his own crew to arrive. However, that day, no one came. After that, Anshika was called and they all left for some work, leaving Aryan as the only person working in the company.

While he was working, he felt a familiar aura and followed her scent to Tanisha's cabin. He waited for a while until the perfume started fading, then unlocked the door and entered the cabin. However, by then, she had already left. He was about to leave, but then he paused and glanced at the small recorder he had previously broken.

He appears silent while Tanisha claims, "It's the same recorder the CEO destroyed, but I restored it, and all its data is secure."

Tanisha asked Aryan if he still liked it or if it no longer mattered to him. Aryan responded, "You can choose whichever option suits you best," and then left. Tanisha mentioned that the old Aryan would do anything for the recorder, but this new Aryan didn't seem to care.

Aryan's eyes narrowed in anger as he turned towards Tanisha, closing the distance between them. "Yes, I've changed," he retorted bitterly. "And it's all because of you. Your betrayal, your deceitful tricks, and your web of lies have not only wounded me, but they've also shattered the trust I once had in you. Now I'm scared of myself for trusting you blindly, even fighting with the CEO for you, but you hurt me deeply, and the damage can never be healed."

He handed the recorder to Tanisha, saying that he didn't need it anymore because one person destroyed it and the other person fixed it. Ironically, both of them were people he used to care about, but now he hates them both.

He left Tanisha broken and found Yogesh waiting at the TRUST main gate. They stood silent for a moment, then Yogesh spoke up, "I already warned you to stay away from Anshika, but you do as you please. However, today I will put an end to this since no one is here to interrupt us."

Aryan said, "Well, then what are we waiting for?"

They sprint towards each other and engage in a colossal fight, using everything around them to strike. Eventually, both were badly injured but refused to give up and prepared to attack each other with sharp objects. Then, Tanisha intervened by firing a shot to halt them. Despite both stopped, Yogesh refused to quit and hurled the pointed rod at Aryan. To protect Tanisha, Aryan took the blow on his back.

Tanisha held Aryan tightly, his mouth filled with the taste of blood, as he defiantly whispered, "Only a coward strikes from behind."

Yogesh acknowledged, "I picked up that trick from you," while Tanisha fired additional bullets and threatened him not to advance and said, "If you move forward once more, my aim won't fail this time."

"Do you really think I'm scared of you?" Yogesh replied. You were both free until the CEO supported you, but now you have nothing, you are nothing.

Tanisha, while listening, lowers the gun and says, "Even if you had the opportunity, you still couldn't save your mother. Aryan saved you from that guilt a long time ago, but instead of being grateful, you keep hurting him over and over." Yogesh became annoyed and cautioned, "Stop right there or things will get worse for you as well."

Tanisha responded, "I am far superior to you, and I have the power to defeat you right now." She then gathered all her men and the DIVINE armed forces to surround Yogesh with guns, leaving him anxious. Tanisha noticed his tension and said, "Don't worry, I won't let you off that easily. You'll have your revenge, but for now, he's mine. Nobody can touch him until I've dealt with him." Before leaving, Yogesh informs Aryan that he's saved today because of this girl.

Tanisha wanted to help Aryan after he left, but he got up on his own and walked out of TRUST. Urvashi arrived just as he barely walked a short distance, but he refused her help and fainted before leaving on his own. Urvashi supported him and took him to a secret place for three days of medical treatment while Aryan was unconscious.

Aryan finally wakes up and discovers himself bandaged in an unfamiliar location. He asks Urvashi, "Where am I?"

Urvashi explained, "I brought you to a hidden location instead of a hospital to prevent any potential problems." Aryan stood up and approached, his voice filled with gratitude as he said, "I never properly thanked you for always being there for me when I needed help, but I worry that my presence might have a negative impact on you. Please, allow me to take my leave."

Before he could leave, Urvashi's voice trembled as she spoke, "I know our families are at odds and it seems impossible to reconcile, but in you, I see a glimmer of hope. You're the one who brings Mayra back to life, and I fear that will fade if things get worse."

Aryan gently held her trembling hand, reassuring her, "I promise to never leave you, Mayra. I will protect and care for you as if you were my own daughter." Saying this, he gently pressed his lips against her forehead and continued, "I give you my word."

50
Chapter Fifty

Urvashi arrived at the palace and Tanisha asked, "Is he okay now?" Urvashi shared his health status and went to her room. She locked the gate and stood in front of the mirror, gazing at herself. Recalling Aryan's words, she undressed and examined the bruises he had given her last night.

While touching herself, she recalls the previous night when she took care of Aryan while he was unconscious due to excessive drug consumption. Suddenly, his heart started racing and his health deteriorated. Unsure of what to do, she clung to him tightly as Aryan, feeling down, pulled her closer and planted a gentle kiss on her neck, leaving Urvashi both bewildered and comforted - a sensation she hadn't experienced in a while.

She gazed at Aryan, his longing for her evident in his eyes. She slowly began to remove her clothing, pressing herself against his warm body. Aryan mistook her for Cassandra and began to nibble and kiss her body, gradually gaining control over her as she surrendered to his touch. Suddenly, she snapped back to reality and hurriedly dressed herself. She glanced at the mirror before responding to Aryan's question, "You've already thanked me."

Aryan, having left the secret place, headed straight to the TRUST where Cassandra eagerly awaited him, tightly gripping him and asking, "What happened to you?" "Nothing much," Aryan replied casually, his voice tinged with nonchalance. "Just had an accident, but I'm fine now. Let's get back to work; we can't afford any more delays."

The entire crew and staff pause their work, erupting into cheers for his tremendous achievement in the last project. Aryan, who had nearly given up and was summoned by the board of directors, is left astounded and inspired by the display of support.

Aryan entered the meeting room and saw only Tanisha. He asked, "I was told the directors wanted to see me."

Tanisha replied, her voice filled with authority, "As a fellow member of the board of directors, I have called you here because I have an offer that can't be refused." With those words, she swiftly transferred 60% of the profit to Aryan's bank account.

Tanisha suggested to Aryan, who seemed quiet, "This could be a way to save the MAYRA foundation as the deadline is approaching."

Aryan stated that he would rather destroy all money than use it to save the MAYRA foundation before leaving. Tanisha received news while working in her cabin and hurried to Aryan, who was with the crew. Tanisha's annoyance drove everyone away before she questioned, "What did you do with half of the money?"

Aryan nonchalantly responded, "I donated it to help local communities since the CEO reneged on their promises. Someone needs to take responsibility, but I don't expect it from the person who caused harm. If I've made myself clear, you can go now, as I have to finish this work before the deadline."

Aryan's carelessness makes her tense, while he remains focused on his work. However, for the past month, he has been leaving work early without anyone knowing where he goes or when he returns. She asked Cassandra, but even she has no information. Aryan, working late at a restricted site, secretly felt someone following him. He turned around and discovered it was Aditya. Seeing Aryan working like a laborer with others made Aditya furious. He asked, "You don't have to do this. Your worth is much higher than what you're doing. Come with me."

Aryan responded, "I can handle my work without anyone's help or suggestions."

Aditya appears to be stubborn and refuses to leave, standing with his men until Aryan finishes. When the dust settled, he appeared shocked by what he discovered about the site he was working on, but he remained silent, his gaze fixed on Aryan. Before leaving, while the work ended, he said, "Today, I am proud to call you my son. As the CEO destroys on one side, you try everything to protect on the other. I pray that what you started will finish well."

Aryan works at 2 sites without any issues, until one day he visits the secret site and finds unfinished work. However, he refuses to give up easily. While busy contemplating his next move, he sensed Aditya's presence and asked if the CEO had sent him.

Aditya said that our relationship hasn't been good since that day and every time I come here, it's not because of the CEO's orders, but to see how my son is doing. Aryan responded, "Don't call me son. If you had cared earlier, many things could have been saved, but you stayed silent." Aditya interrupted and said, "You can always correct your mistakes, all you need is a second chance." He then handed a cheque to Aryan.

"I don't need help from you or anyone," Aryan said as he looked at it. Aditya held his hand and said, "You used to call me grandfather from your childhood until things got messed up. I couldn't sleep, my patience wearing thin, knowing my grandson was relying on me. If not for the promise I made to your late mother, I would have left my work at the CEO already. Despite the risk of going against the CEO, she pleaded with me to look after you, willing to take any chance. But before that, I would like to ask, if you could forgive your loyal servant."

Aryan embraces Aditya and declares, "You are, and will always be, my grandfather. Never refer to yourself as a servant." Aditya finally feels calm and convinces Aryan to take the cheque, but Aryan refuses, saying, "It's your life's savings. I can't accept it." Aditya gave it to his hand and said, "I would do the same if I had a son, because I've always treated you like my own."

Upon hearing this, Aryan took the cheque to reduce expenses, which had caused the work to be halted. Aditya returned to the palace where the CEO awaited him, asking, "You spent all your savings at once. What did you buy that was so expensive?" Aditya calmly explained that with trust, assurance, and an unbreakable bond, he no longer expects anything more from life.

The CEO said, "It's been so long since I've seen you happy and I want it to stay that way forever." He gave Aditya his credit card and said, "You're lucky to have someone to look out for. Do whatever it takes to keep them safe."

Aditya, seeing the CEO worried about the kids, said, "You'll be proud of your son soon, but what about Tanisha?" The CEO paused and inquired, "What about her?"

Aditya replied, "Just a few days ago, Yogesh and Aryan had a heated argument that Tanisha managed to intervene in. However, Yogesh insulted Tanisha by suggesting she had no one to care for her." listening this, CEO left silently.

51

Chapter Fifty One

❦

Next day,

The CEO and his team paid a visit to TRUST, causing terror among the employees because of his destructive presence. Tanisha walks up to greet him and he asks about the progress of his assigned project. Tanisha stated that Akash is in charge of the project and will soon submit the final report to the board members.

"Would you mind giving me a tour of the site?", asked the CEO. Tanisha was about to enter her car when the CEO intervened and presented her with a new luxury car, stating "it's for the DIVINE successor."

Upon arriving at the site, Yogesh and his seniors were already there. The door opened to greet the CEO, but instead, Tanisha stepped out of the car. Yogesh appears shocked by what he is seeing. The CEO later exits the car and is greeted by everyone, holding Tanisha's hand to show she still holds power. While inspecting the project's progress, the CEO informed the senior officer about a recent attack on the site and requested the best officer from their department to protect the site and his successor.

Senior responded, "Our best officer is already assigned to you. We'll find another person for your request." The CEO confidently stated, "She is no ordinary girl; she is the successor of DIVINE, so everything must be top-notch for her, and she will never settle." He ordered the seniors to find the best person immediately, until then Yogesh would be in charge.

As soon as he spoke, Yogesh walked from the CEO's side to stand behind Tanisha. The CEO told him, "It is your responsibility to protect her, not only physically but also to fulfill all her wishes before she even asks for them. If she encounters any trouble, I assure you I will take legal action against everyone. Consider this my only warning." It made Yogesh feel insulted.

Before leaving, he settles Tanisha's pride issue and then takes a solitary walk. He pauses and gazes at Aryan, who works diligently with the crew at the back of the site. He stood and stared at Aryan for a while, who was later joined by Aditya. Despite his happiness, he concealed something within, leaving him feeling helpless and unable to ask for help. Tanisha witnessed everything and felt guilty because she believed she caused a rift between CEO and Aryan.

Aryan has been consistently working at both sites for 4 months without fail, and one of the tasks assigned by the CEO is nearly finished. It filled everyone with joy from the positive results of the product, except Aryan who isn't happy. He invested whatever he had left into improving the livelihood of local people and a significant amount of money into construction at his secret site. However, he falls behind because it holds more value to him than any other task, yet it remains unfinished and requires additional investment. Unfortunately, he has already depleted all his resources and now only has one person who can assist him.

Aryan entered Tanisha's cabin, surprising everyone by asking for a large loan, but Tanisha explained that she couldn't help as she had already given him a significant amount and the TRUST didn't have enough funds due to investments in two other projects.

Aryan appeared silent as Tanisha mentioned, "If you're truly in dire need of money, I can ask the CEO to lend at a minimal interest rate."

Aryan held his breath as he took out the last item he had left of his late mother, studying it for a moment before passing it to

Tanisha. "Maybe this can resolve the problem," he pleaded, "please use it and lend me the money." With that, he departed.

The room is filled with shock as they see the expensive pendant, especially because it bears the late wife's signature of the CEO. Yogesh asked, "I despise him, but what he lent you is not a possession; it's his heart. If he can release it easily, then his problem is not ordinary; it takes immense courage to let go. The CEO didn't have the courage to take it from Aryan, but he lent it to you. If it's found anywhere else, except with Aryan, it will cause unstoppable destruction. Only the CEO can prevent it. Think carefully before deciding.

Tanisha pondered over Aryan's situation while Cassandra chased after him, eventually catching up. She looked into his pained yet hopeful eyes, knowing he could set things right. With gentle care, she held his hand and assured him, "I am by your side in your plans, and I know you will succeed in whatever you have planned." Aryan thanked Cassandra by kissing her hand and acknowledging her constant belief in him. He vowed to avoid disappointing anyone this time.

The CEO has been clueless about Tanisha and her ongoing project for 5 days. Suddenly, his spies informed him about Tanisha's unexpected plan to sell 20% of her shares. At TRUST, everyone appears tense as they observe the dealer accepting Tanisha's conditions.

In desperate need of money, Tanisha agreed to sell her shares at a lower price and signed the papers. As the dealer was leaving, he spotted the CEO in front. The CEO quietly raised his hand for the papers, which the dealer silently handed to him. As he held the papers, the CEO approached Tanisha, who appeared calm but confident in her actions. He asked her, "If something is out of your reach, why not let it go?"

Tanisha raised her hand, revealing the asset, causing the silent CEO to notice his late wife's pendant. Tanisha mentioned that Aryan has never asked her anything before, instead he has always given so much that even if they counted, they couldn't afford 10% of it. Today, he asked her for help for the first time. He offered nothing in return for security and gave away his most precious possession, which I am determined to protect at any cost as it is the only thing that can stop him at TRUST.

The CEO noticed Tanisha's despair and picked up the pendant. When the CEO glanced at Aditya, a smile appeared on his face as he disclosed, "Since my wife's passing, this is the first instance I've held this pendant. Aryan's trust in you is unshaken, as you were the sole individual he permitted touching it. He acknowledges you are the only one capable of keeping it safe, as you showed today."

He returned her shares and placed the pendant around her neck, remarking that it had found its rightful owner. He kissed her forehead before leaving. Tanisha asked if he wanted anything in return.

The CEO responded, "I achieved what I desired, and today I'm able to touch it for the first and last time because of you. If viewed as an asset, it holds no value; but if seen as emotions, it becomes a priceless gift that I've longed for and paid dearly, now bestowed upon a successor by a godfather."

In her final plea, Tanisha whispered, "Perhaps one day, Aryan will seek your assistance. I implore you, fulfill his wishes without hesitation." CEO agreed and left with his crew.

52
Chapter Fifty Two

Aryan visited TRUST and found everyone gathered in the hall. He noticed Tanisha holding the pendant as he passed by. He remained silent as he studied her, then glanced away before taking the papers from her. Shocked, he pondered what she had done to protect the pendant and offered to cancel the deal and to take back her belongings, saying, "I don't want the money if it came at such a high cost to you."

Tanisha responded by saying that the buyer desired to touch it once and ended up paying me twice the amount of my shares before finally gifting me the pendant. Aryan asked, "Who is the buyer?" seeming surprised.

Tanisha responded, "It's a present from my godfather to his heir." Aryan appears heartbroken and asked if you let him touch the pendant.

Tanisha remained silent; Aryan smiled slightly and continued, "Today, he emerged victorious, just as he had always claimed he would. He bought the pendant at a price you could never fathom. I never shared the last sign of my mother with him. This pendant wasn't expensive, but he desired it so much and bought it at an unattainable price. I misjudged his desire to take this from me. He wanted to give it to the rightful owner, and today he finally succeeded. You're fortunate to have a godfather like him."

Aryan approached Tanisha and requested permission to touch the pendant one final time. As she agreed, Aryan gently brushed his fingers against the pendant resting near her heart, remarking, "I guess the CEO gifted it to you because it truly suits you. You look like an angel holding it." As he was about to leave without taking the price, she asked, "Aren't you interested in your money?"

Aryan pauses and says, "I can't put a price on what you have, it's priceless." Tanisha's said, "I knew you would never part with this pendant, but you gave it up for something worthwhile. I wish you luck in seeing it through to the end." She handed the cheque to Aryan, and everyone praised Tanisha for her generosity.

Aryan now has enough funds to complete the construction, but first, he needs to gather a large workforce and seek help from the community. All those who previously paid the large sum to support Aryan have agreed to assist him, and work is commencing rapidly with great effort. Aditya assumed responsibility for everyone's safety and keeping the work secret until completion. After working for a month and a half, Aryan finally finished the job. He looked at the newly built building and smiled, a moment that Aditya captured to commemorate his first solo success.

Aryan finished the final task in the project and submitted the last report to Tanisha before the deadline, then asked one final question before the project began. She couldn't meet the request, stating that the desired location is under the CEO's authority and that you should inquire with the CEO to reclaim it. Aryan took back the project details from Tanisha and left.

Aryan stood before DIVINE, glanced at it, then entered. As he entered the premises, memories of the moments spent with his father flooded back. Everyone at the office is shocked to see Aryan, and he line up to meet the CEO with his project file. The CEO, learning about this, requested the staff to allow him entry. Aryan entered the cabin where everyone was present and handed the project details to one of his staff members. Boldly, he asked, "Can I have the FAITH back area on January 8th?"

The room fell silent as everyone listened to the date. The CEO stayed quiet for a moment, recalling Tanisha's request, and then said, "granted."

Aryan looked into his father's eyes, unsure of how to express his gratitude. As he was leaving, the CEO stopped him and returned his musical belongings, saying, "On that special day, enjoy every moment as if it's your last chance to live life freely." Aryan vanished for 2 days until a text arrived revealing the celebration venue, FAITH back area, where his secret work would be unveiled.

At the venue,

As everyone arrived at the venue, they saw the FAITH building completely covered, with a massive music celebration organized at the entrance, featuring artists from various countries. People of various age groups and social classes gathered for the celebration, and the concert began with a variety of music until the main guest of the show was still expected to arrive.

Tanisha and her family, along with Akash and his family, Yogesh as the security in charge, and Aditya with his troop, all attended the Aryan mega concert in support. Suddenly, Aryan and his music troop appeared on stage, making the whole concert seem silent.

Aryan played a beautiful melody as a way of thanking everyone gathered here. Eventually, the large screen on his back began showing pictures of motherly love with the children as the concert started. As the show progresses, the picture changes, showcasing special moments of different families with their children. The pictures gradually transition from Akash's family to Yogesh's family and finally to Tanisha's family, capturing their special moments with their mothers. As the music gradually intensifies, everyone's eyes seem to fill with emotion.

Media and crowds flocked to the event, making it even more massive. The event became even bigger when the CEO arrived and more artists joined the performance. The display shows pictures of the CEO and his wife, and it's touching to see Aryan perform with such passion, as if the CEO is reliving his past.

He recalls the words of Aryan, "One day, I will give a performance that will earn me praise from everyone. And when that day comes, I want my father to be in the front, supporting me. That day, I will feel like I've lived my whole life."

Wondering which CEO walks to the front of the stage, with no picture of Aryan and his mother, revealing his lack of maternal affection and melting everyone's heart.

The picture suddenly changed, showing moments with Aryan and each family member, starting with Yogesh, Akash, Tanisha, Aditya, and ending with a large picture of Aryan with people from the locality. Despite not having a mother, he had a big family that made him feel less lonely and he expresses gratitude towards each family member.

As his day ended, he abruptly began breaking his music equipment one by one, marking the end of his love for music. Filled with tears, he went to the CEO to say goodbye, but there was a smile on his face as his father finally fulfilled his dream and presented the gift he had been working on in secret for a long time.

53

Chapter Fifty Three

The CEO unveiled the FAITH building by pressing a button. Tanisha's eyes welled up with tears as she witnessed the building being renovated with a new design, thinking she had done the worst to him. However, he still cared about her dream. The CEO appeared amazed as he saw the new architecture he had built all by himself, and everyone's eyes were glued to the building. The CEO, accompanied by Tanisha, couldn't do anything when they saw Aryan leaving the concert. The CEO expressed feeling helpless as he couldn't buy Aryan's peace, despite having everything.

Late at night, after everyone had gone, Tanisha remained and admired the building when a voice asked, "Do you approve of the new architecture?"

Tanisha recognized Aryan as he asked, "Can I show you around your new building?"

Witnessing Aryan's tranquility and his desire to share this moment, she offered her hand. Finally, after walking her to every corner, they ended up in the CEO cabin where he made her sit and took a picture. When Tanisha asked him what he saw in the picture, he appeared lost.

Aryan said, "I've never seen that priceless smile on your face until today."

Holding her hand, he prepares to leave, but Tanisha notices a piano in the corner of the main hall and exclaims, "I've never seen this piano before!" Aryan said, "This is one of my musical instruments. It's the only thing I haven't destroyed, so I left it here in case someone can find it useful since I can't."

Tanisha opened the board and glanced at the clock. She asked, "Can you play it one last time for me? There's still some time left." Aryan played the piano for the last time, fulfilling her wish, and asked, "how was it?"

"There's only one more thing left," Tanisha replied. She played the tune on a fixed recorder and asked, "Will you dance with me before the night ends?" Aryan agreed. While dancing, they exchanged glances and Aryan's gaze made her feel cherished; they appeared entranced in that instant. Suddenly, the clock struck 12, and their dance came to a halt.

Before leaving, Aryan kissed her hand and expressed, "Today was the best day of my life. I am grateful for your presence and for fulfilling my dream of having a CEO support me in music. Thanks to you, I have everything I could ask for."

Tanisha's eyes appear emotional as she asks, "Can you forgive me?"

Aryan kissed her forehead and reassured, "I could never hate you. My only fear was losing a friend like you. I did everything to protect you and now everything is fine." He says this and walks away, leaving Tanisha alone with her dream, FAITH.

The CEO walks to Aryan's room in the palace. As he surveyed all of Aryan's belongings, which he had once bought with joy to bring him happiness, he realized nothing could bring him joy anymore. In a fit of anger, he began breaking everything in sight. Finally, when he messed up everything, an eerie silence filled the air as he gazed at the shattered pieces. Aditya comforted him, his voice filled with reassurance, "Just stay strong, time will pass slowly."

The CEO turned, his eyes filled with a mix of sadness and admiration, as Aditya gently placed a hand on his shoulder and uttered, "Your dreams require immense courage, and today, I am proud of you and our grandson Aryan."

Aditya replied, his voice filled with admiration, "Now he won't fully grasp the sacrifice you made for him. But when he does, he'll be filled with pride to have a father like you."

Listening intently, the CEO holds Aditya and sincerely apologizes for his past behavior, saying, "In all this, I have also hurt you. Please forgive me."

Aditya responded, "I have been taking care of my two sons since the beginning. I consider it my responsibility, not just my duty, to fulfill until my last breath, as I have only two people I call family."

The CEO held Aditya's hand and asked, "Promise me you'll always take care of Aryan, whether or not I'm here." Saying this, the CEO held his breath and continued, "eventually, face a situation where you have to choose between us, let it be Aryan." Aditya seemed shocked and his hand trembled as he asked, "why are you saying this? Did you do something I don't know?"

In a reassuring tone, the CEO calmed Aditya, reminding him that although it wasn't happening today, the day would come and he needed to be prepared. Aditya replied, his voice filled with conviction, "Even if you ask or not, I would always take Aryan's side. But what you're asking is difficult for me because I can't distinguish between my two children. It's an impossible task."

With that said, he left. CEO lost in thoughts pulled out his phone. The CEO reviewed a recording from a few years ago when Aryan accidentally caused a catastrophic event resulting in numerous casualties. The CEO closed the video and instructed their spy to eliminate any remaining evidence.

After ending the call, he stared at his wife's portrait and whispered, "No one can harm our son. If anyone tries, I'll eliminate them all." Touching her picture, he concluded, "He's the only part of you that remains." Then he left.

54
Chapter Fifty Four

When Aryan arrived at TRUST the next day, he was greeted with applause and surprises that he didn't anticipate. Finally, Tanisha and Cassandra arrived at the main hall to hand him the fund cheque collected from the previous day's event. Aryan appeared shocked and asked Tanisha if what he was seeing was real. "It's merely a day's earnings, as it's still in the process of growing," Cassandra replied.

Holding Aryan's hand, she said, "Your hard work not only brought TRUST fame but also earned its trust back by making such a profit."

Aryan thanked her and said to Tanisha, "I don't want this, you take it and get MAYRA foundation back. It's a gift for Mayra that I won't share with anyone." Tanisha agreed and said, "You can keep the rest, it's all yours."

Aryan asked, "What about TRUST?" Aryan continued, his voice filled with conviction, "Everyone seems confused. TRUST is still under CEO control. Get it back as well. This company belongs to you and will always be."

Aryan smiled, his eyes twinkling, and asked, "Did you manage to prepare the last thing I asked for before we started working on the project?" Tanisha furrowed her brow, looking confused, and quickly called over the staff to retrieve the items. Aryan looked at all the cheques, each bearing a small amount of money under his name. He handed it back to Tanisha, his voice filled with joy as he said, "get it wrapped up and give it to the CEO, it's a little gift from me."

Tanisha agreed and instructed Aryan to join the crew in the meeting room for a discussion on the new project. Everyone started heading towards the meeting room, except Aryan. Tanisha asked if there was anything else, seeing him stuck at his place.

Aryan quietly handed the envelope to Tanisha, surprising her. She asked, "How long have you been planning to give this to me?" Cassandra revealed the contents of the envelope: a resignation letter. Tanisha approached, looking into his eyes and asked, "You've resolved everything, and now you want to go?"

Aryan said that everything is temporarily fixed, but if he stays, the CEO will return eventually. You won't just be his successor, but also his daughter, a relationship that has been damaged because of me. Letting one person go will secure local people, the MAYRA foundation, your enterprise, and its staff, so it's best if I leave.

Tanisha appears possessive and inquired, "What about you? You're doing awesome and soon you'll have the CEO's trust. That's why he sent you here. At least consider what the CEO thinks." Aryan replied, "I think about him all the time. And when I reach this point, what if he finds out that my success isn't just mine, like everyone thinks?"

"What do you mean?" Tanisha asked, confused.

Aryan gave her his phone and revealed, "Since day 1, I've had a mysterious friend who has supported, guided, and handled everything for my project without me even asking. The ironic part is, I don't know who this person is or what they look like. The only thing I gained from solitude is the trust of others, a family, a helpful colleague, and an incredible boss to learn from. I came here to inform the CEO about my recently fulfilled dream, but TRUST faced many issues along the way that I can't afford to repeat."

Tanisha reassured, "We'll start fresh and help you accomplish everything, so you won't have to feel ashamed." Tanisha took the paper from Cassandra and handed it back to Aryan, who ignored it and instead held her hand, saying, "I paid a lot to regain your trust and patience. If anything happens after this, I won't be able to forgive myself. Let me go and end this relationship here."

Tanisha pleads, "You can't leave, remember? You said you wouldn't until I asked, and I won't let you quit." Just as she was about to tear the letter, Aryan embraced her and pleaded, "Please don't make it difficult for me and allow me to leave in peace."

Tanisha seems quiet and won't push him anymore. Before leaving, Aryan holds her hand and says, "I will always miss you, my boss," blinking with a smile before leaving behind many cherished memories.

Tanisha silently watches Aryan before he leaves TRUST and dismisses everyone for the day. Cassandra wanted to comfort her, but she also asked to be left alone. After everyone departed, she remains alone at TRUST, gazing at the gift he left for the CEO and the checks he left for Mayra and the TRUST foundation. She had finally gotten rid of Aryan, everything she had always wanted, but now she didn't feel fine. She started angrily breaking things, overwhelmed by the realization that he wasn't just leaving her, but her family as well.

55

Chapter Fifty Five

Sitting alone in the main hall, the CEO's fingers traced the faded photographs in the family album. Suddenly, a voice called out, "Father!" Listening intently, the CEO stood in disbelief, unable to comprehend what he was hearing. "Do you have a moment for me?" Aryan inquired.

The CEO abandons everything and embraces his son tightly, saying, "It's been too long since I've heard the word 'father' from you."

The CEO appears pleased that his son has returned and is already showing off his purchases. He starts by showing the new music instrument, then leads him to the garage where a brand-new Mustang awaited, something Aryan had always desired. Aryan then interrupts, saying, "I wanted to talk to you, it's been a while since we last conversed."

Aryan stands and starts discussing his past life, then moves on to his present life and shares his experiences, while the CEO sits calmly. "Being Aryan, he formed strong connections during that period, but ultimately he reached the main point, stating, "I have gained valuable knowledge and during this time, our family has caused harm to many lives, which I have now rectified. I not only acquired valuable business strategies, but also demonstrated my capabilities, just as you desired. Now, there is no reason for me to remain here."

Saying this, he gently grasps the CEO's hands and pleads, "Please, let me go." The CEO observes Aryan's miserable state, silently acknowledging his pain but concealing his own emotions. Finally, he asks, "Are you truly determined to leave?"

Aryan replied, his voice filled with confidence, "it's better for everyone, and I am sure the relation and company I have set up, you will look after it. If you won't help the less fortunate, think about how they have never let down your son and treated me like their own. It never feels like I was separated from my family."

CEO agreed.

Aryan, who appeared calm, wanted to leave. The CEO asked, "Won't you ask me the main reason for your visit instead of asking unrelated questions?"

Aryan stops and turns, silence engulfing him. The CEO locks eyes and asks, "What about your guilt?" Aryan appeared surprised as the CEO mentioned the incident when Tanisha, who despises you immensely, spoke to you at the hospital without informing me. However, I was somewhat aware and heard about your feelings of guilt at that time.

Aryan showed the picture he took of Tanisha at a music event to the CEO, saying, "Her smile is priceless, and I only saw it when she sat in the FAITH CEO chair. Working in TRUST, being with local people, colleagues, and staff, I feel guilty every second. Despite treating them poorly, they still treat me like family."

Aryan grasped the CEO's hand and proceeded, "My excitement was unbearable after I acquired that prize for you, but now all is well since you remain the CEO, an unmatched business person whom no one dares to challenge. You've achieved what you desired, so let's conclude this and enable everyone to live peacefully."

The CEO silently handed Aryan papers containing FAITH, MAYRA, and TRUST, which he had already given rights to the former owner, and said, "There is nothing my son wished for that I couldn't fulfill." Aryan embraced his father, who reciprocated the hug, saying, "I can handle anything, but I can never stand to see my son in pain. You took FAITH from Tanisha, so you should be the one to give it back to her."

Aryan agreed and was about to leave, but the CEO knew it would be difficult for Aryan to say goodbye, so he asked him one last thing: "Son, will you, like Akash, enter the palace for the last time?"

Aryan gazed at the CEO one last time, eyes filled with emotion, and expressed gratitude for having a father like him. In response, the CEO turned around, allowing Aryan to leave peacefully. After some time, the CEO received a text from Aryan, causing the CEO to suspect that Aryan was not leaving. He found out that Tanisha has Aryan's private number. Curiously, she asks, "Are you the mysterious friend who aided Aryan in his journey to success?"

Seeing the CEO silent, Tanisha continued, "I feel envy of Aryan to have a father like you who parted him from himself but always looked after him, which you never do for me. You refer to me as your daughter, yet never showed the same affection you had for Aryan. Please clarify why you think he is superior to me. Is it because I am not your real blood?"

Seeing Tanisha broken, the CEO replied with a heavy heart, "You are right. Despite calling you my daughter, I cared for Aryan the most. But I couldn't stop him, and he left."

Tanisha was shocked when the CEO said, "I know he didn't want to leave, but he has to because he can't bear any more pain from me. Even before leaving, he couldn't confide in me about his pain because he lost faith in me. I ruined our relationship by my own actions, for something he never wanted to do, but he did it because of my wish. Now he is successful, not because of my support. I gave him the resources, but he learned the implementation and strategies from you. He made me proud by proving his worth to the world, but in the process, he lost himself, and I fear I will never regain it. I feel like I've failed as a father, but before leaving, he fulfilled every duty of a son, reminding me of all that I had. Now, I can't buy back his happiness, and I'm left alone with my pride and success."

Tanisha comforted the broken CEO, her voice filled with sincerity. "I was mistaken about you, and even more so about Aryan.

I thought you had sent him to seek revenge. Instead, he joined TRUST to show his capabilities and gain your confidence. He had a burning desire to absolve his cousin's wrongdoing, and he achieved just that. In fact, he not only rectified everything but also surpassed your wildest expectations."

Saying this, she carefully retrieved the gift that Aryan had left for the CEO. CEO appears silent as he opened the gift. Tanisha continued, "I couldn't understand why he refused to take the profit earned by his event for such a small amount."

CEO looked at Aryan's monthly salary cheque and replied, "It may seem like a small surprise, but he gave me the most extravagant gift. This is no regular check because he worked for it. Throughout his life, he always received what he desired even before asking for it, as I never wanted him to work. However, he always wanted to prove his value, a conflict I couldn't resolve until I finally gave him a chance. That opportunity was his only shot at demonstrating his capabilities to the world. Despite the hardships, he aimed to protect the success he gained."

Tanisha expresses amazement at Aryan's dedication to saving all checks and remarks, "You're an amazing person, and Aryan will continue to fulfill your wishes, so you don't need me anymore."

As Tanisha was leaving, the CEO's voice trembled with hurt as he asked, "Will you abandon your father too, like Aryan did? Am I truly that terrible?"

Tanisha tightly embraces the CEO as he forgives her, stating, "You have always been my daughter, and now you are all I have because he still sees me as a threat to you and your people, and has abandoned everything."

The CEO, regaining composure, proceeded, "Daughter, it's true that my son has bound us in an unbreakable bond, one that only Aryan can release. I never wanted this to happen because it will not only make me lose you but also cause Aryan to sever all ties between our families, ultimately losing himself forever."

Witnessing the CEO's miserable state, Tanisha makes a solemn vow: "I refuse to let him depart in such anguish, and if I fail, I will never show my face again." Before leaving, Tanisha paused and reminisced, "Your son once gave me a dreadful gift, but little did he know, it led me to Aryan, for whom I forgave him a long time ago. Aryan's happiness matters more to me than revenge, so I won't let him break this bond easily," and left.

56
Chapter Fifty Six

Aryan arrived at the airport and just as he was about to check in, he received a text from his secret friend on his personal phone asking, "Why are you leaving so early?" Aryan paused while reading a text from his secret friend, then replied, "I am grateful for everything you've done for me. It not only resolved my problems but also transformed my life."

Secret friend replied, "Could we meet one last time before you depart forever? Today holds a special significance for me, and I would be delighted if you could join me in celebration."

Holding the ticket, Aryan rescheduled and replied, "Okay, but I'm short on time, we have until midnight."

Friend responded, "It's sufficient for me, but I have a condition before we meet." Aryan was amazed. "Today's event is traditional, so dress accordingly." By asking, he disclosed the gift location that Aryan followed and arrived at the upscale makeover place. The showroom was empty, as he had booked it for just one person, making Aryan even more curious about his secret friend. Once he was ready, a luxury car arrived, and he left for the destination.

Aryan is in awe as he gazes at the beautifully decorated building, where people from TRUST, DIVINE, MAYRA, and the local community have gathered. This intensifies his curiosity to discover which guest is his secret friend. Aryan was greeted with applause as he entered the main door where everyone was dressed traditionally and waiting.

As Aryan passed by everyone, he gently placed his hand on Mayra's head. Aryan, while giving Mayra's hand to Urvashi, he stated, "Mayra is safe with you." After saying this, he handed Urvashi the papers of MAYRA Foundation. Aryan wiped away the tears from her eyes, his touch filled with tenderness, as he reassured her, "I promise to protect Mayra's future, which is safe in your hands."

Urvashi was about to return the contract due to not wanting the responsibility, but Aryan stopped her, saying, "I trust you completely. No one else could handle Mayra like you can, not even me. Please accept this and show everyone what you're capable of." Urvashi agreed. Mayra asks Aryan if he's leaving.

Aryan kneels down and presents sweet dishes to her, saying, "I can't leave the city without you." He pulled out a new phone and gave it to Mayra, saying, "Whenever you're lonely, call me. I'll come for my angel, no matter where I am." Then he turned to Tanisha and declared, "Today is your lucky day."

Handing her both contracts, TRUST and FAITH, he said, "Today, you are liberated from the bond my brother created between our families. You have regained your freedom. Today, I returned everything my family took from you and your people. Now, I am free and can leave peacefully."

Aryan, after returning her rights, was preparing to leave. However, before departing, he embraced Tanisha and quietly said, "Once I'm gone, the CEO will be alone. Please take care of him. Consider this my final request, as we will never cross paths again."

Aryan held Tanisha's hand and said, "I hope you will always be happy." While departing, he scanned every person in search of his secret friend, but to no avail. As he was leaving through the main gate, he received a text saying, "Are you leaving without saying goodbye?"

While Aryan was reading the text, Cassandra approached him from the front. He believed she was his secret friend, but before he could react, he received another text saying, "I am waiting behind you." As he reads this, he turns and sees Tanisha holding the CEO's secret phone. He texts her back, "I saw you." The phone in Tanisha's hand rings, making it clear she's his secret friend.

Back to CEO palace when Tanisha was leaving to stop Aryan,

Before Tanisha could leave, the CEO discreetly slipped her a piece of paper with his secret phone number, a last-ditch effort to stop Aryan.

Tanisha couldn't help but embrace the CEO tightly, her gratitude and determination overwhelming her saying, "I promise as a daughter to bring Aryan back, and if I fail, I'll never show my face again."

As Tanisha spoke the word "father" for the first time, the CEO kissed her forehead lovingly. Aryan gifted him the most precious gift and expressed confidence in Tanisha, saying, "I never doubted you. Do whatever it takes to bring Aryan back."

Present time,

Upon discovering that Tanisha is his secret friend, Aryan abandons Cassandra and approaches her. However, before he can say anything, Tanisha presents him with the FAITH contract, expressing that while she once desired it greatly, she no longer wants it if it will sever the bond between their families and themselves.

She was on the verge of tearing the contract in front of his eyes, but Aryan intervened and took it back. Tanisha, annoyed, forcefully pushed Aryan against the wall and declared, "I won't allow you to abandon me because you mean everything to me. I finally understand your importance, and if anyone tries to separate us, I will obliterate them, even if it's you."

Aryan boldly replied, "There's nothing left for me here."

While Cassandra watched, Tanisha kissed him desperately, until Urvashi came searching for Tanisha. Cassandra was visibly shocked and heartbroken, and she left silently. Urvashi observed the scene and realized that Tanisha got everything she desired, but in the end,

Urvashi was happy for her because she made a good choice. Urvashi was happy for Aryan because Tanisha gave him a compelling reason to stay.

Urvashi glanced at Aryan before leaving, reminiscing their precious moment. She saw them together and all her feelings for him vanished, so she returned to the event. Aryan, trying to regain his composure, firmly grasps Tanisha's arm and gently guides her towards the wall. He asks, "Why are you making it difficult for me? You were the one who wanted to sever all ties, so why now?"

Tanisha interrupts him, her voice filled with determination, "Now I want you, and whether you like it or not, you can't escape me until I decide otherwise. You belong to me."

Witnessing Tanisha asserting her dominance, Aryan defiantly ripped the contract apart before her, solidifying his commitment and sealing it with a kiss that Tanisha reciprocated. Aryan's lips trailed down her body, leaving a trail of kisses and gentle bites. Suddenly, Tanisha stopped him, her fingers gripping his hair tightly. She looked into his eyes and asked, "Do you still want to leave me?"

Aryan's gaze lingered on her, and he murmured, "I want to make you mine forever."

Tanisha pushed him off herself, leaving Aryan confused. "I wanted this moment to be special, where we could truly be one," she said, her voice filled with anticipation. As she said this, she extended her hand towards him. Aryan, in silence, retrieved the flight tickets and whispered, "I'll be waiting for you whenever you're ready, but I can't wait too long after you made me fall in love with you." He handed her the tickets, only for her to tear them up immediately.

After Aryan left, Tanisha quickly sent a text to the CEO, proudly stating, "I kept my promise," before returning to the event. The CEO is amazed that Aryan couldn't leave because of Tanisha's love, which is exactly what he wanted. Aditya asked him what he had in mind on the FAITH anniversary day when he ordered his men to prepare a great event. In a determined tone, the CEO explained, "To make their bond permanent, I've chosen to tie them in a knot on the FAITH anniversary day."

Aditya replied, "The pace is a bit quick, let both children have some time to enjoy their freedom." The CEO turned and cautioned, "Time is running out, so everything must be executed according to my wishes." He shifted his gaze to the other side and added, "Ensure that the management is taken care of. I want this wedding to be unforgettable, not just in the business world, but throughout the entire city. And until all the arrangements are complete, keep it confidential."

Before leaving, Aditya suggested, "I think it's important for both of them to know your plans." The CEO, deep in thought, whispered, "No one will have a chance to escape this marriage. What I've decided will happen, no matter what."

57

Chapter Fifty Seven

Everyone gathered to celebrate the re-opening of FAITH, unaware of the CEO's master plan. The CEO and his crew waited at the designated spot for his children while Tanisha prepared for the event. However, today she brought out the box given to her by the CEO's son instead of wearing Aryan's mother's pendant. She wore the dress Aryan had given her, put on both the outfit and pendant, and went to meet him at their favorite spot before going to the FAITH event. Meanwhile, Aryan, who had also dressed formally as Tanisha had always wished, left for their meeting spot.

Aryan is astonished to discover that Tanisha, his mysterious girl, was the one who wore his gifted dress and stood before him with a gun. Just as he was about to move forward, the main hall's big screen revealed the accident recording that the CEO had kept hidden.

Aryan watched a video where a racing car recklessly crashes into Tanisha's car, which had her parents and brother inside. The accident was so massive that it resulted in the death of all her family members on the spot, while the other car was also severely damaged and saved by the CEO's guards. Aryan stepped out, covered in blood and injured, just as the CEO's guards destroyed everything and set the area on fire to eliminate evidence of Aryan's presence.

Aryan remains silent as he looks at this, then turns towards Tanisha. He gazes into her eyes, intending to explain everything, but before he can say a word, Tanisha shoots him. Aryan was shot at close range and then shot again, forcing him to kneel. Tearfully, Tanisha uttered, "I loved you, but you are responsible for my parents' death. I can't forgive you." As she was about to fire the third bullet, she stopped upon hearing the sound of open fire. It was Cassandra who protected the injured Aryan by pointing a gun at Tanisha.

Tanisha asked, "Don't interfere, this time it's personal. I don't care if you love him because he killed my parents." Cassandra interrupted, saying, "I don't want you to make the same mistake as Aryan."

Lowering the gun and clutching her stomach, she reveals that she's already three months pregnant. Tanisha, feeling heartbroken, expressed, "He not only destroyed my family but also betrayed both of us." Tanisha didn't abruptly halt, causing a large armed force to appear, which wasn't affiliated with either Tanisha or the CEO. Tanisha appears shocked and inquired, "Who are you? I won't quit today, even if it costs me my life."

Cassandra gave Tanisha a drive, saying, "Take this. It contains all the records needed to demolish DIVINE's vast empire in one go. However, I want Aryan's life in exchange." Tanisha couldn't believe Cassandra when she found herself surrounded by a collection of loaded guns. Tanisha asked Cassandra, "Even after all the times he betrayed you, you still want to help him?"

"If you take him today, then our relationship will also come to an end," Tanisha warned her. Cassandra stopped abruptly and retorted, "The relationship was over long ago when you attempted to separate Aryan from me." She defiantly took Aryan with her, causing her immense army to disband as well, much to Tanisha's surprise. Tanisha had the power to dismantle DIVINE, just as CEO's son had dismantled FAITH, and she promptly shared all the information with the police and legal authorities.

The CEO and his crew received information from their spies that Tanisha has turned against DIVINE and exposed all the secret files that only the CEO had. The CEO couldn't comprehend, and was informed that she killed Aryan, who is now dead. The CEO's tone seemed broken as he asked, "Tanisha, what have you done?"

He carefully held his antique gun, observing as his men geared up and loaded heavy machine guns, preparing for the mission to bring an end to the story Tanisha had started. Tanisha told Yogesh before murdering Aryan and planning to kill the CEO today. If you want to stop me or seek revenge on the CEO, find me at TRUST.

All the seniors and staff who had previously supported the CEO forcefully, now wanted revenge and left. Yogesh also left with his crew. Before the CEO could reach TRUST, he encountered a massive blockade of police, army, rivals, and partners protecting Tanisha.

Without hesitation, the CEO commanded his army to attack, transforming a part of the city into a battlefield where no one showed any signs of retreat. The CEO became ruthless and joined the battle, swiftly taking down many opponents with strategic moves. However, his army suffered significant injuries and couldn't hold on for long. Unexpectedly, CNH group also came to support the CEO.

As more forces arrive to take down the CEO, CNH CEO Giriraj instructs the CEO to leave, saying "I'll handle things here." The CEO, before departing, assured, "DIVINE will always remember your support and will repay it in the future." Saying this, he departed for TRUST, where Tanisha and her men were already waiting.

The CEO, covered in blood, entered TRUST alongside Aditya who informed him, "You must leave now, CEO, or DIVINE will be destroyed forever." Ignoring the warning, he moved towards Tanisha, but before he could reach her, Yogesh and his men blocked his path, protecting her. Tanisha ordered her men to stay back upon seeing Yogesh at her side.

"If you want to take revenge," Yogesh warned, "now is not the right time. You must leave the city immediately, or you risk losing everything." Aditya covered the CEO, who lowered his gun, as they were being taken away. As the CEO was attempting to flee, Tanisha's men prepared to attack, but Yogesh's crew intervened and prevented any harm.

While the CEO made his exit, Yogesh unveiled, "Aryan once played the hero for my mother, and today, I've returned the favor. Now, we're squared."

As the CEO and his crew made their escape, Aditya bravely shielded the CEO but was shot in the process. Witnessing Aditya's injury, Tanisha immediately commanded her men to halt, prioritizing Aditya's well-being over the escape plan.

58

Chapter Fifty Eight

After CEO's departure, Tanisha walked past the crew and confronted Yogesh, asking, "Why did you do this?" Yogesh responded, "I am aware that Aryan is not dead, and as long as he is alive, I will protect him from everyone, as he is my top priority. He is responsible for my mother's death and needs to pay."

As Yogesh's seniors and staff entered TRUST, the air was tense with anticipation. Yogesh had just helped the CEO escape, narrowly avoiding termination. Tanisha intervened, declaring, "From now on, he works for me." In response, a senior staff member challenged, "Why should we follow you?"

Suddenly, all men and armed forces directed their gun points towards them. Tanisha revealed, "In the past, the CEO owned this city, but not anymore. His successor has taken over, along with his powers."

The whole force surrenders to her and demands the decommissioning of DIVINE. Suddenly, Aditya's laughter echoed through, despite the pain he was in. Tanisha asked, "Are you still alive?"

As she aimed the gun, Aditya bravely walked towards her and confidently stated, "DIVINE cannot be destroyed because his rightful successor is still alive." Tanisha lowers the gun and asks, "Will Akash seek revenge for his father?"

Aditya responded, "This time you made a huge mistake with no one to protect you from him, not even the CEO who always had your back, but you intentionally not only removed the CEO's name and reputation, but you also wanted to harm the CEO, and he won't spare anyone for that. Live your lives until he comes back, because when he does, the entire city will burn and nothing can stop it."

Tanisha responded, "I'll prove you wrong. Stay alive and witness his downfall, just like I did to the CEO." While Yogesh walks beside her, her men took Aditya. Before leaving, Aditya said, "Aryan trusted you, and what you did to him isn't fair because what you knew is only half the truth," which shocked Tanisha. Aditya continued, "Wait for Akash's return, he will finish this story and the half-truth you began."

Once everyone departed, Tanisha examined the pendant, grasped it, removed it, and tossed it aside.

A few days had passed when Aryan woke up to find himself in a luxurious cage, surrounded by others in separate, less favorable cells. The only thing they had in common was being slaves. Aryan, shocked, yelled for help upon seeing a place filled with murderers, thugs, and terrorists, wondering where he was.

Witnessing Aryan's misery, Cassandra shuts off the live recording and calmly takes her seat on the throne, surrounded by heavily armed guards, whose numbers far exceed those of the CEO. Additionally, the guards bear a secret symbol on their attire, matching that of the CEO's antique gun.

Cassandra took out the box and extracted the antique gun, which happened to be the exact same one as the CEO's. Looking at the CEO portrait, she softly uttered, "I've waited patiently, and now I possess what you hold dear. I will train him to go against you. Enjoy every moment until he's ready to take back what you took from me."

To be continued...

www.ingramcontent.com/pod-product-compliance
Lightning Source LLC
Chambersburg PA
CBHW051147130726
47988CB00005B/2030